Books by Sean Wolfe

Close Contact

Aroused

Taboo

Published by Kensington Publishing Corporation

Taboo

Sean Wolfe

KENSINGTON BOOKS
http://www.kensingtonbooks.com

KENSINGTON BOOKS are published by

Kensington Publishing Corp.
850 Third Avenue
New York, NY 10022

ISBN-13: 978-0-7582-2512-2
ISBN-10: 0-7582-2512-1

First Kensington Trade Paperback Printing: December 2008
10 9 8 7 6 5 4 3 2 1

Acknowledgments

Thank you to all of the guys who served as inspiration for these stories and more. Ricky, Erick, Miguel, Izakk, Morgan, and Rob. All of you are represented in this book, although some of the names have been changed to protect the not-so-innocent. Thanx for all the "happy endings."

Thank you to Jane Nichols, my best friend, second mother, and earthly angel. Even though you'd never read any of my erotica books, you have always supported me in whatever endeavor I chose to embark upon, and your belief in me is unwavering. I love you.

Thank you to Gustavo Paredes-Wolfe. Every good thing about me is because of you, and for that I'm extremely grateful. You have been the love of my life since the day we met, and the fact that you are no longer physically with me won't ever change that. I miss you terribly, and you need to contact and visit me. We both know you can do it . . . stop being so stubborn. Spread your wings and fly my way, please.

And lastly, a big THANK YOU to John Scognamiglio, my editor. Your patience with me and your willingness to forgive a two-months-late submission of this manuscript is much appreciated. Thank you for believing in me and giving me my first break. You ROCK!!

Introduction

Taboo: *tabú n 1: forbidden to profane use or contact because of what are held to be dangerous supernatural powers 2: banned on grounds of morality or taste, or banned as constituting a risk 3: a prohibition imposed by social custom or as a protective measure.*
Merriam-Webster's Collegiate Dictionary

Well, sign me the fuck up!

Most of us, unless maybe we were born in New Orleans, where taboo is a way of life and a rite of passage of sorts, have been told from a very young age that taboo is wrong and is a very bad thing. Stay away from it. It's a sin and you can get hurt by it. I'm not aware of any scientific studies that could undisputedly identify the number of people who have never indulged in the taboo. But I'd be willing to bet that the number is extremely low. And even lower would be the number of people who have never at least thought about and been tempted by the taboo. There might be a handful in the entire world, but I'd venture a guess that that's pretty optimistic. If Christian history is to be believed, our species has been fascinated with the forbidden since the beginning of time . . . or at least the beginning of *our* time.

But as gay brothers and sisters we have a special fascination with the taboo. We identify with it intimately, because according to (the published figure of) nine out of ten people on earth, we are taboo ourselves. We are freaks of nature, something of the supernatural, a sin and an abomination. Our lives and our relationships threaten the sanctity of traditional heterosexual marriage and incite much anger and hatred among otherwise seemingly rational and educated people. We are bad, bad things and we can hurt you.

And so we relate to the taboo. We seek it out often. We embrace it.

This book is a look at several taboos that are imposed upon us by society, much as are restricting a woman's right to choose whether to have a baby and what to do and not to do with her body, the legal drinking age of twenty-one even though you can vote and risk your life "for the good of your country" by going to war three years earlier, and a class and tax system in our country that makes it easier for the rich to get richer and much harder for the poor to dig their way out of poverty to make a decent living.

Some readers may agree with some of the above-mentioned societal norms, and may even agree that some of the taboos listed in this book should remain taboo and not permitted or engaged in. And that's okay. My goal is not to change anyone's mind about what is right and wrong or to dictate what one thinks or how one feels about any subject. There is enough of that in the world today, and in my opinion, that is the true sin and the undoing of any civilization. What I do hope the book will do is allow readers to take a fresh look at established taboos, to examine the who's and the why's and the individual circumstances behind them, and to make up their own minds about what they believe about the taboos.

Universally, very few things are as taboo as sex. Somehow, over thousands of years of human evolution, we've managed to take something very pure and very honest and very pleasurable and turn it into something forbidden and disgusting and sinful. The act of sex itself hasn't changed, but people's moral reactions to it and their fear of it have. And we all know that when we're afraid of something, we either run from it as fast as we can or try to manipulate it to fit into our realm of understanding.

In this book I've divided the taboos into four different geographical areas of the United States. That does not by any stretch of the imagination mean that taboos listed in one geographical area are exclusive to that area. Never is that the case, as a matter of fact. For the most part, taboos are universal and know no boundaries. But certain areas of the United States are perceived to hold certain principles more dearly than others, and I've tried to pair the taboos with overlying principles that are prominent in the given regions. For example, many people in every state of the country believe that interracial relationships are wrong and taboo . . . but because of the history of the deep South, I've included the story dealing with interracial sex in the Deep South section of the book. The West Coast is considered to be very relaxed, both physically and morally, and so the stories in that section reflect that lifestyle. And the East Coast is considered sophisticated and wealthy and "old school," and the stories in that portion of the book deal with taboos that address those values.

Taboo is divided into four sections: West Coast, Middle America, Deep South, and East Coast. Each section opens with a portion of a longer novella, where the main character travels from San Francisco to New York City and details his sexual adventures along the way. As Chance McAllister drives across the country, we follow his journey of self-discovery as he gets closer and closer to the past he left behind several years ago. After the chapter of the novella, each section has three independent short stories highlighting a different taboo sex act.

I truly hope you enjoy the stories in this collection. Although some of these taboos are controversial and might be hot buttons for some, my desire in these stories is to allow you to put aside any judgments or moral values or preconceived ideas of the situations and to look at them with an open mind and determine for yourself how you feel about them. There are way too many people judging us for being who we are. I hope we can remove ourselves from that group and embrace our uniqueness, our intelligence, our talents, and our diversity, and ultimately be proud of who we are, what we believe, and what we do.

THE
WEST
COAST

What do you think of when you think of the West Coast? It's my favorite part of the United States, and I desperately long to move back to my beloved San Francisco. It's such a unique part of the country, and it elicits different images from people who call it home or who have visited it.

For me, the West Coast screams San Francisco. The City by the Bay is quite possibly the most diverse city in the country. People from every ethnic background, social class, education level, and spiritual mind-set call it home. For the most part, everyone gets along, and the people don't just tolerate the diversity of the city, they value and embrace it. It is the home of both the hippie movement and the gay movement, both of which define themselves by the themes of love and acceptance of all human beings in society.

Some people think of the warm and sunny beaches of Los Angeles or San Diego, with blond-haired and blue-eyed and smooth-muscled surfer dudes and gals. They are gnarly and unfazed by the demands of the bustling cities around them, and live only to hang ten and catch the next beach party.

Others see the tree-hugging, coffee-drinking, rain-loving yuppies in Seattle and Portland as the epitome of the West Coast lifestyle.

But whatever picture you have of the West Coast, one overlying theme prevails here. Slow down and smell the roses . . . or coffee. Take life one day at a time. Don't take yourself, or anyone else, too seriously. Live and let live. And most of all, don't judge others. Chill out.

The stories in this section deal with that mentality. Their characters struggle with finding their own identities, with leaving the past behind and moving on, with not taking themselves too seriously, and with having fun while maintaining their sense of self-value. The taboos here are prostitution, incest, and orgies/group sex. Although none of these taboos are exclusive to the West Coast, of course, they might be just a little more common here than . . . say in the hills of the Appalachians.

So, grab a cup of joe, kick off your sandals and let the surf tickle your toes, and let the waves take you to a place you might find oddly familiar.

A Matter of Chance

Part One
The West Coast

"Woo hoo!" someone yelled from inside the kitchen.

Chance wasn't even sure who it was. There were twenty-two men crammed in his tiny apartment. Most of them were gathered around the television, watching the Academy Awards, as had been their tradition for the past four years. But a few, those who'd been convinced by the second commercial that the show was rigged and that their favorites had no chance of winning their categories, huddled in the kitchen around the booze and food.

"Hell will freeze over and we'll elect a competent president before Angelina wins a Best Actress Award." The voice emerged from the kitchen, and Chance saw that it was Reggie. No big surprise there; he was the most vocal of the group by far. "And that is just a travesty of justice. Not to mention an embarrassment to the Academy and thespian-loving fags all across this fine nation."

"It's a good thing you don't lean toward the melodramatic." Chance laughed as he picked the last piece of pepperoni pizza from the box on the coffee table.

"Right?" Reggie said as he kicked several legs out of the way and made his way back to his seat.

From the kitchen behind him and the bedroom just to his left, Chance heard the phone ring. "Oh, hell no," he screamed. "Who the hell would be ignorant enough to call right as they're announcing Best Actress? James, can you get that? And tell them to get a life and call back after the awards."

"Who the fuck would be stupid enough to call in the middle of the most important evening of the year?" James yelled as he answered the phone. "Chance wants you to call back after . . ."

When he stopped in midsentence, Chance looked over to see his best friend turn as white as new snow. The look on his face was a mix of shock, fright, and mortification. "It's your mother," he said as he covered the phone. "She didn't sound amused."

Chance jumped up and grabbed the phone, and then ran into the bedroom.

"Hi, Mom," he said as he closed the door. "Is everything okay?" He closed his eyes and rubbed his temples as he listened to her. "That was my friend James. Sorry, we're having an Academy Awards party, and we got a little carried away. No, he's really a very nice guy. I'm the one who was being disrespectful. I told him to say that."

He kicked his shoes off and lay on the bed. Experience told him that this would be a painful phone call. He hadn't spoken to his parents in more than a year. The last time had ended in a screaming match and his parents hanging up on him. He'd gotten his stubbornness from both of his parents, and so it didn't surprise him when they didn't call him back and try to mend the relationship. And he was sure it didn't surprise them that he hadn't made that move, either.

"Yes, I'm sure you *are* disappointed in me, Mother," he said, biting his bottom lip to keep from saying something they'd both regret. "But in my defense, you haven't called or written in more than a year. I really wasn't expecting it to be you. And my friends here know me well enough to know that answering the phone that way is a joke. And they'd know not to call me during the Academy Awards."

One of his guests knocked softly on the door, and then walked in, pointing to the bathroom. Chance nodded for him to go ahead and rolled his eyes at the phone in his hand.

"Yes, that is a gay thing, Mother. I don't mean to be rude, but I've got a house full of company. It'd be in poor taste to leave them unattended for too long. Why did you call me tonight?"

Normally Chance wasn't this bold. Normally he'd be quiet and listen to his mother without talking back. Normally he'd cringe at the icy tone of his mother's voice and the harsh indifference in his father's. But today was not a normal day, and this entire week had been far from ordinary. Earlier in the week, he'd been passed over for a promotion for the third time in six months. And just a couple days ago, he'd gotten in a horrible argument with his boss. And to top it all off, that blond bitch Cameron won a Best Supporting Actress award earlier in the night, and it looked like goddess Angelina was not going to win her most deserved Best Actress trophy. Life was not fair, and Chance had had just about enough. His mother calling out of the blue and interrupting his evening was just the last straw. And it was quite possible that the six margaritas and mojitos he'd had in the last two hours had emboldened him just a little.

But perhaps he'd chosen the wrong night to assert himself. He'd thought he was strong enough and prepared enough for just about anything. But he was wrong.

"What?" he screeched. "What happened? Is he okay?"

Chance listened without interrupting for the next ten minutes as his mother described, in vivid detail, his father's stroke a couple of days previous. Chance was confused about what he should feel at hearing the news. His mind told him that he should be sad and shocked, that maybe he even ought to cry. But his heart told him that he shouldn't give a damn, that he should remain angry and upset and indifferent with his parents for disowning him eight years ago and sending him to Stanford so that he'd be as far from them as possible.

The reality was, however, that he was numb. He didn't feel a thing when his mother announced that his father was gravely ill. When she started crying and saying she didn't know what she was going to do and how she was going to get through the next several months, he didn't even blink or clear his throat.

And then he felt as if he'd been struck in the throat with a brick, or perhaps a baseball bat. He tried to breathe, but couldn't. He tried to speak, but couldn't. It took him a full five minutes, and the goading of his mother, to squeak out a response.

"That's out of the question, Mother," he said quietly, and then cleared his throat. "There's no way I can go . . . home. I'm very busy at work."

It'd been a long time since his mother had made him feel like a child. His father had always been quiet and somewhat listless, and never had much to say to Chance, either positive or negative. But he never said anything to his wife as she ripped into him, and so Chance always thought that his father might be somewhat afraid of his mother as well. A few times, Chance had seen his father roll his eyes as his mother went on one of her famous rants, but for the most part he kept his eyes on the television and his left hand on the omnipresent can of Bud Light that accompanied him when he was home.

But his mother had always been skilled at making him feel small and insignificant. She didn't even need to speak a word to silence him. Most of the time all it took was one of her patented single raised eyebrows. He could count on one hand the number of times he'd talked back to her, and the number was equal to the number of times he'd been on the receiving end of her wicked backhand. Now, even three thousand miles away, he swore he could feel the sting of her hand across his cheek.

"Yes, Mother, I know you didn't raise me to speak to you like that," he said as he peeked into the living room. The ending credits were rolling across the screen, and his friends were moving the leftover pizza boxes, beer bottles, and potato chips into the kitchen. He knew from experience that that was as far as they'd go. They wouldn't actually clean up. "But I'm not the little boy that you used to smack around. I've grown up and become my own man, and I make my own decisions, including how I speak and to whom."

He held the phone a few inches from his ear, fully expecting to hear his mother scream. Her rants and raves were known coast to coast, and anyone who knew her made a point of not incurring them. He also expected a long string of expletives, some of whose origin were suspect, at the least. And he was certain the conversation would end with the click from the other end of the line, as their last call had.

What he was not prepared for was the soft moan of his mother's cry, or how quickly that simple whimper made him agree to return home.

It took him a couple of days to get everything lined up so that he could take off, and he honestly thought that given a couple of days to think about it, he'd have chosen to back out of his word and not leave. But he had three weeks of vacation and personal leave available at work, had asked James to house- and plant-sit for him, and now, two days after his mother's phone call, he was throwing his packed bags into the trunk and sliding behind the wheel of his new Saturn Sky.

The sporty convertible had been his one indulgence on himself in the past five years. He'd always wanted to own a fun sports car but had never entertained the idea of actually owning one. His parents had instilled in him very successfully the common sense and value of driving a fuel-efficient four-door sedan, and he'd obliged by tooling around first in a run-down Geo Metro for a few years, and then upgrading to a Saturn Ion. He loved the Saturn so much that when he finally grew his backbone and decided he was going to make his next car a true reflection of himself, the Sky was an easy choice. It was cute and funky and sporty and fun . . . just like him.

Chance's mother had balked at the idea of him driving all the way across the country, making a big fuss about how dangerous it was. He knew she was really only concerned about the amount of time it'd take him to get there. She'd tried to talk him into flying, even offering to pay for the ticket. But he'd insisted on driving his new car to New York. He needed some time to think and prepare himself for the next couple of weeks, and the fresh air from driving across the country would be perfect.

He looked in the rearview mirror as he pulled away from the curb, not really sure what he was looking back at, or what he expected to look back at him. James wouldn't be coming over until after work later that evening. None of his friends had gotten up early to see him off. He didn't have a dog or a cat. So he just stared at the single empty window with the tasteful and expensive mauve and teal treatment as it got smaller and smaller in the mirror. When he could no longer see the window, or his apartment complex, or even his neighborhood, he took a deep breath and ran his fingers through his hair as he gained speed and exited the city.

San Francisco had been his home for the past eight years. It hadn't been his first choice of a home, and he ended up there by accident, really. He'd been quite happy attending NYU back home, and discovering himself and his newfound sexuality. And when he met Dylan, he'd felt as if he'd found the part of him that he'd always known was missing and just waiting to be discovered. They spent every spare moment of every day together and had started talking about possibly moving in together.

But when Chance finally worked up the nerve to tell his parents that he was gay, and to introduce them to his boyfriend, his home, and in fact his entire world, collapsed around him. Nothing in his nineteen years of living with his parents had led him to believe that they'd welcome the news with open arms and a congratulatory cigar. But neither had it prepared him for the fury with which they unleashed their disgust and hatred.

Within a week, Chance was ripped out of NYU and on a plane to Palo Alto to live with his father's brother and sister-in-law. He started Stanford the following term and never heard from Dylan again. San Francisco was less than hour away, and so it didn't take long for Chance to discover it, and once he did, he came out with a vengeance. Before the school year was over, he'd moved out of his uncle's house and into a tiny studio in the Mission District.

That was four apartments, two cars, six jobs, and a dozen two-month stands ago, and he'd never once been compelled to return home. He'd become strong, he'd become independent, and he'd become proud. Yet with his father's typically silent stroke, and the anything-but-typical quiet whimper of his mother, he was putting his life on hold and driving three thousand miles alone to face his demons, as his mother would say.

"God*damn*, why do I let them get to me like this?" Chance said as he slammed his fist into the steering wheel. "I'm not a fucking kid anymore. I have my own life to live and to worry about."

He hadn't let them affect him in a long time, and resented

the helpless feeling it brought to the surface. He took a couple of deep breaths and drank in the warmth of the sun on his face and the wind blowing through his hair. Just north of Santa Barbara he noticed a sign announcing a rest stop and realized he'd been driving for three hours without stopping.

He pulled into the stop and took a few moments to stretch. It was one of the larger rest stops he'd seen along the six-hour drive down California's scenic Pacific Coast Highway, with a small park, plenty of parking spaces and RV hookups, a long line of vending machines, and a huge cinder block building housing the men and women's restrooms and showers.

There were only four other vehicles parked there: two eighteen-wheelers, a minivan, and an old beat-up convertible Jeep Wrangler with a surfboard tied to the frame and numerous bumper stickers extolling the praises of surfing, boarding, and "hanging ten." One of the big trucks was quiet, and sheets covered the windows from the inside. Several feet away the other truck had the driver door open, and Chance could hear the twang of Willie Nelson coming from the stereo. On the other side of the long lot was the minivan, parked right next to the playground, where a man and women played with three young children.

Chance loved the smell of the ocean, and he took a deep breath. The crash of the waves somewhere in the distance made him realize how badly he had to pee. He locked his car and walked into the men's room.

He was surprised at how clean it was. He'd heard and read stories of roadside truck stops and rest stops that had made him cringe. This place didn't live up to that reputation at all. His shoes didn't stick to the floor as he walked, the walls weren't covered in graffiti, and it didn't smell like the entire homeless population of New York City had relieved itself there recently. The gray walls were clean and graffiti free, save for one "Jesus Loves You" proclamation right next to the paper towel dispenser. The counters and trash cans were emptied and looked newly cleaned. There were three urinals and three stalls in the room, and all of the stalls had their doors intact.

Chance walked over to the urinal bank and unzipped. About halfway through his flow he heard a rustling sound to his right. He looked over at the wall to the stall a few feet away. There was a crude hole, about four inches in circumference, somewhat resembling a circle cutout about three feet above the floor. From the other side of the wall Chance could see a naked thigh and a hand covering part of the guy's crotch. Below the wall, a pair of orange and yellow beach shorts crumpled around the ankles of the stall's occupant. Long legs stretched out and made a production of thumping the big sandals on the concrete floor.

Chance's heart sped up, and he quickly finished peeing and shook his cock. Just the sight of the long tanned legs on the other side was causing his cock to respond. He looked harder into the hole and saw the guy was beating off. He couldn't make out any details, but the hands were moving a great deal over the crotch. Struggling to catch his breath, Chance stroked his cock as he took a step closer to the wall to get a better look.

Before Chance could reach the wall, a long, thick cock poked through the hole and hung heavily down the wall. It was not fully soft, but nowhere near hard either. It was plump and pink and covered in a thin layer of foreskin. Chance thought he might never have seen a more beautiful cock, not even in pictures or videos, and licked his lips. Even from the moment it peeked through the hole, it was impressive, but as it lay there exposed to the air and to whoever happened to be standing outside the stall, it began to pump and grow larger and even more remarkable.

"Come on dude, suck it," the guy on the other side of the wall said impatiently.

Chance dropped to his knees. Face to face with the cock now, it seemed monstrous. He was barely able to close both fists around the thick cock, and there was still room for another fist, if he'd had one. It was hot, and throbbed in his hands as he squeezed it. He felt the fat veins press against the tender skin of his palms. A clear drop of precum oozed from the tip, and that was all Chance could take.

He licked at the precum, and when the guy moaned loudly, he took the whole head of the cock inside his mouth.

"That's it, dude."

Chance flicked his tongue around the hard head as he sucked another inch or so of the giant cock into his mouth. God, it felt so good . . . sweet and hard and soft all at the same time. He felt his face flush as the head pressed against the back of his throat and then slid down his esophagus. His mouth was filled and his lips stretched to their limit as he swallowed the last couple of inches deep into his throat.

"Fuck yeah, man," the guy on the other side of the wall said. "Suck my dick."

Chance did his best at breathing through his nose and not choking to death, and prayed that it passed as the stranger's idea of having his dick sucked. The huge cock slid slowly in and out of his mouth for a few moments, and then began pounding him with more force. It knocked him off balance and to the floor as he struggled to keep it in his mouth. His own cock was hard and begging to be freed, but he didn't dare reach for it. The guy was fucking his face seriously and would knock him over if he didn't hold on to the floor and wall with both hands.

"That's it, dude, you're gonna make me cum. Keep sucking my dick like that."

Apparently he was a better cocksucker than he'd given himself credit for, because he had no idea that the guy could've been anywhere near close enough to cumming. But as hot as this all was for him, it was not the way he wanted it to end. He slowly and carefully pulled his mouth off the big cock and kissed the head gently before pulling himself to his feet.

"Aww, come on, man," the guy moaned from the other side of the wall. "You can't stop now. I'm so close." His giant cock bounced up and down several times and dripped a long string of precum to prove his point.

Chance quickly unbuttoned his jeans and slipped them down his legs. His cock sprang free and bobbed painfully in front of him. He moaned loudly as his fist wrapped around it, and he leaned forward and pressed his ass against the hard cock still sticking through the hole and begging for attention. A million thoughts flew through his head at once . . . the guy on the other side could be an ugly troll with warts and hair on his face, he might be really fat or horribly disfigured, he might be seventy years old, for crying out loud. Or heaven forbid he be a cop. But none of that mattered then. The only thing Chance cared about was sliding his ass onto the hard thick cock and riding it like a champion bull rider.

"Fuck me," he barely whispered as he pressed his ass against the hot head of the big cock.

"What?" the guy asked.

"I said fuck me," he said louder, and impaled himself onto the fat rod in one quick move. When the head slid inside the sphincter, it made a popping sound, and Chance took a deep breath as he slid his ass all the way down the length of the rod until it rested against the cold wooden wall behind him.

"Damn, dude, that's fuckin' amazing," the faceless stranger grunted as he slammed the big cock deeper inside Chance and wiggled it around.

Chance bit down on his lower lip to keep from yelling out in pain. Tears formed in his eyes as the cock began sliding in and out of him, and he wondered if he'd ever be able to walk normally again. *It hurts, it hurts,* was all he could think. Yet, instead of pulling off it and running away, he thrust himself back onto the fat cock harder each time. And instead of begging the guy to stop, he moaned deeply and begged him to "Fuck me harder, man. Fuck my brains out."

The thin wooden partition between the two creaked and moaned in protest as Chance took every deep and furious thrust. It echoed throughout the empty restroom, and Chance worried that their moans and the sound of the wood being torn apart like a tornado ripping through it would carry out into the parking lot and draw attention to them.

"Maybe we should try not to make so much noise," he said softly.

"Fuck . . . that . . ." the guy said in a staccato tone as he slammed his cock deeper into Chance's gut with each word. "I'm . . . gonna . . . fuck . . . you . . . until . . . you . . . fuckin' . . . drop."

That might not be as long as the guy hoped for, Chance thought. Each time the huge cock slid deep inside him, it banged his prostate and sent pleasure waves throughout every inch of his body. His t-shirt scrunched up around his neck and down his arms awkwardly, and his ass clutched and squeezed and massaged the big cock. It felt to Chance as if his ass were dancing along the big pole. His own cock throbbed painfully and begged for attention, but when Chance grabbed it, he knew it was all over.

"Fuck, man," he screamed, "I'm gonna cum!"

The guy on the other side of the stall quickened his pace and pulled his cock all the way out of Chance's ass and then slammed it all the way back in a couple of times, with lightning speed.

"Ungh . . ." Chance grunted, and his load shot from his

cock and sprayed in every direction as he continued to get fucked. Some of it landed on his face and chest, more of it on his arms, and some on the floor and the urinal a few feet in front of him.

"Oh God, man," the stranger yelled, "here I cum!" He ripped his cock from Chance's ass in a brutal withdrawal, causing Chance to whimper.

A second later he felt the first wave of the stranger's cum splash hot across his neck and shoulders. Five or six more shots landed on his back, and several others dribbled across his ass cheeks and down his legs. He couldn't see the load, but it felt like there was much more there than was possible from one guy.

When the last of the cum had landed on him, and Chance heard the guy on the other side of the wall begin to pull up his shorts, he stood up and grabbed a handful of paper towels to wipe himself off. When he heard the door to the stall begin to open, Chance sucked in his gut and quickly pulled the t-shirt down to cover his chest and stomach.

The guy walked out of the stall and glanced briefly at Chance. He was taller than Chance had imagined, easily six foot five, with a smooth, tanned, and muscular chest. Chance could count the lines on his abs, and a thick, dark blond trail of hair started at his navel and disappeared into his orange and yellow surf shorts. He had a thick, full head of blond curly hair and the deepest blue eyes Chance had ever seen.

Chance was struck speechless with the beauty of the young man and stuck his hand out stupidly as the guy walked past him and to the bank of sinks to wash up.

As he washed in the sink, the surfer glanced at Chance in the mirror and winked at him with the slightest trace of a smile. "Thanks, dude," he said with a nod as he walked toward the door. "That was hot."

Chance just stood there and blinked several times, and brought his breathing back to normal. Then he ran to the window and watched the sexy surfer dude with the huge cock slide into the front seat of the Jeep Wrangler and peel out of the parking lot and onto the highway without a glance back.

He walked over to the showers at the other end of the room and started to undress. But he stopped after kicking off his tennis shoes and halfway through removing his socks. On second thought, he decided against a shower. He could still feel the huge thick load from the surfer dude drying against his skin, and decided to leave it there. It was going to be a very long drive back to New York City, and a little reminder of this hot afternoon would be a good thing.

He tied his shoes, ran a couple of handfuls of cold water across his face, and left the restroom. He could still feel the big cock in his ass, and he prayed to God that the little boy and girl watching him leave the restroom could not see the huge smile on his face.

The drive across the desert was every bit as painful as he'd imagined it would be. It was well over one hundred degrees with not a cloud in the sky, and so he wasn't able to ride with the top down but instead had the A/C full blast. This was not what he'd had in mind when buying the cute little sports car, and he was in a bad mood the entire ride from Santa Barbara to Las Vegas. But perhaps that was a blessing in disguise. It'd prepare him for the visit with his parents.

All his life his parents had been strict and cold and unloving. He'd heard stories of gay men and women whose parents had been loving and supportive of them before they came out, and then became the opposite with the news of their children's sexual orientation. But that wasn't the case with Chance. His parents had been that way since he could remember. Not once could he remember his mother having a kind or encouraging word for him as he grew up. Never did she tell him he could fly to the moon or be the next president of the United States if he wanted to be. Instead, she focused on all of the thousands of things he *couldn't* do. In addition to astronaut and president, the short list included asking out Cyndi Manheim to the eighth-grade prom—because she was out of his league; applying to Harvard—because he wasn't smart enough and shouldn't be so far from home (never mind the fact that they shipped him off to Stanford in a moment's notice, where he was easily accepted); and having any chance at anything more than mediocre happiness—because who did he think he was anyways, Donald Fucking Trump?

His father hadn't been any better a supporter. He never directly told Chance that he couldn't do anything or couldn't become whatever he put his mind to. But his silent indifference and the disgust with which he accepted his own miserable existence spoke volumes. Chance grew up believing that life was a series of wretched events to be tolerated and overcome and that happiness was something invented for children's books and Hallmark cards. People were meant to be unhappy, uncomfortable, and disagreeable.

By the time he approached the Las Vegas city limits sign, he had a headache and was more depressed than he'd been in years. Perhaps the let's-be-miserable-to-prepare-for-the-visit-with-the-parents thing needed to be re-evaluated. The thought of a migraine and the overwhelming sense of dread he was currently experiencing lasting for three days was more than he could take.

It was just approaching dawn, and Chance was tired. He hadn't planned out his trip at all—not which highways and routes to take, which hotels or motels to stay in, or which gay hot spots he really shouldn't miss. He hadn't really had time to plan that much, and all other excuses cast aside, he just hadn't been able to bring himself to think about the trip and its inevitable destination.

He'd been to Vegas several times and had stayed in a few of the hotels on the Strip. Sahara was his favorite, and the one where he'd stayed the most often. It was modestly priced, had good and inexpensive food, and always seemed to have rooms available, even without a reservation. He drove there from memory, checked in, and threw himself on the big bed.

He hadn't meant to fall asleep, really—just thought he'd lie down and rest for a few minutes before going down to dinner. But when he finally opened his eyes and rolled over to look at the clock, three hours had passed. It was almost midnight.

"Fuck," he said, and jumped out of bed and into the shower.

He grabbed a sandwich and salad at the hotel's twenty-four-hour Caravan Café and asked the waitress about any good shows in the hotel.

"Well, currently we have a really amazing magician appearing in the Congo Room. I haven't seen the show yet myself, but I hear it's really good."

Chance scrunched his nose. "I'm not really into the whole magic thing," he said.

The pretty blond waitress looked down at his t-shirt, which had a large rainbow flag on the right chest and "Proud Fag" embroidered into the left short sleeve. "I don't blame you," she said, as she sat on the chair across from him, and winked. "The Sahara Theater has a show called 'Matsuri,' and it's really amazing. I've seen it, and it took my breath away. Lots of really hot and half-naked guys doing gymnastics and martial arts tricks and stuff. I don't know what all of it was about, but it was incredible to watch, and I couldn't take my mind off all the beautiful men."

Chance laughed. "Yeah, that's much more what I'm looking for."

"I thought so." She smiled and patted his hand. "The performers come in for dinner and breakfast a couple times a week. I happen to know that several of the male cast play for your team, because they asked me to refer them to some gay bars. They usually only do one show a night, but tonight they're doing a special fundraising show at 1:00. I doubt they've sold out. If you hurry, you can probably make it."

"Thanks," Chance said, and slid a ten dollar bill toward her. "You're a lifesaver."

The waitress laughed. "Have fun . . . and be safe!"

The show was every bit as entertaining as Missy had promised. Not quite Cirque du Soleil caliber, but with a comparable style and smaller, more intimate environment. They had aerial acrobats, martial arts presentation artists, and gymnasts performing feats that Chance had never imagined. And Missy was right, the men were stunning. Their bodies were smooth and tight and tanned, and glistened in sweat and the theater lighting. They were all shirtless, and most of them wore tight shorts or tights that left absolutely nothing to the imagination.

There was one performer in particular, a gymnast, who caught Chance's attention immediately and wouldn't let it go. He was short, about five foot six, with a body right out of a Michelangelo sculpture. His skin was dark and smooth and perfectly muscled. He looked to be of an Asian/Latino mix, with strongly defined bone structure, black hair and dark eyes, and a smile that lit up the large room. His nipples were tiny and stood at attention the entire time he was on stage. His abs looked like a Bowflex commercial, and Chance was mesmerized by the way the tiny drops of sweat rolled down his chest and stomach and rode the ridged muscles on his abs like a raft rolling along a whitewater rafting adventure.

The gymnast's tights were sheer to the point of being almost translucent, and they hugged his massive thighs like a second skin. They didn't even come close to concealing the huge bulge that protruded from his crotch. Chance couldn't stop staring at the guy, and especially at the big bump right below his waist, and halfway through the show the bulge began to grow noticeably.

Chance was sitting in the second row and had an unobstructed view of the protuberance. It caused his own cock to swell in his jeans. When he glanced up and into the guy's face, he was surprised to see the gymnast matching his own gaze as he caught his breath between stunts and acknowledged the audience's accolades. Chance's heart raced as he watched the guy finish his last couple of routines and then bow gracefully as the audience gave him a standing ovation. As the gymnast strode off the stage, he locked eyes with Chance and winked, and Chance felt his knees quiver with excitement.

The next act was some Chinese acrobat thing with about a dozen demure girls and half a dozen nondescript guys. Chance couldn't keep his mind on it and was deep in his own world fantasizing about the gymnast. He didn't even notice the usher tapping him on his shoulder.

"Sir," the young man whispered into Chance's ear as he tapped him harder.

Chance jumped a little and looked at the usher.

"You've been invited backstage by one of the performers. Would you like to come with me?"

Chance was up and out of his seat even before the college kid had finished the question. He followed the usher behind the stage and through a winding hallway.

"Second door on the right," the usher said, and turned to leave.

Chance walked the last few feet to the door, took a deep breath, and knocked tentatively.

"Come in," he heard from behind the door.

He opened the door and closed it softly behind him. The room was empty, but a light lit up a hallway to the right, and Chance walked toward it. The dressing room was to the left, and when Chance walked in, he gasped.

The gymnast was completely naked and leaning against the counter. His cock was fully hard and bouncing in front of him. It was long and thick, with blue veins snaking the entire shaft, and big shaved balls hung below the big cock.

"Come over here and suck my dick, dude," the young man said.

Chance walked over to the counter and dropped to his knees. He wrapped his fist around the thick cock and shivered as the heat from the throbbing dick pulsated through his hand, up his arm, and across his chest. He licked the fat head for a moment, and then sucked it into his mouth.

"Oh yeah, man," the gymnast said.

Chance sucked just the head for a couple of minutes, and then slid his mouth down the big cock a couple of inches. He loved the way the thick veins pulsed against his lips, and flicked at the head as he swallowed more and more of the cock deeper into his mouth. When the head bumped against the back of his throat, he yawned and swallowed at the same time, which opened the back of his throat and allowed the giant cock to slip past and farther down his gullet.

"Fuck, dude," the guy moaned as he leaned back and thrust his cock all the way into Chance's throat until his balls rested against Chance's chin. "That's so fucking hot."

The fat cock leaked a good amount of precum, and Chance swallowed it hungrily as the gymnast thrust his big dick in and out of his mouth. Most of it pumped down his throat as the mushroom head slid past his tonsils, but a few drops landed on his tongue, and Chance loved the sweet taste and silky texture, and savored it in his mouth as long as he could before the sliding cock forced it down his gullet.

"God, man, that feels incredible," the guy moaned. "I'm really close."

Chance was torn. On one hand he wanted to keep sucking the big dick for hours on end, teasing it and getting it close, and then pulling back and keeping him right at the edge. But on the other hand he wanted more than anything to drain this hot man of his load and to swallow every last drop of it.

The gymnast wasn't torn, though, and knew exactly what he wanted. He grabbed Chance by the back of the head and pulled his face closer to his crotch. When his cock was buried deep in Chance's throat, he moaned and his knees began to shake.

The first couple of shots splashed against the back of his throat and caused him to gag as he tried to swallow all of it without letting any of it drip from his mouth. It was warm and sweet, and there was so much of it that it felt as if he were swallowing a tepid milkshake. The last few drops oozed out of the dick head and slid languidly across his tongue, causing the hairs on his arms and legs to stand at attention.

"Damn, dude, that was amazing," the gymnast said as he caught his breath. "You've got a fucking incredible mouth."

"Thanks," Chance said as he wiped his lips.

"I'm starving, but I'd love for you to fuck me if you're game. We could grab a bite to eat and then head up to my room."

"Oh, I'm definitely game," Chance said.

"Cool. Let's go."

When they walked into the Caravan Café, Missy smiled and gave Chance the "thumbs-up" sign and pointed them to one of her empty tables as she went to get the coffeepot.

Blond Ambition

"She scares me."

Ricky laughed at his friend. "Why?"

"Because she's fuckin' hot, dude," Dean said nervously, and reached down to rearrange the thickening bulge in his jeans. "I wanna fuck her brains out."

"You do know that *she* is a *he*, right?"

"Yeah, that's why she scares me," Dean said as he swallowed the last of his beer. "Keep it away from me."

"She's not an 'it,' and if she hears you say something like that, she will probably kick your ass all the way back to campus," Ricky whispered as he grabbed his roomie by the arm. "Lady Chablis is an icon not only at R Place but in Seattle. Hell, all over the country. Didn't you see *Midnight in the Garden of Good and Evil*?"

"What's that?"

"Man, you need to get some fuckin' culture. Anyway, she's famous, and she considers all these performers 'her girls.' Including the one that is giving you that boner. Don't let all the dresses and the rainbow décor fool you . . . these girls can hold their own, and the guys here won't hesitate to jump in when needed. Not to mention, Lady Chablis is the host of the contest tonight and I need the money. So do us both a favor and keep your fat trap shut, okay?"

"Whatever, dude," Dean said, and left to get another beer.

"Ladies and . . . well, let's face it, those of you who aren't classy enough to be ladies are still just a bunch of Marys anyway."

The large crowd roared its approval as the icon batted her eyelashes playfully.

"Please take your hands out of your crotches for a moment and put them together for our next amateur contestant . . ." She looked at the small piece of paper in her hand. "Ricky!"

The audience clapped politely but drifted away from the stage indifferently as the host disappeared behind the curtain. Ricky strutted onto the stage anyway as the opening bars of "Love Is a Battlefield" blared over the sound system and across the room. He didn't need to have every guy in the room drooling over him . . . just enough of the older, lonelier ones to clap louder for him than they did for the other contestants. It wouldn't be difficult; Ricky was the last stripper of the night, and he'd seen all the others and heard the reactions from the audience.

He swaggered across the stage slowly and deliberately, and allowed only the slightest hint of a smile to crack the sultry pout on his lips as he took in the crowd's reaction. The applause started out tentative but didn't take long to crescendo to overpower the loud music. Then they began hooting and whistling, and the undercurrent of men who'd floated toward the bar just a couple of seconds earlier now stopped in their tracks, turned back and took a moment to assess him, and then surged forward as a single entity toward the stage.

Ricky's father was Spanish and his mother was Venezuelan.

He was blessed with his father's strong, masculine jawline and bone structure and his mother's full, pouty lips and seductive, sultry eyes . . . one brown and one green, with thick black lashes. He wished he was just a little taller but couldn't complain too much. At five foot ten and 165 pounds, his long, muscular legs made him look taller than he was. He played tennis regularly and was captain of the wrestling team at the University of Washington, Seattle, so every muscle on his body was solid and ripped. His copper-colored skin was naturally smooth, and he kept his head shaved to match it. He wore a diamond stud in one ear and a small gold hoop in the other. One large tattoo of a naked angel with his wings spread covered two-thirds of Ricky's back and shoulders, and he had a tribal band tattooed on his left bicep.

None of this went unnoticed by the appreciative audience. When Ricky shrugged off his leather jacket apathetically and tossed it to the floor, they shouted and pounded their beer bottles on the wooden tables. His tiny nipples stood at attention, and the six lines that crisscrossed his abs glistened with sweat as the spotlight caressed his torso. He was the perfect image of a hardened street kid, maybe even a gangbanger. And then his full, pink lips parted to reveal a sparkling white smile that would melt the heart of a serial killer and make any grandmother pull his picture from her purse and show it proudly to strangers on the street. His eyes sparkled in the lights, and his facial features softened to show his sensitivity even as his muscles hardened and flexed seemingly of their own accord as he shucked each layer of clothing.

"Oh, honey!" Lady Chablis gasped into the microphone as she appeared suddenly from behind the curtain. "I felt your heat all the way back in my dressing parlor. You're makin' it hard for the Lady to hide her T, do you know what I mean?"

She fanned herself with an ornate Japanese fan. "Go ahead, child, you just keep doin' what you're doin'," she said as she leaned against the wall and watched.

Ricky winked and blew her a kiss, then turned his back to the audience and kicked his jeans from his legs and across the floor to her. Now, in nothing but a skimpy, almost see-through white g-string, he commanded every eye and every breath in the bar. His ass was round and hard and smooth as marble. He bent forward and wrapped his fists around his ankles, and smiled and winked at the audience from upside down between his legs, and they whistled and clapped louder and yelled for him to take it all off.

He teased them a little longer, dancing with his back to the crowd, and shook his ass quickly. His booty bounce was legendary. When he slipped his thumbs into the waistband and dipped the back of the thong down a couple of inches, the audience went into a frenzy, and Ricky knew the $200 prize was his.

"Oh my God," Lady Chablis breathed heavily into the mic as she stared at Ricky's crotch, "you guys should see the package on this hottie."

"Turn around," the mob yelled.

Ricky laughed, and turned around. The thin pouch failed miserably at containing his cock, and it bulged out impressively in front of him. When he looked down, he saw the thick patch of black hair that started at his navel and dipped beneath the extended waistband of his g-string. His naked cock began to throb and grow as he looked at it lying barely concealed in the skimpy pouch of the g-string. He blushed and quickly covered his crotch with one hand as he reached for his jeans with the other.

"NO!" the crowd yelled as they clapped and stomped their feet.

Lady Chablis bent down delicately and picked up his jeans, and made a production of teasing him with them before relinquishing them. "Sorry, boys," she yelled backstage to the other contestants. "There's no need to vote tonight. Ricky, baby, go collect your rent money. Or better yet, come live with me. The Lady Chablis will not charge you rent, baby."

McMahon Hall was the residence that everyone at UW Seattle wanted to call home. Its unique layout and design made it the perfect place to party for the uber popular and the perfect place to hold study groups for the computer geeks. Suites of four double rooms clustered around a shared lounge and bathroom. Almost every room had a spectacular view of Lake Washington and the Cascade Mountains. Guys and girls shared floors but had separate suites, which made it convenient to mingle and make friends. The waiting list was long, and even though it was against school policy to discriminate against anyone for any reason, it was widely known that with the exception of a couple of suites for the super brainy to give the illusion of noneliticism, only the elite were selected to call McMahon Hall home.

Dean and Ricky shared a room, and the other three rooms of their suite were occupied by members of UWS's tennis, gymnastics, and swimming teams. The boys thought nothing of hanging around the lounge watching TV or playing video games in nothing but their underwear, and even completely in the nude if they were doing laundry and all their underwear was dirty.

A few of the guys were in the lounge playing a game of quarters.

"Dude, you going to that freak bar again tonight?" Dean said as he tossed a handful of popcorn into his mouth.

"Why?" Ricky asked as he stepped out of the shower and

dried himself. "You want me to give your little girlfriend a note or something? It's only been two weeks since you were there. I'm sure she'd remember you."

"Fuck you, Montoya."

"In your dreams." Over the past few weeks Ricky had noticed his roommate was around a lot when he finished showering and had caught a few of Dean's glances as he took his time patting the water from his body. Twice in the past week, he'd known that he was being watched as he beat off in bed. He pretended to fall asleep quickly after cumming but was wide awake as he watched Dean beat off frantically just a few feet away. "No, I'm not going to R Place tonight. I'm going out with a couple of friends. Don't wait up."

He took his time getting dressed, making a production of slipping his tight jeans over his long, muscular legs and smooth, hard ass. He wasn't wearing any underwear and saw Dean staring at his ass from the reflection in the large mirror on the wall. The dude had no clue as to how to be discreet, and Ricky felt sorry for him.

"Can I go with you?" Dean asked.

"No, not tonight. The place I'm going to is not for rookies." He walked over to the built-in bureau and pulled a blond woman's wig from the bottom drawer. "Don't ask," he said with a raised eyebrow, and tossed the wig into his backpack as he left McMahon Hall.

The Cuff Complex was indeed not a place for rookies. It had long been known as Seattle's main cruise bar, and the current resurgence of "backroom" action in gay bars across the country made The Cuff one of the most popular hangouts in the city. Tall, cold, gray concrete walls formed a narrow maze-like walkway that connected the patio with the main upstairs bar. It was known as the Dog Run and was the reason for the bar's now-legendary status. Men lined the Dog Run every night of the week as the evening drew closer to last call, and it was here that most of the guys picked up their one-night stands that they would regret upon waking the next morning.

But Friday nights at the Dog Run were special. Five years ago, the owners of The Cuff Complex had started a night of entertainment called StarStruck. Local amateur performers would dress up as famous celebrities and compete on the patio for a meager cash prize. One night one of the contestants dressed up like Marilyn Monroe, and his performance got a little out of hand. He was drunk, his dress was short, and the men watching the show were even drunker. His performance turned into an orgy on the patio, and after that night, StarStruck transformed into the largest and most successful underground public sex forum in the Northwest.

The crowds quickly grew too large for the Dog Run to accommodate, and it didn't take long for the management of The Cuff to realize they could make a fortune with StarStruck. They struck up a cash deal with a couple of the more motivated performers and started charging a cover to get into the dark back alley. For the first couple of years they charged twenty bucks and split the take evenly with the performers. Most of the action was handjobs and blowjobs, and fairly low maintenance.

But one Friday night Ricky Montoya happened into The Cuff, and StarStruck was forever changed. He'd only stopped in for a quick drink before heading over to R Place. But several of the big men in black leather urged him to head outside to the Dog Run, and when he did, all eyes were on him. Marilyn got pissed when the men moved away from her and began migrating with their hard cocks in their hands toward the hot muscled stud with the shaved head. She threw her blond wig to the floor and stormed out and never returned.

As the group of men closed in around Ricky, he knew exactly what to do. He picked the wig up, placed it on his head, and stripped. As his cock grew hard and thick, the crowd grew larger and thicker, too. The bouncer at the door waved a fistful of bills around above his head. Ricky stroked his cock and spread his smooth ass cheeks apart for the men to see, and they went wild.

His first show netted him five hundred dollars. He took over Marilyn's spot for the last Friday of the month, and every time his earnings increased significantly. In less than three months The Cuff was drawing more men than they could contain on the last Friday of every month. Something had to be done, and so the management increased the cover charge to fifty dollars. No one even blinked, and Ricky was taking home between fifteen hundred and two thousand dollars a night after every show.

He thought the wig was a little silly and had tried to discard it after the first couple of times. He never wore a dress or high heels like Marilyn did, nor did he sing and bounce about giggling like a schoolgirl. So he didn't see the point of the wig. But the men who beat off as they watched him strip let it be known that they liked beating off to a ripped, tattooed, exotic college jock with a cheesy platinum wig, and for a couple grand a night, Ricky was willing to beat off for the men and pout like Marilyn.

When he walked into the bar, the applause was deafening. "Ricky's here, everybody," the bartender yelled above the noise. "The party has officially started."

Ricky laughed. "Thanks, Arnie, but I think I might need a couple of drinks before I get started. It's still early. We're in no rush, are we, boys?"

They gravitated toward and around him as if he were the Pope in a crowd of elderly Catholic women. But with big bushy mustaches and black leather vests and chaps that barely covered their cocks and didn't even pretend to cover their hairy asses. They all clamored to push a drink his way.

He always played a couple games of pool and had two or three drinks before his show, and the men at The Cuff watched him play pool with the same fanaticism with which they watched him masturbate. Ricky appreciated their admiration, and tossed his shirt aside early on, and made a point of flexing his muscles and groping his crotch every couple of minutes. He was never at want for a drink.

"Showtime," he said once the third Long Island Iced Tea kicked in. His cock was already starting to respond.

There was already a line of about forty men at the door to the Dog Run. Gary the bouncer was standing at the entrance, ready to collect the fifty dollars from each of them, and directed the other fifty or so men following Ricky around like lost puppies to the end of the line. Before the night was over, Ricky would do two shows, and the second was always as hot as the first. The size of the paying crowd would range between 100 and 150, and Ricky would walk into McMahon Hall with at least $2,500 more than he had walked out of there with earlier in the evening.

His first show quickly sold out and even packed in more men than the Dog Run could comfortably hold. He had about a four-foot circle roped off around him, which allowed him room to stroke his cock, move around just a little, and make sure everyone on all sides of him got a good look at both his front and back sides. For an extra twenty bucks tucked into his white socks, the guys right up front and closest to him could give his cock a stroke or two, or glide their hands across his smooth, muscular ass. This was above and beyond his take of the door money, and Ricky was generous with the men who were charitable with their hard-earned money. They knew he was a struggling college kid who needed to earn a living, and he knew they were men who worked hard to earn theirs. They had mutual respect for one another. A few of the men from the first show stepped right back into line for the second show later in the evening, and Ricky made sure to pay special attention to them and let them know he appreciated their kindness.

Halfway through his second show, as he was bent over and letting one of the repeat customers lick and kiss his ass and cheeks, he looked out across the mass of men and saw Dean staring wide-eyed at him. Ricky jerked up suddenly and reached for his clothes, but they weren't where he'd dropped them earlier. One of the waitstaff had picked them up and taken them to safety behind the bar. He panicked for just a moment, and then noticed that Dean's cock was out of his jeans and hard as stone.

He stepped from behind his roped area and walked through the crowd over to Dean. Without hesitating, he wrapped one hand around Dean's thick cock and squeezed it gently as he leaned in and kissed him on the mouth. This brought moans of approval from the audience, and Ricky knew what he was going to do next.

He continued kissing his roommate as he guided him through the crowd and to his staging area. He moved Dean inside the roped space and kissed his way down his strong, muscular chest and tight, flat stomach. He pulled Dean's jeans off and threw them aside, and licked the head of the thick, cut dick in front of him.

Ricky sucked on his friend's cock for a few minutes, savoring the taste and feel of it in his mouth. Dean stood perfectly still and seemed like he wasn't even breathing, so Ricky looked up and winked at him, and massaged his ass cheeks playfully. That seemed to relax Dean a little, and he smiled and began thrusting his cock slowly in and out of Ricky's mouth.

The crowd responded with a loud moan of approval and moved in closer to get a better view of the action. Ricky noticed several new guys had paid the cover and joined the already-packed Dog Run. It was going to be a good night for cash, and he decided to give them something special in return.

He stopped sucking Dean's cock, and stood up and kissed him again. "Do you want to fuck me?" he asked as he broke the kiss.

Dean just stared at him and blinked rapidly several times.

Ricky laughed. "I'm gonna take that as a yes." He stood on his toes and waved his hands high above his head to get Gary's attention. "Can you bring me a chair and a condom, please?"

The doorman stared at him questioningly and started to shake his head no, but Ricky knew that he wanted to watch the star of the show get fucked as much as everyone else there did. "It'll be okay. We can shut the door and make sure no one else gets in until we're done here."

Gary disappeared inside the bar and returned a minute later with a chair and a handful of condoms. Then he went back to the door, shut it, and leaned against it so that he could see the show.

Ricky handed one of the condoms to Dean and gave the rest to one of the men in the front to disperse among the crowd. He lifted one leg and rested it on the chair, making sure everyone had a good view of his ass, and then spread his cheeks. "Come on, baby. Fuck me," he said to Dean.

Dean fumbled with the condom, but once it was on, he slipped into autopilot. He grabbed Ricky by both sides of his ass and guided the head of his cock to the pink, twitching hole waiting for him.

Ricky took a deep breath, and then slid his ass backward onto his roommate's big cock. He moaned loudly as he felt the hot shaft tear his ass tunnel wider apart to accommodate its thickness. The initial pain quickly gave way to intense pleasure, and Ricky slid his ass up and down the length of Dean's cock, first slowly, and then quicker and with more fervor.

He looked at the men all around him. There were easily fifty or sixty men on the Dog Run, and all of them were beating off as they watched him take Dean's big dick deep up his ass. A few of the men came right away, but most tried to stop themselves too early and make the moment last as long as possible.

Ricky wanted it to last, too. He'd had the hots for Dean ever since they'd become roomies a year and a half ago. The guy could be a little naïve sometimes, and more than a little insensitive most of the time. But he was really sweet at heart, and was smart and funny and ambitious. Not to mention hot as hell. He was tall and very powerfully built, with legs that went on for days and abs that should have been patented by Maytag. And Ricky had fantasized about sucking that huge, thick pink cock since the first time he'd seen Dean step out of the shower.

Now that it was buried deep up his ass, Ricky meant to make the most of it. He squeezed the thick cock with his ass muscles, and when Dean moaned in appreciation, he rocked back and forth on it wildly. He'd already shot a load a couple hours earlier, and so he could have held out a little longer. But the men around him were spraying their loads in every direction, and the patio was beginning to look like the Drumheller Fountain back at campus, spraying giant jets of jizz up into the air. And Ricky could tell that Dean was about to lose it, too.

"Ready, boys?" Ricky yelled out to the crowd.

The few men who were able to vocalize their affirmatives did so, and everyone took a step closer.

"Pull out, baby," he whispered to Dean. "Let's spray our loads all over these guys."

Dean pulled out quickly and ripped the condom from his

cock. Ricky stood up and wrapped one fist around his cock, and his other arm around Dean's waist. The two roomies stroked their cocks teasingly for a moment, and then more fervently.

"Oh sweet Jesus," Dean yelled. His entire body stiffened as eight or nine huge jets of cum flew from his cock and out into the sea of men in front of him.

A unison moan of lust and desire and approval erupted from the crowd, and the few men who hadn't already emptied their loads did so.

"On your knees," Ricky ordered quickly.

Without thinking about it, Dean dropped to his knees in front of his roommate.

"FUUUUCK!" Ricky yelled.

His knees shook uncontrollably as stream after stream of jizz sprayed from his thick, uncut cock and across Dean's face. It seemed to go on forever, and when it finally did finish, his roommate's face was covered in thick, white cum. Ricky thought Dean would wipe it away hastily in disgust but was surprised when he licked as much as he could from his lips and mouth, and then rubbed the rest of it across his face and neck and chest.

The crowd stood completely still and quiet for a moment, trying to catch their breath and take in what they'd just witnessed. Then they slowly began to pull up their jeans and began looking for the rest of their clothes, which had been knocked around the small patio recklessly. Dean opened the door, and the crowd meandered back inside without saying a word to Rick and Dean or to one another. The code of silence had been established. There was safety there.

"What just happened?" Dean said. He looked dazed and confused.

"You fucked me in front of about a hundred guys," Ricky said as he collected the money from his socks and picked up the chair.

"But . . ."

"Did you like it?" Ricky asked softly as he set the chair down and looked into Dean's eyes. "Did you enjoy how I sucked your cock and how your dick felt inside my ass?"

"Yeah," Dean said awkwardly. "I loved it. I've been dreaming about it for over a year."

"Me, too. So now we don't have to just dream about it anymore. You can fuck me all you want, and I expect for you to learn how to get fucked too, because I love that sweet, hot ass of yours."

"Thanks," Dean said shyly, and blushed. "But, what about this?" he said, and looked around the patio.

"Last Friday of every month," Ricky said evenly. "Couple thou a night when it was just me. I can easily see that increasing significantly if we continue to double up. Those men were eating you up with their eyes. And I think they liked seeing me brought down to size just a little bit by getting my ass fucked long and hard. I can be a little cocky, sometimes."

"No shit." Dean laughed. "What about the other contest at that other place?"

"Just a teaser to get the guys in here for the bigger money. So what do you say? You game?"

"Only if I get to wear the wig when you fuck me in front of the group," Dean said, and grabbed the wig from Ricky and put it on his own head.

"Deal," Ricky said, and leaned in and kissed his roommate passionately. "Now let's go in and get a couple of drinks, then we can go home and do this the right way."

Dean reached down and entwined his long fingers with Ricky's, and led him back inside The Cuff.

My Brother's Keeper

"It's uncanny how much they look alike," President Daniels said as he stared at the cake sitting on the table in front of him.

"Yes, it is," Martha said. "The girl at the cake shop thought the picture was of the same boy. That it had been . . . oh, what do you call it?"

"Doctored."

"Yes, that's it!" she said excitedly. She balled her hands into fists and then unclenched them quickly as she glanced around the crowded kitchen. "I have no idea why they would use that term."

President Daniels watched her rush around the room, moving the cake from the table to the counter and then back again, rearranging the punch bowl and glasses for what must have been the third time in less than an hour. "They can use computers to superimpose an image of someone onto another, so two different pictures of the same person can be morphed together and look like . . . well, look like this. Or they can take a picture of a celebrity and another one of you or me and make it look like we're together, having dinner or discussing politics. Can you imagine having a picture of you and Brother Callahan having dinner with Frank Sinatra or President Reagan, God bless his soul?"

"Amazing," Martha said in a distracted tone, and then shook her head to emphasize her confusion. "But I suppose if they can make a cake frosting from an actual photo, then I shouldn't be surprised at anything."

He smiled at her and nodded his head in agreement. She was one of the sweetest people he'd ever met, and one of his most devoted parishioners. When he stepped down as stake president in six months, her husband would become the new leader of the second largest Latter-Day Saints district in Nevada, and President Daniels couldn't think of a better replacement. Sister Callahan might not have a master's degree in graphic arts, but that was okay. She was always right where she was supposed to be . . . a couple of steps behind her husband, and she supported him unconditionally. They were the perfect picture of the perfect Mormon family, and President Daniels was proud to have been their pastor and mentor for the past twenty years.

"Well, in the cake girl's defense, I've known Darren and Warren since the day they were born, and I still can't tell them apart." He looked at the translucent photo that was the cake frosting. The two boys were perfect and indistinguishable—six foot two; 180 solidly muscled pounds; light blond, neatly trimmed hair; and naturally tanned smooth skin that accentuated their ocean-blue eyes and made their blindingly white smile seem . . . well, doctored.

"Me either, and I'm their mother!" Martha laughed. "I swear, if Warren didn't have that adorable mole on the bottom of his earlobe, I'd never call them by their correct name."

"At least it keeps you on your toes, Sister Callahan," he said as he smiled and patted her gently on the shoulders.

"Oh, that it does, Elder Daniels," she agreed, and moved the punch cups half an inch farther from the bowl one last time. "That it does."

Just then the kitchen door swung open and Martha's best friend bounded into the room. "Hurry, everyone," she said breathlessly as she grabbed the cake. "They just pulled into the driveway!"

"SURPRISE!!"

Darren and Warren Callahan pretended to be just that as they walked through the living room door. Darren clutched at his heart and Warren braced himself against the doorjamb dramatically, and they both elicited an almost believable gasp of shock. It was their birthday, and not one of the past fifteen of their eighteen years had passed without this exact same surprise party. The same gift of ten dollars from each of the same twenty-six adult guests, all of whom were friends of their parents and not of the twins. The same Hawaiian Punch and ginger ale "spiked" cocktail served in the same glass bowl and cups. The same cars lined up down the couple of blocks leading to their house, which they'd feigned not to notice since the age of seven.

And up until today, the same German chocolate birthday cake. It was the first thing the two brothers noticed when they walked into the room full of people they couldn't pretend were strangers no matter how hard they tried. They walked over to the six-foot foldout banquet table borrowed from their church and stared at the full-sheet cake with the blinding white frosting and an edible photo of themselves taken for their high school yearbook only a couple of months earlier.

"Wow!" Warren said.

"You remembered," Darren said.

Both boys put on their patented movie star smile and

blushed as if on cue as their guests closed in around them, patting them on the back and congratulating them on another birthday. They were duly gracious, and humble and appreciative of everyone's gifts, and of their love and support over the years.

"I know it's *your* birthday," Brother Callahan said in a booming voice from atop the ledge of the slightly raised fireplace, so that he could be heard and seen by everyone in the room. "But you two boys have given me the best gift a father could ever hope for. I can't begin to tell you how proud of you I am," he said with a crack in his voice.

Their mother rushed to her husband's side and hugged him lovingly as the other women dabbed at their teary eyes and the other men stared at the floor and shuffled their feet as they mumbled their unintelligible support.

"Today we are privileged to be witness to the birth of an historic event," President Daniels said grandly to the crowd, who was eager to have their attention diverted from the uncomfortable moment of emotional display. "It has been my extreme pleasure to serve as your stake president for the past nine and a half years. I think I have learned more from you than you have from me, and I thank you for that. But I'm going to be seventy years old in a few months, and they tell me I'm getting senile."

Everyone laughed and cleared their throats and finished wiping their eyes quickly, then formed a prayer circle around the boys without being told to do so.

"And so I will soon be passing the torch to the very capable Brother Callahan. I'm very proud of you, Bruce," he said with a nod toward his protégé. It was a bold and unorthodox use of his friend's first name, and one that was not given or taken lightly. "You've been like a son to me, and I know you will lead this stake with great dignity and intense devotion. God has shown me a vision of you as a great Mormon leader, and I doubt that anyone here will be surprised to hear that in that vision I saw your two sons not only following in your footsteps but guiding us strongly on our last leg of the journey and through the pearly gates of the Celestial Kingdom."

Everyone clapped and cheered loudly. A vision was not something taken lightly in the Mormon Church, and being blessed with one elevated its recipient to Prophet status. The parishioners in the room were appropriately awed and humbled.

"The Elders Callahan have completed their missionary training in Provo, and in a couple of days they will take their first steps to becoming men and becoming God's chosen leaders of His people into His Kingdom. They will leave for their two-year missionary assignment in Seattle, where they will be tested and strengthened to fulfill God's purpose for their lives and for all of us. I ask now that we all reach one hand out toward our sons and the other hand up to the Heavens as we pray for God's blessing and guidance and enlightenment for them."

In a move eerily reminiscent of *The Stepford Wives*, everyone in the room bowed their heads and raised their right hand toward the ceiling and stretched their left hand toward the center of the room, where the twins had magically been maneuvered.

With every head bowed and every eye closed, Darren and Warren knew they would not be seen. In that supernatural twin telepathy they'd shared since birth, they smiled mischievously as they looked over at one another and winked.

They'd shared a bedroom all of their lives. Not because they had to; there was a den and a spare bedroom in the Callahan home. But because they wanted to. They were best friends, and no one who knew them could remember a time when they weren't inseparable. The room was filled with baseball gloves and footballs and basketballs and soccer balls. Numerous trophies lined shelves and bookcases, and banners from several colleges were thumbtacked to the walls. There were a few family photos scattered about as well, and a full-sized poster of Joseph Smith carefully adhered to the back of the door.

Two twin-sized beds occupied opposite walls of the room, and identical ornate metal crosses hung above each. One of them was empty and perfectly made. Both boys lie naked in the same bed.

"I can't believe the time has finally come," Warren said as he snuggled closer against his brother. He loved the way Darren's solid muscles and warm, smooth skin felt against his, and his cock began to stir when Darren hugged him tighter across the shoulder and kissed him lightly on the head.

"We should've done it sooner," Darren said quietly. "Before going to the training center, and definitely before President Daniels could publicly disclose his 'revelation' about us as the next savior to a room full of our friends. It just makes it seem like that much more of a lie."

"That was not a roomful of *our* friends, babe," he said, as he propped himself up on one elbow and leaned in to kiss his brother tenderly on the mouth. "That was a roomful of 'Brother and Sister Callahan's' friends. And all of this is a lie. Our entire life has been a lie. But remember what Dr. Beck said. It's not our fault. What kind of parents raise their kids the way we've been raised? I mean, seriously, even at our own birthday parties we've never been permitted to have our own friends. It's always their friends and people from the church. And you know that if it weren't for the Mormon school here, we'd have been home schooled and never seen the outside of this house. I swear, sometimes I think even Carrie had it better. At least she got to go to her prom."

Darren laughed softly. "I know, you're right. But maybe we don't have to actually tell them. Maybe we can just sneak out before they wake up tomorrow morning and never look back."

"No," Warren said. "We're not kids anymore. They've told us what to do with our lives long enough. Remember what Dr. Beck said. We have to stand up to them and start living our own lives."

"Yeah, I know. But it's gonna break their hearts. I don't want to hurt them."

Warren slapped him playfully across the cheek. "Snap outta it," he said in his favorite Cher impersonation.

"Okay," Darren said, "but we can't tell them in stereo. One of us should be the spokesperson and . . ."

"Spokesperson?" Warren raised an eyebrow. "Jesus, you sound just like them now."

"You know what I mean. I think you should be the one to tell them."

"Wanna wrestle for it? Loser has to be 'the spokesperson.' "

"Get ready to lose," Darren laughed, and rolled onto his side and straddled his brother's chest.

They'd been wrestling one another their entire lives, and both boys were in the best shape of their eighteen years. But Darren had almost always won their bouts. He had an innate talent for strategy and for predicting Warren's moves a couple of steps ahead of even Warren himself, and was always prepared. And his strength couldn't be overstated, either. Nine times out of ten, Darren overpowered his brother and was triumphant, and that night was no exception. After several minutes of playful but intense grappling on the bed, he still sat naked atop Warren's chest. Both boys were sweating and struggling to catch their breath.

"You call it, dude?" he asked with a grin, already knowing the answer.

"Yeah, I give," Warren gasped. He couldn't take his eyes off of his brother's half-swollen cock just a few inches from his face, and he licked his lips in anticipation.

"Open up, bitch," Darren said, and scooted up the last couple of inches on Warren's body and slapped his cock teasingly across his wet, pink lips. "Suck my cock, baby."

Warren did as he was told and stuck his tongue out to lick the salty head of the thickening cock. He waited until Darren moaned, and then leaned forward so that he could wrap his lips around it. His tongue darted around the big head as he pushed his head a couple of inches deeper onto the shaft.

"Oh fuck, bro," Darren whispered in a deep guttural cry, and slid up even closer, so that his cock disappeared inside Warren's hot throat. He stayed completely frozen as his brother lapped and sucked hungrily on his dick.

The two siblings had never been with anyone else sexually, and so they had nothing to base a comparison on. But Warren didn't need a ton of experience to know that he was one hell of a cocksucker. It was like chess to him, or tennis . . . you either "got" it or you didn't. One could practice at chess or algebra or cocksucking, and might even become less clumsy and maybe even somewhat decent at it. But it was obvious when someone was just a natural at it. And Warren prided himself on being the Martina Navratilova of giving head. He got it.

He waited until Darren's cock was buried deep in his throat, then tightened his muscles around it. The moan from above him let him know it was appreciated, and he slid his lips up and down the length of the long cock, and then pulled it back into his throat and sucked on it some more. It grew thicker in his throat and pressed against the walls of his esophagus. Whenever Darren tried to do this same thing to him, he choked and gagged, and Warren basked in the power he currently held over his brother. He might be the one pinned on the bed, but he was definitely in control. He could get Darren to do just about anything at this point.

"Holy shit, man," Darren gasped in a high-pitched squeak. "We gotta slow down or I'm gonna cum." He pulled his cock slowly from his brother's mouth and watched as a clear string of thick precum oozed from the tip of the head and slid across Warren's tongue and lips.

Warren licked at the sweet fluid and lapped it back into his mouth. He loved the taste of his brother's seed, and he smiled as he looked up and saw Darren's entire body shaking as he tried to hold back his orgasm.

"I wanna fuck your ass," Warren whispered. He knew that right then was the time to strike. If he waited another couple of minutes and continued blowing Darren like he was, it'd be too late. Darren would be like a runaway train and would not stop until he was the one doing the fucking. But right now, and this precise moment, Warren had the power and could still call the shots.

"What?" Darren said groggily, shaking his head back and forth slowly.

"Lay down on your stomach. I wanna fuck you."

Darren crawled off of his brother's chest and lay on his stomach. Warren maneuvered around him and between his long, muscular legs. He spread them apart with his knees as he leaned forward and spread the smooth, hard globes.

"I'm not sure . . ." Darren said hesitantly. The boys had played with each other quite a bit over the past four years, and they had each been in the active and the passive role. But Darren much preferred to top, and he was the one to fuck his brother three times out of four.

But Warren was in the rare mood to pound some ass that night. He bent down and kissed Darren's ass cheeks and spread them a little farther apart. He smiled as he felt them tighten, and sensed every muscle on Darren's body constrict in response. Then he licked between the crack slowly, making sure plenty of spit slid from his tongue and between the smooth, warm crevice.

"Oh my God," Darren moaned, and instinctively moved his legs farther apart.

Warren stuck his tongue out even farther and licked and kissed around the hole. Thousands of chill bumps sprung up all across Darren's body as Warren nibbled and blew softly on the twitching sphincter. He darted his tongue quickly across it, and smiled to himself when his brother moaned loudly, grabbed the comforter on either side of him, and raised his hips to allow him easier access. Then Warren slid his tongue slowly but forcefully inside the warm tunnel and flickered it even more teasingly.

"Fuck me, baby," Darren growled quietly. "Please."

Warren reluctantly left the warm, smooth ass that smelled and felt undeniably like baby oil, and he laid his body across the back of Darren's. "I love you," he whispered as he kissed the back of his brother's ass and nibbled on his earlobe.

"I love you, too," Darren panted. "Now fuck me!"

Warren's cock was already throbbing against the crack of Darren's ass. He shifted his hips a couple of inches and closed his eyes as he slipped effortlessly between the two mounds of muscle and slid inside the hot, wet tunnel. He continued kissing and licking Darren's neck and back when his brother tensed up involuntarily and struggled to catch his breath. But Warren didn't slow down or stop until he was buried deep inside the clutching ass.

He lay there completely still for a moment, allowing Darren time to relax and get used to having his insides stuffed with Warren's big cock. His heart was beating fast and hard, and he knew without even thinking about it that his twin brother's was as well.

It didn't take long for Darren to warm up to the idea of being fucked. He tightened his ass muscles and wriggled his waist and legs around, forcing Warren's cock deeper still inside and eliciting a moan from both of the boys.

Warren slid slowly in and out of his brother's ass for a few minutes, and then pulled Darren up to his knees by his hips. In this position, his pelvic bone was pressed into the soft, warm skin of Darren's ass, as deep and intimate as he could get. An electric tingle surged through his body, and he tried to count backward from 100 to keep from shooting his load too soon.

"Fuck me, baby," Darren growled roughly as he flexed his ass muscles again and slid up and down Warren's cock. "I need your big dick all the way inside . . ."

"Are you boys all right?" Their mother's voice seemed to enter the room from a long tunnel.

"What's all that noise?" Brother Callahan quickly followed. "Are you having a night . . ."

The light blazed across the room and splashed across the twins' naked and sweating bodies. Warren stopped halfway through his withdrawal, a few inches of his cock still buried in his brother's quivering ass. Both boys stared wide-eyed and unblinking at their parents' horrified faces and struggled to find enough saliva to swallow.

"I'm sorry to interrupt, guys," Brian said as he poked his head inside the doorway. "But your father's on the phone."

It had been five years since Darren and Warren had left home. Brother Callahan went completely ballistic when he saw the two brothers fucking on their eighteenth birthday. After covering their mother's eyes and sending her into the other room, he'd slapped the boys around for a few minutes and then literally kicked them out of the house and onto the front lawn. Five minutes later a single suitcase packed with a few of their clothes was thrown out the front door as well, along with the keys to their car.

"Get the hell out of here. Get in that car and drive as far away from here as possible, and don't ever come back. You are dead to us." Those were the last words the twins had heard from either of their parents.

And that suited the boys just fine. They'd already decided they were not going to Seattle to do any missionary work. For the six months leading up to their eighteenth birthday they'd been in talks with a porn studio in Los Angeles to star in a new film. After viewing their audition tape, the studio owner called them immediately and offered them $25,000 each for their first movie. He also agreed to sign them on for another three movies upon completion of the first, as long as they all agreed it was a mutually beneficial relationship and a direction they wanted to pursue.

No one could have predicted the success their movies would generate. Their first two films broke every sales record on the books. For their third movie the boys were paid $50,000 each, and on their fourth and final deal with the studio, that figure doubled. When they finished with their contractual obligations, they decided to start their own production studio. Investors were knocking at their door even before the idea had been completely fleshed out. Within three years Gemini Studios became the largest and wealthiest in the industry.

Brian was their first discovery. The chemistry between him and the brothers was instant and explosive. His mocha-colored skin; shaved head; goatee; pierced ears, eyebrows, and nose; and his absurdly muscled body were the perfect complement to the twins' All-American golden boy picture. And his thick, eleven-inch uncut cock with a Prince Albert piercing soon became legendary. Their sex scenes burned themselves onto the DVDs and catapulted all three of them into superstardom. The chemistry continued off screen as well, and the three quickly evolved into a trilogy.

"You know we don't . . ." Darren started to say.

"I know," Brian said as he held out the phone to them. He knew all about the church and the family and the night they were caught. "But he says it's important. It's about your mom." He handed the phone to Warren and lay on his stomach between the brothers on their bed.

"What?" Warren asked coldly into the receiver. He listened quietly for a moment and closed his eyes and pinched the bridge of his nose tightly.

Brian saw a tear fall down Warren's right cheek and hugged both brothers tightly.

"No, we won't come home," Warren said, looking at Darren to confirm that they were in agreement. They'd discussed this exact scenario before and had agreed they'd never go back home, under any circumstances.

Darren wiped a tear from his eye and nodded.

"No," Warren repeated calmly. "We do *not* have to listen to you. We listened to you and did every stupid little thing you told us to do and to believe for the first eighteen years of our lives." He pulled the phone from his ear and winced as his father yelled obscenities across the line. "We're not your little boys anymore," he said once Brother Callahan stopped long enough to breathe. "Yeah, he's here, just a moment."

Darren took a deep breath as he accepted the phone from his brother. "What?" he matched Warren's icy tone. "No. I'm sorry to hear about Mom, but we already told you we aren't coming home."

His knuckles turned white as he listened quietly as his father ranted. And then he'd heard enough.

"How dare you say that to me. *You're* the one who turned your back on *us*. All our lives we tried to make you happy. We did what you told us to do, we believed what you told us to believe, and we ate and drank what you told us to eat and drink. We were your perfect little puppets performing in your perfect little Mormon puppet opera. Not once did you care enough about your sons to ask what *we* wanted. What *we* thought about anything. What we *felt*. It was always all about you and your goddammed self-righteous Neanderthal beliefs. When you finally did get a tiny glimpse about who your sons were, *you* turned your back on *us*, not the other way around. You beat us up and you threw us out on our asses and you said we were dead to you."

Darren stopped to take a breath, and when he did his father began yelling into the phone again. He listened politely until his father finished. "We're not little kids who have to believe everything you tell us anymore, Brother Callahan. You turned you back on your own children, Daddy Dearest. Don't think that you can come running back with open arms now that you find yourself alone. You cooked your own meal, now you have to eat it. Isn't that what you used to tell us?"

Brother Callahan began another tirade loud enough for all three young men in the room to hear. Warren grabbed the phone from his brother.

"Fuck you, Dad. Happy eternity." He clicked the phone off and set it on the nightstand, crawled up to join Darren at the head of the bed, and motioned for Brian to join them. "It's gonna be okay," he whispered as he wiped a tear from his brother's eye.

"I can't believe she's . . ."

Brian stretched up and kissed Darren on the lips, and then pulled Warren in to join them. The three men tore at their clothes. When they were undressed, they lay on their sides in their favorite daisy chain position. The trio had been lovers for three years, and each was intimate with the intricacies that brought the others to climax.

"Oh God, Warren," Brian moaned as he cupped Darren's big shaved balls in his hands, "that feels so good. Keep sucking on the head like that."

Warren flicked his tongue around Brian's fat cock head, lapping at the precum that dripped from the tip. The fat, veiny brown cock never ceased to amaze him, and he couldn't get enough of it. He licked the head some more, then wrapped his lips around it and sucked gently. When Brian grunted and inched his hips forward, Warren slid his mouth all the way down the long shaft.

"Fuck, dude," Brian moaned. "Swallow my big cock."

Darren loved the sound of Brian's deep, sexy voice. Especially when he was making love. But he had a better idea for the use of his lover's mouth, and he slid his cock inside Brian's slick, warm lips. At the same time, he massaged his brother's heavy balls in one hand and deepthroated his giant cock in one effortless move.

"I can't take it much longer, guys," Warren gasped. "I want you to fuck me."

"Which one?" Darren asked, pulling his cock from Brian's hot mouth.

"Both of you."

Darren and Brian looked at one another uncertainly, and then looked back at Warren.

"Are you sure?" Brian asked. "You've never taken us both before. That's usually your brother's position."

"I know." In the past five years, he'd become much more versatile, and actually liked getting fucked now. Both Brian and Darren had fucked his ass many times in the past. They'd often "skewered" him—one fucking his ass while the other fucked his mouth—but he'd never taken them both up his ass before. He wanted to change that. "But why should he have all the fun?"

He motioned for Darren to lie on his back, and then he straddled his brother's waist. He felt Brian's bald head tickle the small of his back as the "third twin" sucked Darren's thick cock. A second later Warren was pushed forward by Brian's big hands, and his ass cheeks were spread apart.

Brian stuck out his tongue and licked around Warren's ass for a moment, and then wiggled his way inside the rosy, puckered hole. He loved eating out his twin lovers' asses. They were so smooth and hard and hot. The first time they'd done a shoot together, he blew his load all over himself just from rimming the brothers. He hadn't even touched his own cock—it just erupted before he even knew it was happening!

"I want you inside me," Warren moaned. He leaned down and licked Darren's lips for a couple of seconds before slipping his tongue inside his warm mouth. He felt Brian's hands moving his hips around, and a second later he felt the hot, wet head of Darren's cock as it rested against his hole. His entire body was quivering, and he felt his asshole twitching—begging to be fucked. He kissed Darren harder, cupping his face in his hands, and slid his ass down the full length of his brother's cock in one slow but deliberate move.

"Jesus, that feels fuckin' incredible, bro," Darren moaned as he raised his hips off the bed and forced his big cock deeper inside Warren's ass. He slid in and out slowly for a minute or so, and then began fucking him harder.

"You sure you wanna try to take both of us?" Brian asked from behind Warren.

"Yeah, I'm sure."

"All right. You ready then?"

Warren leaned all the way forward so that his stomach and

chest were resting against Darren's. His brother's cock felt so hot inside him, and he tightened his ass around it lovingly. "I love you," he whispered.

"I love you, too," Darren whispered back.

Brian pressed his cock head against Warren's ass, and when he felt Warren inhale, he pushed just the head inside.

"Oh FUCK!" Warren yelled. He shook his head quickly a couple of times, as if to clear the cobwebs or knock back a fainting spell.

The other two lovers knew better than to pull out or ask Warren if he wanted to stop. Warren was the most determined and stubborn person that either of them had ever met. When he set his mind to something, he did it. And so when he took a deep breath again and nodded his head, Brian slid his big cock all the way inside, not stopping until his balls rested against Darren's below him.

The three boys remained motionless for a moment, waiting. One . . . two . . . three . . .

And there it was. Warren moaned softly and tightened his ass around both cocks inside him. When his two lovers responded in kind, he lifted his ass a couple of inches up, and then back down on them again. It didn't take long at all before the three found their rhythm. Darren slowly slid his big cock deep inside his brother's ass as Brian withdrew his equally slow, until just his head remained inside—then Brian inched his way deep inside the ass as Darren pulled almost all the way out. Once they got the rhythm established, they sped up a little, working like a machine. Warren realized quickly that it was best for him to just keep his balance and let his two lovers do all the work. And that suited him just fine.

"Fuck me harder," he barked.

Darren took hold of either side of his brother's waist and Brian grabbed a handful of Warren's hair as both men took no mercy with their lover. They pounded his ass relentlessly, sliding in and out of him faster and deeper with every stroke.

"Oh shit . . . I'm gonna cum!" Warren yelled. His body was sliding up and down both big cocks and rocking all over the bed. Both hands were reaching for a bedpost, a body, a pillow . . . anything to keep his balance. His cock bounced up and down with the pummeling of his lovers. So when his orgasm came, it shot all over the place—Darren's face and chest and stomach, the headboard, the pillows, his own stomach.

"Me too," Brian said, and pulled out of Warren's ass quickly.

Warren rolled over onto his back on the bed and motioned for Darren to get on his knees. He licked his lips.

"FUCK ME!" Brian yelled. His body tightened and a second later a geyser of semen sprayed through the air. The first couple of jets flew across Warren's body and landed on Darren's smooth abs and his thick cock. Several more landed on Warren's chest and stomach.

"Oh God," Darren moaned. He inched a little closer to Warren's face and let go with a gush of cum that showered his brother's entire face. It seemed to go on forever, and even after his knees gave out and he fell on top of Warren's body, a few last drops oozed out and onto the bed.

Brian collapsed onto the brothers and the three lovers hugged tightly.

"I love you guys," Brian said softly, after he had time to catch his breath.

"We love you, too," the twins said in stereo, and all three of them laughed.

They lay quietly for several minutes, and then it was Warren who broke the silence. "I'm gonna miss Mom," he whispered.

"I'm gonna miss the idea of her," Darren said.

"I kinda wish I could have met her," Brian said as he

squeezed the brothers lovingly. "Sounds like I can do without meeting your dad, but your mom sounded nice enough."

"She'd have liked you, I think," Warren said as he yawned.

"Me too," Darren agreed. "Come to think of it . . . I think Dad might even like you."

"Don't get carried away," Brian laughed.

"I'm serious. I think he'd have to approve of this relationship."

"How do you figure?" Warren said.

"Think about it. He's the quintessential Latter-Day Saint and he taught us very well. The prodigal sons return to the true teachings of the Mormon Church. Just how many spouses were our Founding Fathers allowed—hell, almost expected—to have? It's one of the building blocks of the Church. We're fundamentalists!!"

The three lovers laughed and then fell asleep entangled in one another.

Sexual Pursuit

"You do realize that Alpha Cum Epsilon is the most presti-gious fraternity on campus, right?" Jarryd said as he leaned back in the highback executive chair in the library of the frat house and stared unblinkingly at the four potential pledges in front of him. "We don't accept just anyone to be an ACE brother. We're quite picky."

"Yes, sir," the pledges said in unison. They looked duly in-timidated by Jarryd's presence and demeanor, and that was not by accident.

"We're very aware of ACE's solid reputation," Brent said. He was the most outgoing and talkative of the group. It had been his idea to get the four together and pledge for the fra-ternity. They'd become friends their first semester, and the friendship had grown over the next two years. "That's exactly the reason we've chosen Alpha Cum Epsilon."

"That's your first mistake right there, punk," Jarryd said with a snarl. "You do not choose Alpha Cum Epsilon. ACE chooses you. The sooner you realize that, the better off you'll be."

"Yes, sir," Brent said, and squirmed in his chair.

"I'm not sure we've made the right decision on our choice of pledges this year," the president said.

"Please, sir. I meant no disrespect whatsoever. I just meant that we actively chose to try to pledge for ACE because of the stellar reputation for excellence and character of its brothers. I'm sorry. Please give us a chance."

Jarryd leaned forward in his chair and stared down each of the pledges one by one. Few young men had ever been able to meet his stare, and those that did never made it into the fraternity. He enjoyed the power he held over the young men and their spirits. It gave him a rush and a sense of superiority and irreproachability. And it gave him a fucking raging hardon.

"I will give you another chance," he said as if he were disgusted with his own decision. "But only because I have faith in the discernment of character of my fellow Alpha Cum Epsilon brothers. They feel you four represent what we value in a brother and were the only candidates even worth considering. And I agreed with them. I just hope we weren't wrong."

"No, sir, you weren't wrong," Brent said quickly. "We are what you're looking for, I promise."

"Initiation is tomorrow evening at six o'clock sharp. You must absolutely do anything and everything that is ordered without question and without debate. Is that clear?

"Yes, sir," the pledges said together.

"Good. Now get out of here before I change my mind."

Brent was the first to stand up, and the others quickly followed him out the front door. No one said a word until they were several blocks from the house.

"Shit, man," Tim said as he finally allowed himself to catch a deep breath. "I don't know about this, guys. I didn't get a very good feeling in there. I'm not sure I'm comfortable doing 'everything and anything' that guy tells me to do. He seems a little disturbed to me."

"Me too," Rodney said. He was the biggest of the four by far, standing at six foot four and weighing 250 pounds. He had been the star athlete in his high school, and was quickly rising up the ranks of the university's track and field team. But his caramel-colored skin, hazel puppy dog eyes, and full, pouty lips revealed his true shy and gentle nature. It was obvious to the other three that Rodney was more than a little uncomfortable with the whole pledging process in general, let alone one in which a potentially sadistic president had free reign over the initiation.

"Look guys," Brent said as he stopped walking in the middle of the sidewalk. "That's just the game they play. All of the frat initiations are going to be the exact same thing. They're all going to try and humiliate and degrade and embarrass us. That's what they do. ACE won't be any more difficult or more painful than any of the lesser fraternities in that respect. They can't do anything illegal. With all the scrutiny over hazing and inappropriate initiation practices in the public eye today, they have to be careful. We'll be safe. They'll probably just make us clean the toilets with a toothbrush or run around the block in the nude or something equally silly."

"Brent's right," Perry said. "We didn't come this far just to back down now. We knew there was going to be an initiation, and we went into it willingly. We can't back down now. We have to just get through the initiation tomorrow, and then we'll see how silly all of this seems now. Don't let that jerk back there get to us."

The four guys huddled together, clasped hands in the center of the circle, and gave their "all for one and one for all" cheer. Then they went their separate ways to their remaining afternoon classes.

* * *

"Okay, guys, they're going to be here any minute now. Is everything ready?" Jarryd paced around the room, making sure everything was in its place.

"Yeah, dude. We're cool," Matt said. "Just chill. You're the one who's supposed to be the one in charge here, remember?"

"I *am* in charge here," Jarryd said defensively. "I'm cool. I just wanna make sure we've covered everything and that nothing goes wrong."

"Yeah, cuz *that's* never happened at a frat initiation," Mark said sarcastically.

The doorbell rang, and Jarryd jumped. "That's them," he whispered excitedly. "You guys take your places in front of the fireplace. I'll get the door." When he reached the front door, he looked to make sure the three other officers of the house were in place and indicated for them to cross their arms across their chests.

He opened the door and motioned for the pledges to make their way into the library.

"So, you actually had the balls to show up," he said with a snarl. All it took was a fresh audience for Jarryd to switch into his sadistic, controlling fraternity president role in the blink of an eye. He knew that his brothers behind him were probably rolling their eyes at him, but he hoped they were doing it inwardly, and not in a way that was visible to the new pledges.

"This is your initiation," Jarryd said, and pointed to the game board laid out on the coffee table.

"Trivial Pursuit?" Brent said, and looked around for hidden cameras.

"Not exactly. This is Alpha Cum Epsilon Pursuit."

"Seriously? Our initiation is playing a board game?"

"No questions!" Jarryd yelled as he leaned to within an inch of Brent's face. "One more stupid remark like that and you'll never see the inside of this fraternity again. Is that clear?"

"Yes sir!" all four pledges answered, even though Brent was the only one to have spoken out.

"The rules are very simple. You roll the dice and move your playing piece forward on the board accordingly. When you land on a colored square, you pick the top card in that color pile and you do what the card says. You do not ask questions and you do not say no to any card. The moment any player refuses to go along with what the card says, he is no longer a member of this fraternity. Period. The first person to reach the center on the board with a full pie is the winner and the game and the initiation for all players is over. Is that clear?"

"Yes, sir!"

"No questions!"

"Yes, sir!"

"No saying no or passing on a card."

"Yes, sir!"

The four existing members of the ACE leadership team sat alternately between the new pledges and stared at them unblinkingly, without the most minuscule trace of a smile.

Brent rolled the die first and moved his plastic playing piece forward four spaces, landing on a green square.

"Green cards are Dare spaces," Jarryd said grandly. "I'll read your card." He picked the top green card from the pile and read it to himself first, and smiled. "You must strip all the way naked and play the next three rounds in the nude."

"Wha . . ." Brent started to say, and then stopped. He looked around and noticed the four frat brothers watching him expectantly. His friends had a horrified expression on their face and looked as if they might get up and run out the door any minute. "Okay."

He kicked off his shoes and pulled off his socks, and then stood up and removed his shirt. Brent had never been the star jock of his high school and was never even in the running for Homecoming King. But he did like to play tennis and swim and hike and be active, and his body bore witness to that. His chest was not overly muscular but solidly muscled and had a dusting of black curly hair spattered across both pecs. His nipples were constantly hard and poked out dramatically from his chest when he was excited. The coarse hair weaved its way down his torso and past a flat tummy before it disappeared into his jeans.

He took a deep breath and then shucked his jeans and briefs off in one quick move. His limp cock swung three or four inches below his big balls. It didn't look excessively impressive soft, but Brent knew that as the game went on and he relaxed a little, the other players would envy him. He had been in very few situations in which nudity was a factor where that was not the case.

"Your turn," he said to Mark, who was to his immediate left.

Mark rolled a five and landed on a yellow space. Dale read the card out loud:

"While innocently shopping for a porn magazine in a sleazy adult bookstore, purely for research purposes only, of course, your spot your minister's eighteen-year-old son going into one of the stalls in the back room. You follow him in and take the stall next to him. The next day, confessional has never seen so much action! Move ahead two spaces . . . and wipe your lips. There's something sticky there."

The frat brothers laughed as Mark moved his piece forward two spaces, and the pledges all breathed a sigh of relief at knowing that not every card would involve nudity.

Perry went next and landed on a purple space.

"Truth card," Dale said, and read the card silently. He was the secretary of the fraternity. "How old were you when you had your first sexual experience, and who was it with?"

"I don't really think . . ." he started to say. But when all four frat brothers looked at him sternly, he changed his mind. "I was fifteen, and her name was Monica. She was my preacher's daughter."

Everybody clapped and gave Perry a high five.

"Was she good?" Matt asked.

"Nah. She had braces and scraped my dick when she blew me."

"Ouch!" Jarryd said as he rolled the dice for his turn. "Another Truth card."

"How big is your cock when fully hard?" Tim read aloud from the card. "Ten inches."

"LIAR!!" Dale and Mark said simultaneously.

"Okay," he conceded. "It's about seven."

"That's more like it, dude."

The game continued like that for about an hour. The guys all warmed up to one another, and it didn't take long to figure out that the night was all about having fun. Some of the cards involved drinking alcohol, some of them involved making prank phone calls to sorority houses, others challenged the guys to kiss one of the other players. Everyone knew they couldn't say no, but as the evening wore on, that option entered their minds less and less frequently, even though they were all naked after a couple of turns. But that changed when Jarryd had a full pie and neared the center of the board and Brent drew a Dare card.

"Choose any player," Mark read out loud. "If you can get his dick hard in less than three minutes without using your hands, you get to do whatever you want with him and either switch places with him on the board or move ahead five spaces, whichever is higher. If his dick stays soft, you move back to Start."

Brent looked down at the board. "I choose Jarryd."

The other players clapped and whistled. Jarryd leaned back on his elbows and spread his legs wide. "Come on, bitch. You think you can get my dick hard? Come suck it and then watch in awe at my willpower. It's not gonna budge."

Brent had remained naked for the entire game and had started to get a boner a few times when he saw the other guys naked and in various states of arousal. But he'd concentrated on not allowing his cock to get fully hard for one reason. Shock factor. He wanted to surprise everyone at just the right moment, and he knew at once that this was that moment.

He crawled between Jarryd's tanned legs and licked his low-hanging hairy balls. Jarryd laughed and tried to tell him to stop, but the other players reminded him that he couldn't say no or deny a card.

"You gotta do better than that, dude," he relented. "I've been blown by some of the best bitches on campus."

A full minute had already passed, but Brent wasn't worried. He licked the head of Jarryd's cock for a few seconds, then pulled it into his mouth and rolled his tongue across it. When he felt it thicken and grow inside his mouth, he knew he'd won the challenge. He swallowed the cock to the base and tightened his throat muscles around the shaft as it grew longer and fatter in his mouth.

"Fuck, man! No, this can't be happening," Jarryd protested and tried to pull Brent from his crotch. But Brent wrapped his arms around the frat president's waist and deepthroated his cock.

"It's almost three minutes," Matt announced.

Brent pulled away and pointed at Jarryd's cock. It was red

and fully hard and throbbing. It looked as if it might shoot a load at any second.

"He did it, man!" Dale announced.

"That means I get to do whatever I want with you, right?"

Jarryd was speechless, and looked back and forth from one of his frat brothers to another quickly.

"That's what the card says." Matt laughed. He was enjoying this. Jarryd had had this coming for a couple of years, and he was glad it was finally about to happen.

Brent pulled himself up from the floor and stood. His cock swung up and down about ten inches in front of him with the beat of his heart. It was so thick that his fist didn't fit all the way around it. He smiled as he watched the other players stare at his massive cock and gasp as the realization of what was about to happen sank in.

"Just stay right there where you are, *punk*," he said, and kicked Jarryd's legs farther apart. "I'm gonna fuck that sweet jock ass long and hard. You might wanna close your eyes and go to your happy place."

"No way," Jarryd said, and tried unsuccessfully to sit up on his elbows. He was still shaking from the blowjob Brent had given him. "I'm not taking that thing up my ass. Forget it."

"You can't say no," Dale reminded him.

"Like hell I can't. I just did. I'm not taking that cock."

"Anyone who refuses to follow the cards is no longer a member of this fraternity," Matt said. Nothing he'd ever said as ACE vice president satisfied him more than this. "No questions and no debate. Your own rules. You developed the game. The card says if you don't play along, then Brent switches places with you on the board. And according to your own rules, you would no longer be a part of this fraternity. I think it would be appropriate for us to name Brent as the incoming prez."

"You can't be serious," Jarryd said as he tried hard not to cry.

Matt looked at Brent.

"I'm dead serious . . . bitch. Now take a deep breath and bite down on this if the pain gets to be too much," he said, and threw a pillow to the floor next to Jarryd.

The six other guys stood in a circle around Jarryd and Brent and stroked their cocks as they watched the new pledge serve the frat president a big slice of humble pie. Brent took his time licking around Jarryd's puckered hole, making sure there was plenty of lubrication for his thick cock. When he pressed the head against the sphincter, Jarryd let out a yelp and pulled the pillow to his mouth. Brent slid the head inside and let it rest there for a moment, then pushed forward slowly until his balls rested between Jarryd's ass crack.

Jarryd bit down on the pillow, groaned loudly into it, and shook his head back and forth as Brent slid his huge cock in and out of his ass slowly at first and then with faster and deeper strokes. He was putting on a good show of resistance for his buddies, but Brent knew a show when he saw one.

"You love the feel of my fat cock up your ass, don't you," he whispered softly into Jarryd's ear so that the others couldn't hear. They were all moaning and stroking each other's cocks anyway.

Jarryd's eyes widened with fear, and he nodded slightly and flexed his ass muscles tighter against Brent's cock inside him.

"Don't worry, baby," he whispered again, and kissed Jarryd's ear as he slammed his cock harder and deeper inside the hot tunnel. "You just keep putting up a fight if it makes you feel better. It turns me on. No one will ever have to know the truth. And we can do this as often as you like."

Jarryd smiled with the pillow still in his mouth and put up a believable struggle to get free as he cried out in mock pain when Brent began pounding his ass harder and faster.

"You want their cum all over you, don't you," Brent mouthed silently to Jarryd's flushed face beneath him.

Jarryd blinked and nodded, and pulled the pillow from his mouth as he cried out and begged for Brent to stop fucking him. He couldn't take any more. Brent was too big and hurting him. He had to pull out. All the while, he was squeezing the pledge's thick cock and thrusting his ass deeper onto it, bringing them both closer to climax.

"Come here, guys," Brent said. "I want you to splash your loads all over our bitch of a president."

"No, please," Jarryd pleaded, and then licked his lips.

The other players inched in closer to the fucking couple and beat at their cocks furiously. Matt and Tim moaned loudly and shot their loads all over Jarryd's face and chest at the same time. Rodney was next, and his legs gave out right before he blew his load. He dropped to his knees, and when he realized how close his huge cock was to Jarryd's face, he leaned forward and shoved it roughly in the president's mouth.

"Fuck yeah," Rodney yelled as his entire body trembled.

Brent could see Jarryd swallowing what he knew had to be a huge load from Rodney's giant dick. The other three players yelled out various profanities and showered both Brent and Jarryd with warm, fragrant loads, then leaned against one another for structural support.

"I'm gonna shoot, punk," Brent panted. He pulled his cock out of Jarryd's ass quickly and with an audible plop. Cum flew everywhere . . . straight up in the air, onto a couple of the other players, and over Jarryd's head onto the floor behind him. Several spurts landed on Jarryd's face, and he lapped at it hungrily.

Brent collapsed on top of the frat president and struggled to catch his breath as the other players scattered to find various sinks for rinsing off. When they were alone in the library, Brent rolled onto his side and looked at Jarryd.

"You okay, man?"

"Yeah. But how did you know?"

"I didn't, really. Not until I slid my cock inside you and felt your hot, sweet ass milking me dry. I know a power bottom when I fuck one."

"The others can't know."

"Yeah, well good luck with that one. Because when you're screaming in ecstasy with my cock buried deep inside you, I think they might suspect something."

Jarryd laughed. "Fair enough. But dude, I gotta cum. I'm about to explode."

"I think I can help with that," Brent said.

He scooted down Jarryd's body and sucked the hard cock back into his mouth. He was an expert cocksucker, and it didn't take long before Jarryd sprayed his thick load into Brent's throat. He swallowed it hungrily and kissed the head of his new president's cock head.

"We better get up and join the others in cleaning up, or they might get suspicious," Brent said as he helped Jarryd to his feet. "You do realize that I'm gonna have another go at the most prestigious frat ass on campus later tonight, right?" he said, mocking their conversation the previous day.

"You better believe you are," Jarryd said as he leaned in to kiss Brent on the lips. "That's an executive order."

THE
MIDWEST/
MIDDLE
AMERICA

The heartland. Spacious skies and amber waves of grain. Hardworking men and women driving tractors and cooking homemade bread in wood-burning ovens. Okay, maybe that is taking it a bit too far, but not much. Though I call San Francisco home, I really didn't move there until after college. I grew up and went to junior high and high school in a small Texas panhandle town called Booker, Texas. Population 500. Some of you may have read some of my previous stories and wondered if those stories were real, and if I really did grow up in that godforsaken town. The answer, sadly, is yes.

We did three things in Booker, Texas, and I'm sure it's not all that different from what is still done in a majority of the Bible Belt middle America. We played football (and I use the term "we" very loosely and very figuratively), we farmed the land, and we went to church. Try to picture me driving a tractor as a young high school and college-aged faggot, and magnify the comedic image by ten, and you might be close to what I really looked like bouncing around on the tractor seat and trying to keep the tractor riding in perfect lines and not to run anyone over.

It's not hard to get a visual and mental image of the Midwest and the people who live there. We picture pale white folk with freckles and red necks and farmers' tans. We see conservative churchgoing people who go to bed early, get up early, and work long and hard hours in nonglamorous jobs. We can easily envision them picketing abortion clinics, writing letters to their senators urging them to vote against gay marriage, and faithfully tithing ten percent of their income to their church to support their important ministries and to ensure the annual church picnic will be a huge success.

And that wouldn't be a wrong picture of this part of the

country. But as easy as it might be to generalize our views of the Midwest, it's important to recognize the good traits of our heartland, too. They really do work very hard and provide us with the food that we need to survive. They are some of the nicest people in the world. If you have a flat tire on the side of the road, someone will pull over and help you change the tire or drive you to the nearest station. And they . . . okay, that's all I can think of.

Truth be known, as much as I've sworn never to move back and live in the Midwest, and as much as I disagree with so much of what they believe and the actions they do to promote their beliefs, I am thankful that I grew up there. And I can't tell you how many very liberal and very enlightened people who grew up in that part of the country have told me the exact same thing. It made me a very strong person and it taught me the importance of questioning what I was told and not to go on blind faith. And it taught me to think for myself. It also taught me the importance of being a nice person, to have a good heart, and to work hard and help others.

We can't dismiss the fact, however, that because of their conservative views and lifestyles, the Midwest has some very strong opinions of some of the most controversial taboos. In this section of the book, I address the taboos of authority figure abuse, sex with a minor, and sex in public.

Do you see yourself in any of these characters? Look closer.

A Matter of Chance

Part Two
Midwest Bible-Belt Mentality

The early morning romp with Marco, the gymnast, turned into a late morning romp with Marco, and right in the middle of their third go-around of the morning, the phone rang with an automated checkout message. He and Marco hurriedly showered and dressed, and, as they were leaving, promised to stay in touch and to get together again on Chance's return trip home after his visit in New York.

But Chance was acutely aware of the fact that Marco didn't invite him back up to his room, only two floors above his own, and so he was pretty certain that the hot gymnast had no intention of following through on his promise to fuck his brains out again in a couple of weeks.

Not that he was overly concerned about it. He'd never really had a boyfriend. He never had a problem hooking up, and even had some success with second and third dates. But never anything more than that. When he went on vacations alone he never wanted for company, though just about every night of the week the company had a different name. He wasn't completely unfamiliar with the phrase "vacation boyfriend," and over the years he had grown quite comfortable with it.

He knew the rules of the game and played well within their constraints.

As he drove away from the hotel, he noticed how quickly Marco dashed back inside once he'd pulled away from the driveway. He smiled, and admitted that he couldn't blame the kid. As hot as the gymnast was, he probably had another guy waiting for him already. Maybe even a boyfriend in the troupe who was okay with Marco playing with the occasional trick from out of town staying at the hotel.

One of Chance's closest friends, Jeremy, had moved to Denver a little more than a year previously, and Chance had called him and arranged to stay with him one night on his way across the country. He was really looking forward to seeing Jeremy again, and quickly put all thoughts of Marco and his hot cock and beautiful ass and body out of his mind as he jumped on Interstate 15. A little over three hours later he was on Interstate 70, which was a scenic and mountainous drive through the Rocky Mountains.

Eleven hours later Chance pulled into his friend's driveway. He'd never been so happy to arrive at a destination. He dragged himself out of the car and across the lawn, and then sat on the wooden swing on the porch after ringing the doorbell a couple of times.

"Oh . . . My . . . God, Becky!" Jeremy yelled as he threw the door open and ran across the porch to hug his friend. "I was expecting you over an hour ago."

"Yeah, I know," Chance said with a grin. "I got a little . . . sidetracked. You do know that you're standing on your front porch dripping wet with nothing but a skimpy towel wrapped around your waist, right?"

"I was in the shower," Jeremy said, brushing his hair from in front of his eyes. "When I heard the doorbell ring, I didn't want to miss you, so I just jumped out of the shower, wrapped the towel around me, and rushed downstairs."

"It's not like I'd take off and leave if you didn't answer right away." Chance laughed. "I don't know anyone else in Denver, or know where anything is. Where would I go?"

"I know, I know, I didn't think it out all the way. So let's get inside before I get arrested for indecent exposure."

Both men were hungry, so Chance took a quick shower to freshen up and Jeremy dressed, and then they went to Little India, Jeremy's favorite restaurant.

"I still can't believe you're going back home," Jeremy said as he scooped large spoonfuls of Chicken Tikka Masala, Dal Makhani, and lamb curry over a mound of Basmati rice.

"I know, but she cried," Chance replied as he filled his plate with the fragrant entrees. "I've never in my life seen or heard my mother cry."

"So the Ice Queen broke, huh?"

"Yeah, and it took me completely by surprise. I couldn't say no."

"Well, you're a bigger man than me," Jeremy said as he scooped some of the food into a fold of cheese naan bread and popped it into his mouth. "Literally," he mumbled through a mouthful of the food, and winked.

He and Chance had dated a few times before realizing that they made much better friends than lovers. But Jeremy was a notorious size queen and never passed up a moment in which he could comment on the size of Chance's cock, or anyone else's for that matter.

"Oh please," Chance said as he tried not to smile at the compliment. He was now certain that he and Jeremy would be sleeping together that night. He had been pretty sure before, when he noticed his friend glancing at his cock several times, and when he felt Jeremy's knee pressing against his own. But now he was positive. "It's not like I'm doing this out of some weird sense of nobility or anything. I'd just feel horrible if my father died without my having a chance to say good-bye. I know that sounds weird to you, but I wouldn't be able to live with myself if I didn't at least make an effort."

"It doesn't sound weird to me," Jeremy said, and placed his hand over Chance's. "It sounds just like you, and I love you for that. If it were my old man, I'd let him croak and never think twice about it."

"No, you wouldn't."

Jeremy shrugged. "Enough of this depressing crap," he said. "I don't want to be sad while you're here."

"Me, either," Chance said, and slipped his foot on Jeremy's chair, right against his crotch. "So are we gonna go back to your place and fuck, or what?"

"Thank God," Jeremy said, and waved the waiter over. "I thought you'd never ask."

The next morning Chance woke to breakfast in bed, complete with mimosa and a single red rose in a glass vase.

"Good morning, sunshine," Jeremy said as he leaned down to kiss Chance on the lips.

"Wow," Chance said, rubbing his eyes as they tried to focus on the spread before him. His idea of breakfast was a Sausage McMuffin with Egg sandwich from the golden arches. As he looked at the bacon, eggs, country potatoes, mini pancakes, milk, and mimosa, his stomach growled with appreciation. "What's all this?"

"Well, it could be a bribe, or it could be just breakfast. Depending on you."

"A bribe?" Chance said as he sat up and pulled the tray closer to him.

"Yeah," Jeremy said, glancing away and finding little figurines that needed to be adjusted on the bureau. "I was thinking that maybe this could be a permanent thing."

"What could?" Chance asked as he shoveled a forkful of egg and potatoes into his mouth.

"Well, this," Jeremy said, and waved his arm across the tray. "And maybe even us."

Chance stopped chewing in midbite and glanced at his friend. "Huh?"

"I really miss you, Chance," Jeremy said nervously. "I've been thinking about it a lot, and . . . well, since you're already away from San Francisco . . ."

"Boo," Chance said, and set the fork down. "You and I would never make good boyfriends. You know that. We tried it once and it just didn't work."

"Yeah, but that was a few years ago. We've both grown and . . ."

"We haven't grown that much," Chance said, and pulled his friend down onto the bed by his arm. "You're just lonely, Jer. When your aunt died and left you this huge house, you just packed up everything and moved out here on a whim, thinking it would be good for you to get out on your own and start fresh. We all go through that phase, and it's not a bad thing at all. But you haven't really made any close friends and you're feeling homesick. I'm just a representation of that home that you're missing so badly."

"It's not that. . . ."

"Yes, it is," Chance said, and leaned over to kiss Jeremy. "That's all it is. You're missing California, you're missing your friends, you're missing . . ."

"I'm missing you."

Chance looked at his friend and stifled the urge to cry. "Jer, I can't move out here. My life is in San Francisco. And even if I could, it wouldn't be the right thing to do. I'm sorry."

"Okay, then it's just breakfast," Jeremy said, and kissed Chance again, then skipped out of the bedroom.

An hour later Chance was on the road again. Had he known the visit with Jeremy would be such an ordeal, he never would have asked to stay with him. It was good to see him, and the sex was incredible. But he could have done without all the drama. He'd have enough of that once he got to New York City.

The drive across the eastern plains of Colorado and the entire state of Nebraska was pure torment. He'd never seen such dry and flat land in his life, and he had to constantly fight off falling asleep at the wheel. But it was the shortest distance to Chicago, and he was determined to make it to the Windy City. So he stopped often, bought plenty of soda and Red Bull, and kept the gas pedal on the floor.

He hadn't expected the heat, though, and hadn't properly prepared his car for it, either. A little more than five hours into his drive from Denver to Chicago, his car began to overheat and smoke.

"Shit," Chance said loudly as he pulled into the small town of Osceola, Nebraska.

According to the sign at the city limits, the population of Osceola was a little more than eight hundred. It reminded him a lot of Mayberry in the old reruns of *The Andy Griffith Show* he watched late at night when he couldn't sleep.

"Please, God," he said as he looked at the huge expanse of corn and wheat fields on both sides, in front of and behind him, "let there be a service station in this hideous excuse for a town."

The entire town had maybe a dozen streets, and halfway through the Podunk town he saw what apparently served as the village's one and only gas station/coffee shop/novelty shop. Husker's Service Station didn't have a single customer filling up with gas, but there were six or seven men, all in overalls, standing over the open hood of an SUV, talking and scratching their heads.

Chance recited the Serenity Prayer as he pulled the smoking Sky into the open lot.

"Excuse me," he said as the smoking car rolled to a stop just a few feet from the open garage door where the men were working. "I seem to be having a small problem here." He prayed that the farmers didn't recognize the HRC equality sticker on his bumper or the rainbow flag necklace draped over his rearview mirror.

"Yup," said the man with the name Merve embroidered onto the chest of his shirt. He opened the hood of the convertible and peered inside for a moment. "Not too bad. I should be able to fix it in about an hour."

"Oh, good," Chance said.

"But it'll be a couple of hours before I can get to it."

"Huh?" Chance said, trying not to sound as irritated as he felt. "Really?" He looked around at the empty lot and the six men standing around one car, and then back at the Merve.

"Yup," Merve said through a chewed-up matchstick. "Workin' on Harry's Explorer right now. He's got an important meeting in a couple hours and we gotta get it up and running again."

"An important meeting?" Chance asked, looking around him at the silo and endless fields of corn and wheat. There wasn't an office in sight. "Serious?"

"Yup."

"You gotta . . ." He started to challenge the red-necked, tobacco-chewing farmer, but noticed his posse begin to move closer to his car. "You gotta McDonald's or Burger King around here? I could grab a bite to eat while you're finishing up here and work on my car."

"Nope," Merve said, and pulled off his cap and scratched his head. "We ain't got no diners in Osceola."

Chance bit his lower lip to keep from saying something he was smart enough to know he'd regret.

"But Bud was just about to head on home for his lunch."

"Bud?"

"My son. Mama made us both a couple o' meatloaf sandwiches before she left for Lincoln this morning. I brought mine with me and already ate it, but Bud was just about to head home to eat his. I'm sure he wouldn't mind sharin' with you."

"Oh, that's not . . ."

"Bud," Merve yelled loudly, "come on out here."

"Really, that's not . . ." Chance stopped when he saw Bud walk out of the garage.

Bud was stunning. A couple of inches taller than Chance, he nearly filled the doorway as he strutted through it. His long blond hair fell to his shoulders, and he brushed a thick strand of it from his eyes as he walked toward Chance and Merve. Even from several feet away, Chance could see his turquoise eyes sparkle, and the dimples crease his cheeks. His white wifebeater stretched tightly across his chest, highlighting his hard nipples, and long legs filled out his faded blue jeans.

"That's not a bad idea," Chance said. "I've been on the road for hours, and I'm really hungry. I'd be much . . . obliged," he said slowly, hoping he'd remembered the line right from one of those old cowboy movies he'd watched at two in the morning when he'd had one of his notorious bouts of insomnia.

He rode with Bud in his pickup to an old farmhouse about five miles outside of "town." The ride itself was torturous. Chance got an instant hardon the moment he laid eyes on Bud, and it didn't go away the entire ride to the farmhouse. He found it hard to breathe normally, and he couldn't help but glance over at the giant bulge between Bud's legs every few seconds.

Bud didn't say a word while they were in the car. He kept his eyes on the road, his hands on the wheel, and his mouth closed. Chance was afraid if he tried to speak that his voice would come out as a high-pitched adolescent squeak and that he'd blabber on and on endlessly, so he decided to go the silent road as well. He figured that when Bud was ready to speak, he would, and he wasn't in a rush.

They pulled up to the expansive ranch-style home and parked the truck. Bud opened the door, and as Chance walked through it, the farm boy pushed him from his back and shoulders inside the house. Chance stumbled and crashed against the kitchen wall. When Bud grabbed him by the shirt and pushed him against the wall, Chance thought he was about to be beaten and opened his mouth to scream.

Bud leaned in, placed his mouth on Chance's open mouth, and slid his tongue inside. He kissed him slowly and softly as he reached down with one hand and squeezed Chance's cock playfully.

Bud's grip and his kiss were strong and tender at the same time, and Chance struggled not to whimper as the hot farm boy worked his cock into a frenzy and melted his mouth.

"Oh God, I need you so bad," Bud moaned as he pressed himself against Chance and kissed his chin and his neck clumsily. "Please tell me you're okay with this."

Chance pushed Bud away from him a couple of inches and held him at arm's length. "Are you kidding me? You're gay?"

"Yes," Bud groaned. "I mean, no. I don't know." He looked at Chance in the eye for a moment and then dropped his eyes to the floor and took a step back. "I don't know."

"And I don't really care," Chance said, and took a couple steps forward and kissed Merve's son on the lips. "Are you sure you wanna fuck me?"

"Hell yeah," Bud said, and looked back into Chance's eyes hopefully.

Chance ripped Bud's shirt off in just a couple of tugs and attacked his naked chest. It was marble smooth and hard. His tiny nipples begged for attention, and Chance sucked them into his mouth and flicked at them with his tongue.

"Shit, that feels so good, dude," Bud moaned as he fumbled with the buttons on his jeans and pressed his chest even harder against Chance's mouth.

Chance dropped to his knees and pulled Bud's jeans down to his ankles in one move. The kid was wearing a pair of SpongeBob boxers, and his cock stuck out of the fly like a fat, veiny mushroom-headed tongue. It was long and thick and bobbed in front of Chance's face temptingly. Chance was barely able to wrap his fist around it, and when he squeezed it, a thick string of precum dripped from the head. He licked the sweet liquid and sucked the fat head into his throat.

"Oh God," young McDonald moaned, and leaned against the wall to keep from crumbling to the floor when his legs quivered violently.

"You okay, man?" Chance asked as he pulled his mouth from the big dick and looked up into Bud's face.

"Yeah," Bud whispered, and clasped his hands tightly into fists. "I'm just really close."

"What?" Chance said. "But I haven't even done anything yet. I barely sucked the head into my mouth."

"I . . . ummm . . ." he stammered. "I've never really done anything before."

"Nothing?" Chance said, thinking he'd heard incorrectly.

"Well, I've played with myself, of course."

"I don't believe this. You've never fucked a guy . . . or a girl?"

Bud blushed.

"You've never even been blown?"

The farm boy shook his head.

Chance felt his cock throb against his jeans. "Come here," he said to Bud, and pulled him closer to him. He wrapped his arms around the boy's long, thick legs, and hugged them against his chest. Bud's long cock pressed against his face, and he leaned back enough to lick and kiss at the head a moment, and then sucked the entire length into his mouth and down his throat.

"Oh shit," Bud moaned, "I'm gonna . . . don't . . ."

Chance wrapped his lips around the thick cock and tightened his throat muscles around it as it slipped deeper into his throat. He slid his tongue across the head and his own dick hardened so hard it hurt as his tongue licked the thick veins that riddled the fat shaft.

"Ungh . . ."

Chance felt the cock thicken in his mouth as Bud's entire body convulsed against him. Several shots of thick cum splashed against his throat and he swallowed as much as he could. He drank a lot of it, but there was so much that some of it spilled from the corners of his lips. He pulled his mouth from the big dick just as the last couple of spurts landed on his lips and chin.

"Oh my God," Bud whispered as he cleared his throat. "That was incredible."

"Thanks," Chance said as he wiped his lips and rearranged his cock in his jeans. "You ready for lunch?"

"Will you fuck me?" Bud said quickly.

"What?" Chance squeaked. "You're kidding, right?"

"No."

"But you've never . . . I mean . . . you don't even . . ."

"I've fucked a cantaloupe a few times," Bud said matter-of-factly. "It felt all right. But when I used a cucumber in my butt, well, that felt really incredible. I've always wanted to have someone fuck me, but I can't ask anybody around here. They'd run me out of town."

"Bud," Chance said softly. "I don't think that's a good . . ."

"Please," Bud pleaded. "It has to be you. If you don't fuck me, no one will. I'll never know what it feels like."

"Are you sure?"

The farm boy blushed, then smiled. His cock was still fully hard and bouncing in front of him. He reached down and held Chance's hand, and led him into his bedroom.

Once they cleared the bedroom door, Chance pushed Bud forward and onto the bed, and pulled his jeans off roughly. Then he shed his own clothes and climbed into the bed next to Bud. The boy's body was beautiful . . . toned and muscular and smooth. Chance caressed him and leaned in to kiss him.

"Fuck me," Bud whispered hoarsely. "Please. Just fuck me."

Chance's cock was hard and throbbing. It felt like it would explode before he even got inside the young farm kid. He rolled over and pressed his crotch and torso against Bud's backside. "Lift your leg," he said, and put his hand underneath Bud's knee to help the process along.

Bud didn't need any help. He lifted his leg high into the air at the knee and scooted his ass all the way against Chance's cock. He reached back with one hand and grabbed Chance's hard dick and squeezed it a couple of times, and then placed the head at his ass crack. "Fuck me," he moaned, and wiggled his ass against the hard cock head.

Chance's heart was beating fast. He wanted to fuck the farm boy more than he could remember wanting anything in a very long time. The feel of the smooth soft skin, the smell of his musk, the flushed red cheeks that were visible when he looked back at Chance were more than he could take. He spit into his hand and slid the saliva across his cock head, then pushed his hips forward, sliding three or four inches inside the hot hole.

"Oh God," Bud yelled. He bit down onto the pillow to keep from screaming louder.

Chance felt Bud's body tense, and his ass clamped down around Chance's cock like a vice grip. He was afraid of hurting the kid and started to pull his cock out of the tight ass.

"Don't you fucking dare take that cock out of my ass," Bud said between gritted teeth. "Fuck me."

Chance rolled onto his side so that he could slide more of his cock inside the farm boy's ass. When Bud moaned louder, Chance took that as his cue to fuck the kid's brains out, and he set about doing just that. Bud's grunts and moans turned him on more than he'd expected, and he slammed his cock deeper and harder into the hot hole, trying to elicit more of them.

"That . . . feels . . . so . . . good," Bud said in staccato as Chance's cock stabbed into him.

Chance slapped the boy's ass hard, and the sound of his hand making contact with the bare smooth ass caused a jolt of electric pleasure to shoot up his body and through his cock. He almost shot his load right there and knew he had to slow down if he wanted the session to last.

He pulled his cock out of Bud's clutching ass and pulled him onto his knees. With Bud on all fours, he spread his ass apart and spit onto it.

"Yeah, man," Bud said. "Rape my ass, fucker!"

Chance was shocked at those words coming out of the quiet farm boy's mouth. He was even more surprised at how intensely it turned him on. He spit a couple more times on Bud's ass and then slammed his cock all the way to his pubic bone deep inside the smooth hole.

"Owwww," Bud cried, and buried his head in the pillow again as he tightened his ass around Chance's cock and slid backward onto it harder. He bucked back and forth on the thick cock, grunting and moaning the entire time. His fake pleas of mercy and for Chance to go easy on him quickly turned to "fuck my ass, man . . . rape me harder."

Chance slammed his cock harder and faster into the tight ass. He grabbed Bud by the waist and pulled him onto his cock and slapped his ass playfully, but with just enough sting to elicit another cry from the farm boy.

"You ready, man?" Chance said as he grabbed Bud by the hair and pulled his head up toward him. "I'm gonna cum."

"Fuckin' shoot your load all over my ass, dude," Bud spat out as he tightened his ass around Chance's cock.

"Oh fuck!" Chance yelled. He ripped his cock out of Bud's ass just a second before his cock erupted in every direction. Two or three shots splashed across his own face before he was able to point his cock in Bud's direction. Several more landed on the farm boy's ass and back, and a couple sprayed over the kid's head and landed on the headboard.

"I'm cumming, man," Bud said.

Chance grabbed him by the waist and flipped him onto his back in one rough movement. He quickly laid on his stomach between Bud's legs, spreading them farther apart as he positioned himself. He grabbed the base of Bud's long, thick cock and brought it to his mouth. He opened his lips and sucked the big dick deep inside his mouth and throat. The cock felt bigger this time, and he had a little trouble swallowing it all, but after a couple of tries, had it buried deep down his gullet.

"Oh my God," Bud moaned, and lifted his hips off the bed.

Chance knew this reaction and was prepared for it this time. He tightened his lips around the cock and sucked harder. A few seconds later he was rewarded with several mouthfuls of warm cum. He swallowed as fast as he could, determined not to spill any this time around. But as skilled as he was at sucking cock and swallowing loads, Bud just produced way too much. There was no way he could swallow all of it fast enough, and he gagged again, spilling another couple of shots of the sweet cum down his chin.

"Damn, dude," he said, wiping the pungent fluid from his lips and chin.

"Was that all right?" Bud asked, pulling Chance down on top of him and hugging him tightly.

"All right?" Chance asked incredulously. "It was fucking amazing. You have one of the sweetest asses I've ever seen."

"Really?"

"Hell yeah, man. And you have one hell of a hot cock, too. I've never known anyone who shot that huge a load. Fucking incredible!"

The two guys hugged and kissed for a few moments and then fell into a light sleep for about half an hour. Chance woke up first and nudged Bud awake.

"You ready to go again?" Bud asked as he rubbed his eyes.

Chance laughed. "No, baby. I gotta get going. But I'm starving now. Do you really have a meatloaf sandwich?"

"Yeah, come on." He led Chance into the kitchen and made them both a sandwich. He watched Chance the entire time they were eating, and as Chance wiped his mouth and finished his glass of iced tea, Bud decided he couldn't wait any longer. "Take me with you," he blurted out.

Chance choked on his tea. "What?" he asked after catching his breath.

"I gotta get out of here," Bud said, and walked over to stand behind Chance and massage his shoulders. "Take me with you. I won't be a pest, I promise. I could keep you company and we could have fun, don't you think?"

"Bud, I can't take you with me. I'm going home . . . a hostile home, at that . . . to New York City. Have you ever been to New York City?"

"No. I've never been out of Nebraska."

"That's what I thought," Chance said. "Let me tell you, it's a whole different world."

"I want a different world. This one is stifling me."

"It's not a good different, Bud. At least it wouldn't be a good different for you. It'd eat you up in less than a week."

"Please," the farm boy begged.

"No, you can't go with me. But I'll tell you what. When I get back home to San Francisco, you can come visit me for a few days. I'm the last person to stifle someone's coming-out process, and San Francisco is a little less intimidating than New York. If you feel at home in the city, then you can stay with me for a couple of months while you get on your feet. Deal?"

"I don't want to go with you to 'come out.' I want to go with you to be with you," Bud said, and walked away from Chance and over to the back door, where he looked out the window.

"Come on," Chance said, and walked over to join young McDonald at the back door. "Don't get all dramatic on me, Bud. You've known me for a little over an hour. We had sex once. It was incredible, don't get me wrong. But it wasn't life changing."

"It was for me."

"Don't do this to me, please," Chance said. "I'm just not in a place right now where I can be responsible for someone else, especially someone who is a newbie. I've got too much on my mind right now, and I have a lot to deal with when I get home. I can't have something else to worry about."

The hurt look on Bud's face said more than his words ever could have.

"Oh, come on, Bud," Chance said quickly. "You know I didn't mean . . ."

The phone rang and Bud rushed over to pick it up. He turned his back to Chance and spoke softly into the receiver. "Your car is ready," he said quietly without looking at Chance.

The ride back to the garage was speechless, and when they pulled up to the stucco building, Bud got out of the car and walked away from Chance without saying a word.

"How much do I owe you?" Chance asked Merve as the elder farmer watched quizzically as his son stormed past him and into the garage.

"Forty-seven dollars," Merve said as he removed his cap and scratched his head.

"Seriously?" Chance asked. "For parts and labor?"

"Ah, nonsense," Merve said. "I'm not gonna charge you for an hour's worth of work. It basically gave me something to do on my lunch break. And besides, you had to wait around a bit. Just forty-seven dollars for the part, and we're good."

"Well, thank you. I'm not used to that kind of service."

"No, I'm sure you're not," Merve said, and replaced his cap on his head. "And you never know when I might need a favor from you, right?"

"Right," Chance said as he climbed into the car and started it. "Thanks."

"Come back and see us again sometime," Merve said, and waved as Chance pulled away out of the parking lot.

Chance looked in his rearview mirror and saw Bud standing at the open garage door. He saw young McDonald wipe at his eye and then walk dejected back into the garage.

"I cannot believe you're behaving like this," his mother said sternly, her thick arms crossed across her ample bosom. "I did not raise you to be a selfish young man."

Chance stared at his mother as defiantly as he could muster and wondered to himself if her arms really were that much more hairy than that of his friends' mothers' arms or if it was just his imagination. And was that a mustache on her upper lip? He was quite certain Johnny's mother did not have a mustache, nor did Amanda's. Maybe that was why she was so miserable and mean; she was beginning to look more and more like Chance's father every day. He'd overheard a discussion among his parents and their friends a couple weeks ago about how "old married couples" started to look alike and take on one another's personalities. Now he understood.

"But it's my birthday," he said, trying his very hardest not to cry or let her see his lips and chin quiver. She hated that.

"Yes, I know it's your birthday," she spat back at him. "I'm the one that was in labor for sixteen hours, remember?"

Chance glared back at her, refusing to look away. But it wasn't easy. Her voice was getting louder and she took a couple of steps toward him. She wasn't an exceptionally tall or large woman, he knew, because whenever she stood next to other grown-ups she looked rather short and a little stocky. But she towered over him, and her crossed arms and straight, rigid back tended to intimidate him.

"But you are not a baby anymore," she continued. "You're eight years old now, and old enough to realize that you can't always get what you want."

"It's just a bike," he pouted, and looked away from her stabbing eyes. Already he was caving in, and he hated himself for being so weak. "All of my friends have one. I'm the only one who doesn't."

"And I suppose you think that makes it right? If all of your friends also went out and committed mass murder, would that make it okay for you to do?"

Chance looked up at his mother and scrunched his eyes quizzi-

cally. It wasn't that he was challenging her or disputing her in any way. He'd never do that. He just didn't get her reasoning. But he knew the moment he felt his brow crease that his mother would take it that way, and the expression on her face confirmed it.

"What the hell was that look all about?" She raised her voice a couple of decibels.

"What?" he asked, and took a step backward.

"Don't get smart with me, young man," his mother scolded. "I did not raise you to be a smartass."

"No, ma'am," Chance said quietly, and dropped his eyes to the floor.

"At your age you should not be so selfish. Jesus H. Christ, all you think about is yourself. You act like money grows on trees or something."

"But you just bought a bunch of toys for that missionary group at church," Chance said softly. "I don't know why . . ."

Her hand swung through the air swiftly and landed hard across his cheek with a slapping sound. Though he wasn't exactly expecting it, he was also familiar enough with his mother's reactions to his asserting himself that he was somewhat prepared for it. His head swerved to the side as her open hand made contact, but his feet were firmly planted on the floor and he didn't sway.

"Oh, for crying out loud," Chance's father said from his La-Z-Boy in the corner of the living room several feet away. "Is that necessary, Martha? He's just asking for a bike on his eighth birthday. It's not like he's asking for a Corvette or anything. Like he said, all of his friends have a bike. It's a perfectly normal request."

Chance looked at his father and felt like crying. Not from the pain of being slapped from his mother, but because he couldn't remember ever having loved his father more than he did at that moment.

"Well, isn't that just great?" his mother said, and placed her hands on her hips. "So now you're going to side with him and gang up against me, huh?"

"I'm not siding with anyone," his father said, and already Chance could hear his resolve weakening. "And we're not ganging up against you. I'm just saying I don't think he's asking for anything out of the ordinary. And certainly not for anything that is worth a slap in the face."

Mrs. McAllister stared at her husband, straightened her back, and raised a single eyebrow. Chance watched as his father's posture slumped in the chair, and he physically saw the will to defend himself or Chance ooze away from his father and float out the door.

It wasn't the first time his father had let him down, and it certainly wasn't the last. But it was the time that Chance remembered most of all. It was the time he felt most betrayed, because in the past his father had never bothered to try to defend him. This time he did stand up to Chance's mother, if only briefly. And when he backed down so easily it felt as if he'd dangled a carrot in front of Chance's eyes and then snatched it away with no hope of ever seeing it again. It was a carrot that Chance didn't see often throughout the rest of his life, but when he did it always ended up being pulled back out of reach.

A large truck barreled past Chance in the passing lane and blared his horn as he did, jolting Chance from his daydream. The drive across Colorado, Nebraska, and Iowa had been a big blur, noteworthy of nothing save for his overnight stay with Jeremy in Denver, and maybe the lunch stop with Bud in Nebraska. But he wanted to put all that behind him now.

But he'd really been looking forward to his visit and overnight stay in Chicago. It was one of the few cities in the United States that he'd always wanted to visit but hadn't been able to. As he drove into the city limits, and the downtown skyline came into view, he felt his heart begin to speed up and butterflies twitter in his stomach. He'd seen photos and articles in the newspapers and magazines, and had even seen a few videos of the International Mister Leather contests in Chicago, and had always been turned on by them. While in Las Vegas he bought a U.S. gay travel guide and had precisely planned his visit to the Windy City.

Or more accurately, he'd meticulously planned out his visits to the bars and clubs, even going so far as to make a schedule for each place. What he'd failed to do, however, was to make reservations for a hotel. He hadn't thought it'd be necessary. With so many hotels in Chicago, surely it wouldn't be a problem getting a room. But he was wrong. He hadn't anticipated the largest evangelical convention in the country being in town the same time he was there and quickly learned that virtually every hotel room in the city, or at the very least every one of them that was habitable, was already rented out.

After being turned away the sixth time in less than a couple of hours, Chance turned to his gay guide and came across an ad for Steamworks, Chicago's famed bathhouse. He'd never been to a bathhouse before; he'd heard about them in New York before leaving for the Bay Area, but he'd been too young and inexperienced to work up the nerve to go. They were banned in San Francisco. There was one in Berkeley, also called Steamworks, and the Watergarden in San Jose, but he'd just never had the need or the desire to drive an hour to check one out.

But now that he was stranded in Chicago, with very little if any other viable option, he found himself getting excited over the idea. He'd stopped in at Nookie's Tree Café for a sandwich and soda, and according to the travel guide, it was only a couple blocks from Steamworks. Chance quickly finished the last of his dinner and walked the short distance to the bathhouse. He paid the $5 one-time membership fee and, after hearing the descriptions of the room choices, decided on the $55 extra large room; for an extra $7 Chance elected to add a sling to his room.

He had no idea what a typical room in a bathhouse looked like, but he was pretty sure that the term "extra large" would be considered a stretch of even the most vivid imagination. Still, it had a clean and decent-sized bed, and the leather sling fit comfortably next to the bed and in front of the door. He reminded himself that he was not staying in the Hyatt Regency that night, and once he'd reconciled that fact, he found himself getting aroused at the smell and feel of the leather sling.

He undressed quickly and changed the channel on the TV to one that was showing a video that he found hot. Then he clumsily climbed into the sling and settled into it. It took him a few minutes to realize what the hanging straps at the foot of the sling were for. But once he figured it out, he quickly slipped his feet through the straps and his cock instantly hardened as the stirrup straps forced his legs apart and exposed his naked ass to anyone walking by his open door.

The feel of the leather straps on the sling pressed against his skin and the musky smell of it permeated his nostrils. Chance had never really gotten into the leather scene and was surprised at the reaction he was having to it. He couldn't remember when his cock had been as hard or as hot, and his heart pounded erratically in his chest as he struggled to catch his breath. He could feel his asshole twitching uncontrollably and wished he'd been able to do that at will on more than once occasion.

He hadn't been in the sling more than five minutes before he got his first bite. But the guy was a little overweight and a little old for Chance's preference, and so he shook his head and said, "no, thanks" when the middle-aged man walked into his room.

The next guy looked to be in his midthirties. He was well over six feet tall, with long muscular legs and a strong, powerful chest. His face was chiseled with a little stubble and a pair of dimples that never went away, even when he wasn't smiling. He had a spattering of short black hair across his muscular chest that almost, but not quite, hid his tiny but hard nipples. He had a clean white towel wrapped around his lean waist, and it tented out several inches down the inside of his thigh.

Chance gasped audibly as the man took a couple of steps into the room. His cock throbbed visibly and his asshole began to do the cha-cha between his spread legs. He tried to control his breathing and make his mutinous ass stop embarrassing him, but it was useless. His body was on autopilot, and he couldn't deny that he wanted this guy to do whatever he wanted with him.

The stranger dropped to his knees, and a second later Chance felt strong hands grab his legs and push them even farther apart. He shuddered as he felt a stream of cool air blow across his exposed hole, and then a second later he felt the guy's face press against his ass cheeks. A loud ringing bounced between his ears inside his head, and he felt like he'd faint as the strong, wet tongue licked around his hungry hole and then slipped slowly inside.

"Oh Jesus!" Chance moaned as he slid his body farther down the sling to give his new friend easier access.

"You like that, man?" the guy asked as he came up for air and peeked around Chance's legs.

"Hell yeah."

"Good," he said with a smile, and dove back in between Chance's legs.

Chance felt his eyes roll back into their sockets as his throat dried up and felt like sandpaper. He couldn't stop his ass from twitching or his legs from spreading farther apart to take even more of the guy's talented tongue. After a while, he stopped trying and just allowed himself to enjoy the workover. His cock bounced across his belly and dripped huge amounts of precum. He wanted to stroke his cock but knew that as soon as he touched it, he'd blow his load all over the place, so he wrapped his arms around the chain restraint that hung from the ceiling right above his head.

"You ready for me to fuck your ass, man?" the stranger said roughly as he stood up and positioned himself between Chance's quivering legs.

"Oh God, yes!" Chance whispered. He looked behind the beautiful man and saw a group of five or six guys huddled around his door and watching them. He started to ask them to leave but then noticed that all but one of them were really hot and were stroking their hard cocks as they watched him prepare to take the studly stranger. The idea of so many guys getting off on watching him get his ass fucked turned him on. "Fuck me!" he said louder and more forcefully than he'd intended.

The man spit a mouthful of saliva onto the head of his cock and rested it against Chance's sphincter. He was being gentle and not trying to press forward, but Chance's ass was hungry and begging to be fed, and it opened up and swallowed the thick cock head like a Venus flytrap.

"Damn, dude," the guy moaned as he slid all the way forward until the last inch of his cock was buried deep in Chance's ass. He grabbed Chance's legs and held them at the ankle as he slammed his cock in and out of Chance's hole first slow and deep, and then faster and with a jabbing rhythm.

Chance glanced over at the men standing just outside his doorway. They were all pretty good-looking and had nice bodies. Under any circumstances, they'd be his type, and he'd not complain about any of them fucking him. "Get over here and let me suck your cock," he blurted out to no one in particular.

The group surged forward like a swarm of bees and surrounded Chance around the sling. One of them stood behind him and slipped his thick, uncut cock into Chance's mouth. Two more stood on either side of him and stroked their cocks close to his face. The last one stood next to his waist, leaned forward, and sucked Chance's cock into his mouth.

"Hell yeah, man," the guy fucking him moaned as he pounded Chance's ass harder and faster.

Chance felt as if he were floating outside and above his body. His ass was being stretched to a point it hadn't often been. Every time the big dick slammed deep inside him and scraped his prostate, he felt as if he'd had a religious experience. The thick cock in his mouth rubbed against his tonsils as it slid deep into his throat. He loved sucking a nice cock although he had never considered himself an expert cocksucker, but the guy was fucking his mouth as hard and fast as the stranger on the other end of the sling was fucking his ass, and Chance didn't gag once.

"Oh fuck!" the guy in his mouth moaned. "He's got a fucking hot mouth, guys." He held Chance by the head and slid his cock deeper into his mouth a couple more times. "I'm gonna cum!"

He stopped pumping his cock and just kept it buried deep inside Chance's throat as he held onto Chance's head.

Chance felt the guy's legs shake violently, and a second later the cock in his mouth grew even thicker and sprayed a huge load into his gullet. He swallowed five or six times to keep from choking on it, and when the guy began to pull out, he was reluctant to let it go. He didn't taste the cum, because the cock was too far down his throat and away from his taste buds, but his throat and esophagus grew warm with the load, and he didn't want the feeling to go away. He sucked it back into his mouth and continued sucking on it as the guy caught his breath.

"Did he drink your load, man?" the first guy asked as he slammed his dick deeper and harder into Chance's ass.

"Fuck yeah, man."

"Nice," the guy said. "I'm gonna shoot!" He ripped his cock from Chance's ass and pointed it toward his head. Several shots of hot cum sprayed across Chance's body and landed on his face and chest, and then the rest settled onto his stomach and balls, and on the back of the head of the guy sucking Chance's cock.

"Oh my God," Chance tried to say, but because his mouth was still filled with cock, it came out as "ungh mmm gnng." A second later his body stiffened as he spewed his load into the mouth of the guy sucking his cock. He convulsed several times as he bucked up and shoved his cock deeper into the guy's throat, causing him to gag.

The man pulled his mouth off of Chance's cock to catch his breath, and the last couple of shots of Chance's load splashed across his stomach.

"Shit!" the guy on Chance's left yelled and shot his load all the way across his chest, landing on the other guy beating off on his right. Both men sprayed their loads all over his face, chest, and arms until he was covered in jizz and all of the men around him panted to catch their breath and leaned against the walls for support of their shaking legs.

The other guys slowly straggled out of the room, leaving Chance and his first friend alone.

"Very nice, man," the guy said as he walked over and sat on the bed. "Are you from here in Chicago?"

"No," Chance said, still struggling to catch his breath and trying to sound like he wasn't completely overwhelmed with the beauty and virility of his new friend. "I'm from San Francisco and am on my way to visit my folks in New York."

"Damn, that's too bad," the guy said. He looked to Chance as if he was truly disappointed, and that made Chance feel like he was some kind of rock star. "How long will you be here?"

"I leave tomorrow. I'm just staying the night here because all the hotels were sold out. I promised my mom I'd be home . . . well, her home anyway . . . by tomorrow, and I'm already a day behind."

"Shit," the stranger said. "Well, I'd really like to make love to you. The right way this time, kissing and holding and cuddling with you in bed. Mind if I stay with you here tonight?"

Chance untangled himself from the sling and stumbled over to the bed. He leaned down and kissed the man on the mouth, savoring the taste of his tongue and lips. "No, I don't mind at all," he said, and wrapped his arms around the guy as he fell forward onto the bed.

Right of Passage

Lawrence Henderson looked out the tiny rectangular window at the landscape below him and struggled to catch his breath. He'd been told to be prepared to have his breath taken away at first sight of the African savanna, and he thought he was. He was wrong. The sun was just preparing to set over the horizon, and it cast an orangish-red hue across the few clouds that were strewn across the deepest and most majestic violet sky he'd ever seen, or even imagined.

Scattered prides of lions sprawled under the shade of shorter trees as giraffes and elephants grazed on the fruit and leaves of the magnificent and much taller wild syringa, leadwood, and marula. The giant cats yawned lazily and watched disinterested as antelope and wild rabbits bounded across the terrain. They seemed in no hurry to pounce, and it looked to Lawrence as if the prey were oblivious to their presence.

As the plane touched ground, he felt tears well up in his eyes and thought his heart would burst in his chest. The lump in his throat made it impossible to swallow. He'd often heard people say that they felt at "home" when they visited Africa for the first time, and he'd just as often thought it was the most ridiculous and trite thing he'd ever heard. How could anyone feel at home in a place they'd never been before, and halfway across the globe from their life and their real home?

But now he understood. Of the forty or so passengers on the plane, only six were black. Lawrence looked around at the faces of those around him. Five other people had that same sparkle in their eyes that he knew he must have, and they had the same irrepressible smile on their lips. They were home, too.

"I know it might not seem like much," Greg said in his deep voice and thick Kirundi accent, "but it is our sanctuary and we take much pride in it."

Lawrence stood in front of the tiny stone and mud building and took it all in. He didn't need to move his head or use his peripheral vision to get the full effect—it was all right there. Four walls, about ten feet tall and twenty feet wide. One room. A modest wooden cross perched atop the rounded straw roof. He allowed Greg to walk a few steps ahead of him and open the single door made of large twigs held tightly together by thick rope. At the front of the chapel was a single black aluminum music stand that he knew would be his pulpit for the next two years. An old upright piano rested against the back wall, and a couple dozen folding chairs were placed in meticulous rows on either side of the narrow aisle down the center of the room.

"It's beautiful," he said, and noticed the proud smile spread across his caretaker's face. "How many congregants do we have?"

"There are about twenty of us who attend regularly," Greg said, and swatted a fly from his face. "But the entire village has been waiting with much anxiety for your arrival. I expect they will all be here. I must remember to bring in a few more chairs."

"And just how many is 'all of them'?"

"There are thirty-two people, including children, in this village." He pointed to the next hill over, about a mile away. "Our neighbors have their own church, but they will be curious, so I expect they will be here on Sunday as well, to satisfy their curiosity. I would be prepared for an audience of about sixty."

"There's no way this room will hold sixty people," Lawrence said as he quickly scanned the room. "Even if they are all standing."

"No. Many of them will stand outside and watch from the door and windows."

"Fair enough," the pastor said. He reminded himself that he'd wanted an adventure and a challenge, and that he'd applied for this missionary position out of selfless love. He didn't need the Crystal Cathedral or the Mormon Tabernacle to preach the gospel and save souls.

"I hope you don't think me too bold," the custodian said awkwardly, "but may I ask why you came to Burundi?"

The question caught Lawrence off guard, but he tried to maintain a neutral expression. "I wanted to make a difference," he said honestly.

"In your life or in ours?"

Pastor Henderson flinched from the question and reached out for the nearest chair, as if he'd been struck.

"I'm sorry," Greg said, and reached for his new preacher. "I'm very rude."

"No, Greg, it's fine. Really, it's a fair question."

"It's just that . . . well, as I stated, we're very curious. All of our other missionaries have been Caucasian. We were not expecting you to be one of us."

"I have always wanted to be a missionary," Lawrence said, and motioned for Greg to sit with him. "I love to travel and to experience the world. I never really gave a lot of thought as to

106 / *Sean Wolfe*

where I would serve. But when this opportunity presented itself, I jumped at the chance. I thought it would be good to connect with my heritage a little. So, to be honest, I guess I came here with a few selfish motives. But I hope that it will prove to be a mutually beneficial relationship. I expect to learn as much from you as you do from me."

Greg laughed heartily. "You are well practiced in the art of diplomacy."

"It comes with the position." Lawrence smiled and extended his hand. "Friends?"

"Friends."

He thought he was prepared but he was wrong. While in training for his missionary work to "the Heart of Africa," he was taught about the recent civil war that had just ended a few years ago, and that was still very fresh in everyone's memory. Almost half a million people had been killed, and that was not something that was easily forgotten or forgiven. Tension was still high among the feuding Hutu and Tutsi tribes, and stress was a way of life, he was told. People walked around with rifles and shotguns and machetes, he was informed. Gunshots and guerrilla warfare still occurred on the streets of Bujumbura, the capital city. And so he could logically expect an even tenser and more violent situation in the rural hilly plateaus between the capital and Gitega, the second-largest city a few miles east.

And so Lawrence had been prepared for the worst and was pleasantly surprised when he arrived in his small village. The land there was a series of rolling hills and narrow valleys, and he was surprised at how lush most of it was. He'd envisioned dry and dusty flatlands and leafless, scrawny trees. Families, or clans, built tiny mini-villages on individual hilltops, staking their claim and farming and cultivating the land. They lived as high on the hilltops as possible, avoiding the valleys because of the devastating tsetse fly infestation in the dried-up riverbed valleys below.

Each small hilltop village consisted of eight to ten *rugos*, or small straw huts, inhabited by immediate family members. Though in much of the country the two tribes could be distinguished and identified by their economic status—the Hutu being peasant farmers and the Tutsi being cattle herders—in this particular small patch of Burundi landscape the two tribes found a way to make peace and support one another. They bartered the scarce cattle and livestock for vegetables, fruit, and pottery. Each clan had its specialty, and everyone respected the communal efforts of the others.

There was no fighting . . . not with guns or machetes or even words. Not in this small piece of paradise. Instead, when they weren't working the paltry fields or herding the emaciated cattle or poultry, the young kids played soccer and practiced reciting poetry, and the older kids and adults told stories and played mancala, a popular board game. There were still Hutu and Tutsi, and they didn't cohabitate, but they got along and they supported one another with trade.

It didn't take long for Lawrence to relax and stop listening for gunshots in his sleep or expecting to be captured and beheaded or eaten alive. The first Sunday morning was and always would be a blur for Lawrence. His heart pounded in his chest and against his ribs. Bright pinpoints of light burst in front of his eyes and floated around his face. A loud ringing in his ears threw him off balance and he struggled not to faint. But as the weeks passed and he became acquainted with the members of his congregation, it all got easier and he began to feel more at home. He began to believe he'd made the right decision, and that all would be right.

Until one Sunday morning about three months into his tenure. It started out like any other Sunday morning and any other sermon. This particular one was about temptation, and it proved to be prophetic. Lawrence had been studying everyone's name and practicing his pronunciation. He just about had everyone's name down and was familiar with which rugo they lived in and what role they carried out in the communal assignments of societal tasks.

But that particular Sunday a newcomer attended his service, and Lawrence's world was shaken to the core. The boy couldn't have been more than fifteen or sixteen years old. He snuck in quietly almost halfway through the service and took one of the few empty seats in the back row, trying to be as inconspicuous as possible. But that was *im*possible. Most of the children in Lawrence's village, and about half of the adults for that matter, wore outdated western clothes donated by various churches from the States. But this young man walked in wearing brightly colored flowing robes and an ornate headdress with a long purple scarf draped down his shoulders and back.

Every head in the small church turned to look at the boy, and it didn't take long before the whispered chatter grew louder than Lawrence's sermon. When he spoke louder to overcome it, the murmur crescendoed to match his volume. He'd lost his audience's attention, and so he wrapped the sermon up and closed the service hurriedly. Before he said "Amen" on the benediction, the people were on their feet and gravitating toward the newcomer like a celebrity.

From his place at the pulpit, Lawrence couldn't make out the boy's features very well. He could tell that he was a young boy and that he was brilliantly dressed. As he put on his glasses and walked toward the boy and the crowd surrounding him to find out what all the commotion was about, he was stopped halfway down the center aisle. The boy was stunning, and when he looked into Lawrence's eyes, the pastor's cock hardened.

"No, God, please," he prayed under his breath. "Not again. Not here."

"Lawrence, you must come here," Greg said loudly over the crowd, and motioned excitedly for the pastor to join him at the center of the circle of his congregation. "This is Gabriel Bhatanyanaku. He is the eldest son of Chief Bhatanyanaku of the most honored and revered Hutu clan in Burundi."

"Nice to meet you, Gabriel," Lawrence said as he extended his hand.

Greg slapped the hand away quickly. "You are not to shake his hand," he whispered.

"I'm sorry. I didn't know."

"Bow your head," the caretaker said, and bowed his as well.

Lawrence bowed his head slightly and felt Gabriel's hand touch his head lightly. It was the slightest touch, yet enough to make the hardon in his slacks throb painfully against his leg. The boy's long fingers caressed the crown of his head and caused an electrical tingle to surge through his body.

When motioned to do so, he straightened up and looked at Gabriel. The boy was about six feet tall, and even with the oversized colorful robe, Lawrence could see he was powerfully built. His facial features were sharp and exotic, with high cheekbones and a strong jawline. His eyes were almond shaped and bright hazel in color with long, curly lashes.

Gabriel whispered something into Greg's ear, and Greg shooed the congregation away quickly. Then he motioned for Lawrence and Gabriel to sit.

"He has traveled by foot for four days to meet you," the custodian said when the boy finished whispering in his ear.

"Well, that's very flattering," Lawrence said with a chuckle. "I like to think I'm a pretty good preacher, but I don't think anybody's . . ."

"You have been chosen," Greg said solemnly. "It is a very big honor, Lawrence, and not a laughing matter."

"I'm sorry," the preacher said. "I didn't mean to offend. But what have I been chosen for?"

"To be Gabriel's *concebena*."

"His what?"

"Gabriel is the last son of the Bhatanyanaku lineage. They are the oldest of the Hutu tribe and date back to the first century. They used to rule over vast tribal territories, but over the past several decades they have all been killed off. His father is the final of the *Bahinza*, an ancient king, almost like the Egyptian pharaoh."

"Wow, that's very impressive," Lawrence said as he stared at Gabriel. He could easily see Gabriel as a pharaoh. "But I still don't get what that has to do with me."

"On his fifteenth birthday, the eldest son of the Bahinza trades in his *dashiki*, this colorful garment Gabriel is now wearing, for a white robe called a *dashira*. He wears this dashira for one year and twelve days while he follows his father's every move and become his apprentice. After that period of time, the boy burns the dashira in a ceremonial bonfire with all of the clan members in a sacred dance, and it is then he is given the *tankshitri*. This is the elaborate gold and green robe of the Bahinza. The boy is now the new Bahinza, and his father becomes the senior advisor on the tribal council."

"That's wonderful," Lawrence said. I'm sure Gabriel will make a great Bahinza."

"Yes, he will," Greg said matter-of-factly. "But before he can become Bahinza, he must mate with a chosen concebena."

"Excuse me?"

"This is a spiritually blessed and anointed elder male not of the immediate Bahinza clan. The union is blessed and the

Spirit of Na circulates through the blood of the concebena and into the Bahinza. It is a rite of passage into manhood and a prerequisite for becoming Bahinza."

"That's ridiculous," Lawrence said before he could stop himself. Greg stared coldly into his eyes. "I'm sorry, I didn't mean to offend you. But this boy is a child."

"Our life expectancy here in Burundi is forty-five, forty-six years old, Lawrence. I am thirty-two, and look how much older than you I look already. At fifteen, a boy becomes a man. For the new Bahinza, part of that ritual into manhood is to partner with a concebena. Once the union is blessed and consummated, only then is the boy ready to marry and create a family, and specifically an heir. It is during this time that he is an apprentice to his father, and eventually becomes the new Bahinza. The concebena becomes the second most trusted and respected advisor, immediately after the father of the new Bahinza. His is a place of trust, and he dwells with the leader for the rest of his life. Without the blessed union with the concebena, the process is stopped and the boy cannot become a man. In Gabriel's case, the Bhatanyanaku lineage would die. There would be no more Bahinza."

"And what about the bride?"

"Her duty is to provide an heir to the Bahinza, to nurture the children and to obey her husband. She sleeps and eats in the rugo with the children and other women, and the concebena is at the side of the Bahinza."

"This is ludicrous. It's a sin. It's not right." Already he could feel his resolve dissipating with each pulse of his cock.

"Blasphemy," Greg said quietly and genuflected.

"Greg, this is preposterous. It is illegal to have sexual relations with a minor."

"You are not in America now, Lawrence. In Burundi, it is

against the nature and law of Eshu if you do not consummate the blessed union with Gabriel. It is preordained that you are the chosen concedena."

"Concubine," Lawrence whispered. "Concedena is concubine, isn't it?"

"Yes. It's a great honor."

"Honor? It's degrading and inhumane and demoralizing. It's a sin and it's illegal!"

"It is not to be debated. It is so. It is a place of honor and dignity. It is the ultimate fulfillment of destiny."

Lawrence looked into Gabriel's eyes and wanted desperately to fulfill his destiny . . . to lean in and kiss him on his full, pink lips. The boy looked like a Michelangelo sculpture, a study in perfection. As hard as he tried, and as much as he argued, he couldn't get the vision of the young boy's cock sliding in and out of his ass or the taste of it in his mouth out of his mind. He'd wanted and desired many things in his life, but nothing as badly as he desired Gabriel.

"But Greg, I am forty-four years old. He's not yet fifteen."

"That is precisely one of the reasons you are the chosen one. Forty-four is a magical number of enlightenment and fulfillment. It is exactly this age at which the chosen one must become one with the young Bahinza. It is not immoral, Lawrence. It is not sin. It is not wrong, it is right. It is destiny. It is law."

The preacher looked over at the young pharaoh, and when the boy looked into his eyes and smiled, he knew he wouldn't deny his destiny. "All right. It is so."

The rugo was lit with a dozen tiki lamps and candles, and strings of bells and wind chimes hung around the door and windows. A musky incense burned in the middle of the small straw hut, with blue smoke drifting lazily to the roof. Outside the rugo, drums were beating in a hypnotic melody, and the chants of a couple dozen tribal leaders from the region were getting stronger by the minute.

Lawrence stared at the young boy in front of him. He knew Gabriel was only fifteen, but only because Greg had told him so. He was tall and muscular and grandiose in every way imaginable. His muscles flexed randomly as he stood quietly in one corner of the rugo. His jawline was strong and pronounced, and suggested a powerful leader in the making. His eyes never left Lawrence's own, and it was hard for the preacher not to get lost in them.

But what really mesmerized the American was the long, thick cock that hung halfway down the boy's legs. Even fully soft it was the biggest cock he'd ever seen, and that was not an insignificant feat. Lawrence wanted to drop to his knees and swallow it in one lunge, savoring its heat and saltiness as it filled his mouth and throat.

He knew the boy was only fifteen, and he was struggling with the intense desire he had for the kid. He'd fled Iowa after the scandal that ensued when his congregation had been informed, by an indiscreet visitor to the town, of their pastor's sexual proclivities. The young man had been overpoweringly beautiful and had come into his life when Lawrence was particularly weak. He'd struggled with his sexuality all of his life but had managed to hide it from most people quite successfully. He went to a Christian college, graduated with honors, and even married his college girlfriend to keep up appearances. He tried to fall in love with Camilla, but never managed to get there. But he had a semblance of happiness in his life as a pastor in the small Iowa town. There was no one there that he was the least bit attracted to, and so temptation was minimal. Once every couple of months he made a trek to Des Moines and visited a couple of their gay bars. More often than not, he spent the time alone, just looking at the lovely young gay men around him. But he did engage with a handful of them over the past ten years.

When Camilla passed away from cancer a couple of years ago, he felt ashamed for feeling like a weight had been lifted from his shoulders. He wouldn't have to hurt her with the truth and he wouldn't have to continue lying to her, either. But the compassion from his congregation after she passed was smothering and made it impossible for him to leave. Impossible, that is, until William Smith roared through town in his red Mustang GT and his breathtaking smile and seductive ass. He'd seemed so nice and sweet while they were together. But after the four-day rendezvous, he left town without a word. Two days later, Lawrence got a phone call from the president of the board of his church. William Smith had mailed a letter and a picture that was "less than satisfactory" for a pastor in Lawrence's position. He would be given a letter of recommendation, but his services were no longer needed at the Council Bluffs Presbyterian Church, effective immediately.

Lawrence fled town in the middle of the night, anxious to get as far away from Council Bluffs as possible. He spent a couple of weeks in a dingy motel room on the outskirts of Des Moines, hiring a number of hookers and taking home a different boy every night of the week either from the street or the bars. He was startled by an early morning wake-up knock at the door by all twelve members of the Council Bluffs Presbyterian Church. They were intervening, and literally pushed him into the church van and drove him 150 miles across the state border to a well-known rehab center. When he finished the program, they continued their support by sponsoring his missionary assignment to Burundi. He needed to be immersed in spreading the gospel to the sinners, get in touch with God himself again, and be as far away from temptation as he could get.

It wasn't working.

"Gabriel, I know you can't understand me," Lawrence said softly, and tried not to stare at the young boy's now-growing cock. "But I have to say this anyway."

"I understand you perfectly," Gabriel said in the sweetest voice Lawrence had ever heard.

"You speak English?" He couldn't believe he was hearing correctly. Surely the incense was tainted with opium or something.

"Yes," Gabriel said, and took a couple of steps closer to the preacher. With each gait, his cock thickened and grew longer and harder. "My mother was British. She met my father while on safari here, and . . . well, here I am. She didn't know she was pregnant when she returned to London. When I was born, she brought me to Africa to meet my father. She had great respect for the African culture and wanted me to share in its wealth. I came back and spent every summer with my father and my tribe, learning their ways."

"Why didn't you say something to me earlier? When Greg was supposedly translating for you?"

"It is custom for the new Bahinza not to speak with his concedena until the night of their marriage."

"Marriage?" Lawrence squeaked out.

"Yes, surely you understand that's what this arrangement is? In our custom, the Bahinza has two partners, two marriages. One with his wife, to provide a family and an heir, and the other with his concedena, to provide spiritual growth, enlightenment, companionship, and esoteric and divine love."

"But if you grew up in London and have had a Western education, then you have to know this is wrong. It is a sin."

"I know that Western education, especially in religion, is more concerned about what they believe is right in the eyes of God than in what God believes is right. I know that they have a strong need to be 'righteous' and to judge others and do not feel they should have to listen or open their minds to the ideas, thoughts, or cultures of other peoples. I believe . . ."

Lawrence laughed. "Okay, okay. I get it. So, you're okay with all of this?"

"Okay with it?" Gabriel said as he leaned forward and kissed Lawrence on the lips. "I chose you. You are my soul mate."

"But surely your mother . . ."

"She died five years ago. That's when I moved here permanently to live with my father."

"I'm so sorry, Gabriel."

"Thank you." He pulled his concedena in closer and kissed him hard and full on the lips. His own cock was quickly reaching full hardness, and when he pressed against Lawrence's torso, he realized that the preacher was not far behind him in arousal.

Lawrence returned Gabriel's kiss and ripped his clothes from his body. When he was completely naked, he laid Gabriel gently on the makeshift bed. His entire body was tingling with excitement, and he couldn't keep his hands from caressing and roaming over every inch of Gabriel's hard, smooth body. He licked the boy's nipples and sucked on them when they grew hard in his mouth. Then he moved his way down the firm, smooth chest and stomach.

Gabriel's cock was fully hard, and his cock head extended a couple of inches above his navel. Lawrence gasped as his mouth reached it. He took a deep breath, and then licked at the throbbing head tenderly.

"Take it all, Pastor Henderson."

Lawrence sucked the fat head into his mouth, and then slid his lips down the huge shaft as far as he could go. With seven or eight inches in his mouth he began to gag, and was amazed to see that he had only about half of the massive dick inside his throat. He was not an overly proud man, and not afraid to admit when he had reached his limit. He wrapped his throat around the big cock and sucked it harder, concentrating all of his oral talents on the half of the cock that he could take.

"Oh my God," Gabriel gasped. "I'm gonna cum."

Lawrence reached down and massaged Gabriel's big balls and sucked harder. A couple of seconds later, he began to choke as wave after wave of warm, sweet cum filled his mouth and slid down his throat.

"Man, that was incredible," Lawrence said slowly as he caught his breath. "But I wish it hadn't ended so quickly."

"Oh, it hasn't ended," Gabriel said. "It's just begun." He leaned over and kissed his concedena on the lips, and then moved down his torso, nibbling on Lawrence's nipples and kissing his belly button.

"Oh Jesus, Gabriel," Lawrence moaned. He reached for the boy's still-hard and throbbing cock, and maneuvered the soon-to-be chief into a sixty-nine position. He licked on the sticky head for a moment and then allowed Gabriel to lower himself farther into his mouth. This time he opened his throat wider, and his eyes bulged and began to water as inch after inch of the boy's giant cock slid deeper into his throat. Gabriel didn't stop until his smooth balls rested against Lawrence's forehead.

Lawrence didn't dare try to be adventurous but instead lay perfectly still as Gabriel slid the big cock in and out of his mouth, and swallowed his own in return. It didn't take long before the young boy was pumping his mouth pretty good and, before Lawrence knew it, was coming, Gabriel released another big load deep into his throat and stomach.

This time, the pastor wasn't far behind. The kid was an expert cocksucker, and Lawrence couldn't hold back any longer. "I'm cumming," he screamed out, as he pulled his mouth from

Gabriel's still-hard dick and thrust his own deeper into the boy's throat. His body quivered violently as he bucked and shot his load into Gabriel's hungry mouth.

"Turn over," Gabriel said softly, and reached under Lawrence to help him move onto his stomach.

"There's no way I can . . ."

"Yes, you can," Gabriel reassured him, and kissed him on the lips as he laid his torso against Lawrence's naked backside. "I'll be careful not to hurt you, I promise."

Lawrence took a deep breath and allowed himself to meld with the mattress beneath him and the sensation of Gabriel's warm, slick body on top of him. He felt the massive dick throbbing against his leg and ass crack, and thought once again that he couldn't possibly take it up his ass. But he knew that he wanted it more than anything he'd ever wanted in his life. More than a normal life, more than his marriage, more than being a preacher. More than salvation.

"Fuck me, Gabriel," he moaned loudly as he tensed his ass cheeks and lifted them so they pressed more firmly against Gabriel's cock and abdomen. Gabriel didn't need any encouragement, and spread Lawrence's ass cheeks apart and slid just the head of his cock inside.

"Oh, FUCK!" Lawrence screamed. "That hurts. Take it out."

"I'm sorry," Gabriel whispered in his preacher's ear, but didn't obey. "It won't hurt for long, I promise."

Lawrence bit down on the pillow and clutched at the sides of the mattress. He took a couple of deep breaths and relaxed. After about a minute, the pain subsided and the huge cock in his ass began to feel incredible. He'd been fucked a few times, but not many. And never any that felt this good. The smell of the incense and the flicker of the candles around him cast a supernatural aura around him, and the nerves in his body felt as if they were being short-circuited as Gabriel slid his cock in and out of his ravenous ass.

"Are you okay?" the soon-to-be Bahinza whispered into Lawrence's ear as he kissed it tenderly.

"Oh yes," the pastor moaned, and squeezed his ass in appreciation. "I'm better than okay."

He leaned backward to kiss Gabriel on the mouth, and as he did his ass opened a fraction of an inch wider, allowing the young boy's dick to slip the last couple of inches inside. Now he was filled with the hot cock, and he felt as if every fiber of his being was ignited with Gabriel's heat. Every sense was heightened. He could smell the sweet breath from Gabriel's mouth and was intoxicated by it. The boy's skin was hot and smooth, but the sweat dripping from it was cool and invigorating. His moans drifted into Lawrence's ear and tickled him from the inside, and as the big cock sped up and slid in and out of his ass faster and deeper and longer, Lawrence thought he might have an out-of-body experience.

"I'm getting close," Gabriel panted as he slowed down. His thrusts became deeper, and hit a spot deep in Lawrence's gut that caused his ears to ring and his head to become light.

"Me too," he moaned, and thrust his ass deeper onto his new lover's dick.

"Oh God," the young Nubian prince screamed, "here I cum!" He pulled his cock out of Lawrence's ass and rested it between the sweaty crack.

A second later Lawrence gasped as he felt the gale force of Gabriel's load spray across the back of his head, back, and ass. It seemed to go on for a couple of minutes, and several long drips of the warm fluid dripped down his ass and onto his balls.

"Sweet Jesus," Lawrence moaned loudly. His body shook all over as he spent himself onto the mattress beneath him.

Gabriel wrapped his arms around the pastor and hugged him tightly, then rolled him over so that they lay side by side. "Was that okay?"

"Okay?" Lawrence asked, incredulously. "That might very well make it into the Guinness Book of World Records."

Gabriel laughed, and hugged his new concedena tightly. "Do you think you can get used to it on a regular basis? Our relationship is regarded as extremely holy, and separation or divorce is not an option."

"Oh, I can definitely get used to this," Lawrence said, and kissed Gabriel on the lips as he squeezed the still hard cock between them. "Does this thing ever go down?"

"If I want it to," the Bahinza-in-training said with a mischievous smile. "But this night is just beginning, and this thing isn't going anywhere anytime soon."

Outside the rugo, the chanting was reaching feverish pitch, and the drums rocked through the small hut with soothing rhythms that set the tone for their lovemaking the rest of the evening. The chiefs of all the neighboring tribes congratulated the outgoing Bahinza on the fine choice of his son's new concedena. With the right wife to bear him many children, and the new spiritual companion by Gabriel's side, the Bhatanyanaku dynasty would grow to be one of the most powerful in modern history.

The Freudian Slip

"How the hell do you *think* I feel about all of this?" Rudy asked. "I'm pissed as hell."

Dr. Livingston crossed his legs at the knee and set the pen and tablet of paper on the end table next to his chair. "That is not an appropriate response, Rudy."

"Why the hell not?"

"We've been over this more than a dozen times over the past couple of months. You know that anger is not a feeling, it's an emotion. An emotion is simply a reaction to the feeling, and it's superficial. I know you're angry. I want to know why. It is the true feeling that is significant, not your response to it."

"I think you're splitting hairs, doctor," Rudy said as he sat up on the couch and rested his elbows on his knees. "I think my angry response is quite significant. Everyone knows that being angry about something you can't change is stupid and destructive."

"So you are feeling stupid and destructive?"

Rudy flinched. "Don't be ignorant."

"I'm just trying to get to the root of the problem, Rudy,"

the psychiatrist said evenly. "When we understand what it is you are really feeling, then we can tackle your reactions to the feeling and make them more appropriate."

The young man stood up from the couch and walked around the office slowly, reading each of the framed certificates on the walls carefully. "All of these fancy degrees suggest that you have an advanced level of intelligence, Dr. Livingston. I can't help but believe that you have a pretty good idea of what I am feeling."

"Maybe, maybe not. But either way, I need to hear it from you."

Rudy lay back down on the couch and crossed his legs at the ankles and his arms across his chest. He closed his eyes and bit down on the molars in the back of his mouth, causing his strong jawline to flex with each bite.

The doctor had seen the stance taken many times in his twelve years of practice. He was prepared for it. "You're feeling neglected, right? You feel abused, like no one has time for you. You're feeling . . ."

"I'm feeling lost, goddammit," Rudy said quietly as he uncrossed his arms only long enough to wipe a tear from his eyes.

"Lost?" Dr. Livingston repeated. Maybe he wasn't as prepared as he thought he was. He picked up the pen and paper again. "How do you feel lost, Rudy?"

Rudy Baylor sat back up and looked the doctor in the eyes. "No one knows me, Dr. Livingston. No one cares enough about me to take the time to get to know me."

"That's simply not true, Rudy. Your parents care a great deal about you. They're concerned about you. That's why they have brought you to see me."

"Bullshit," Rudy spit out, and stood up to pace the room again. "My father has no idea who I am, and he doesn't care. The senator is concerned with one thing and one thing only, and that is sitting his fat ass behind the big desk in the Oval Office in sixteen months and looking impressive for the presidential portrait. He's already started a search committee to select an artist. When I came out to him six months ago, he didn't see a son crying and pouring his heart out to a father. He saw the Oval Office slipping out of his grasp. *That's* why I'm here, doctor."

"But your mother . . ."

"My mother knows that I'm gay, but she doesn't know me. She wants to know who I am, I think. She wants to love me. But she's afraid of the senator. Everyone's afraid of big bad Senator Baylor."

"I don't think that's true, Rudy," the doctor said as he set his pen and paper down again. "Your parents are very busy and very important people, that's true. But I don't believe they are too busy to love you."

"*Love* me?" Rudy laughed. "How could they love me? They don't even know who I am. To them I'm just a faggot who's standing in the way of their almighty dreams and power. They don't even love themselves, Doc. Isn't one of the first things they teach you in those fancy psych classes up at Yale that you can't love anyone else until you learn to love yourself first?"

"Yes, it is."

"Well, they don't love themselves and they don't love me. They don't care enough about me to take the time to get to know me. But you know me, don't you, Doc?"

"I do care about you, Rudy," the psychiatrist said. He didn't feel comfortable with the way this session was heading, though, and so he chose his next words very carefully. "I'm trying to get to know you so that I can help you feel better about yourself."

"I don't mean to be rude, Dr. Livingston, but my father isn't paying you the big bucks to make a faggot feel better about himself. Surely you're aware of his intentions with our little sessions here."

"You're my patient, Rudy. My job is not to make your father feel better about your being gay. . . ."

"He doesn't *want* to feel better about it," Rudy said as he leaned closer to the doctor. "He wants to make it go away."

"My job is to get you to a place where you're not tormented with yourself. Where you know who you are from the core and are happy with that core."

"You know me, don't you, Doc?"

"I'm trying, Rudy," Livingston said with a smile. "I'm really trying to know you."

"I don't mean that you know me because you have all the certificates on the wall saying you know how to interpret me." Rudy pulled a folded and wrinkled newspaper clipping from his back pocket and set it on the table next to the doctor. "You know me."

Dr. Livingston unfolded the clipping and looked at it. His face flushed a deep pink and he felt little pellets of sweat forming around his collar and on his forehead.

"That's a picture taken at the Gay Pride Festival in San Francisco a couple months ago. San Francisco is what . . . a couple thousand very safe miles from Minnesota? Probably a reasonable assumption that no one from the Twin Cities would be seeing this photo. But if I'm not mistaken, that is you standing on top of that float, isn't it?"

Dr. Livingston swallowed hard and wiped at the sweat that was now beginning to drip down his face. "Rudy . . ."

"I would never have guessed that your chest was that smooth and muscular. And that pair of chaps really makes your ass look hot, Doc! I wish I had a view of the front side."

"Rudy, this is really not at all appropriate. Blackmail is illegal and . . ."

"Blackmail?" Rudy reared back as if he'd been slapped. "I'm not blackmailing you, Dr. Livingston. I just want to hear it from your own mouth."

"Yes, I am gay," the doctor said, and unloosened the knot in his tie. "But this is not about me, Rudy, it's about you."

"It's about me knowing that someone cares enough about me to get to know the real me. I know that." Rudy walked over to the Dr. Livingston's chair and knelt on his knees on the floor between the doctor's legs. "And you have been very good about taking the time to get to know me for who I really am, and not for someone else's ideals of me."

"Look, Rudy, this is all wrong. You're transferring your . . ."

Rudy leaned up and kissed the doctor on the lips. At first Livingston resisted and tried to push him away, but Rudy was strong. After a half-hearted effort, the doctor dropped his arms and allowed Rudy's tongue to slip between his lips. His mouth was warm and sweet, and Rudy thought he'd faint from the tingling sensation he felt rushing through his body. He'd only kissed and played around with a couple of guys from high school, and hadn't really felt anything more than curiosity with them.

But this was different, and when Dr. Livingston returned his kiss and maneuvered him over onto the couch, he felt as if he were floating above his own body. He fumbled with his psychiatrist's shirt buttons for a couple of minutes and then just ripped the whole shirt off in frustration.

The older man was much more experienced and patient. He took his time undressing Rudy, and the nineteen-year-old was amazed at how the doc could unbutton and remove his shirt at the same time he was kissing Rudy's naked chest and caressing his back. Chill bumps popped up all over his body, and before he knew it was happening, he felt a warm, sticky fluid dripping down his thigh. He panicked and tried to think of a way he could get his pants off without the doc knowing he'd just creamed his pants from a simple kiss.

Rudy pushed the doctor backward so that he was lying against one arm of the sofa, scooted between his legs, and pressed his body against the naked skin of the doctor's torso. Then he kicked his shoes off and pulled his jeans and briefs off as quickly as possible.

"Rudy, this is wrong. We can't . . ."

"Shut up," Rudy ordered. "This is not wrong, and we can."

He took his time unbuckling the belt and sliding Livingston's slacks down his long and muscular legs. He took in everything his mentor had done and tried to duplicate it. When the doctor was lying on the couch in nothing but his underwear, Rudy ran his hands up and down the long, hairy legs and then worked his way up to the tent at the plaid boxers.

Once he wrapped his hand around the thick cock hidden beneath the thin fabric of the shorts, the fight was gone from the doctor. He kicked the boxers to the floor hastily and pushed his patient backward onto the couch. He pulled off the boy's jeans clumsily and tossed them against the wall.

"Holy shit!" he said as he stared at Rudy's long, thick cock. It was fully hard and throbbing, and by his almost-perfect mental ruler, it was about eight and a half inches long. A thin sheath of foreskin covered the shaft and about a quarter of the bulbous head, which was still leaking a thin string of milky cum.

"I'm sorry," Rudy stammered.

"Don't be sorry," the doctor said, and leaned down to lick the sweet juice from Rudy's hot cock head. He flicked at the piss slit for a couple of seconds and then wrapped his lips around the head and sucked it into his mouth.

"Oh my God," Rudy moaned, and lifted his hips so that another couple inches of his cock slid deeper into his shrink's hot mouth. He'd never felt anything like this before and had to concentrate on breathing and trying to make the buzzing in his ears go away.

The doctor swallowed Rudy's cock and kept it buried deep in his throat as he tightened the muscles around the thick cock. Rudy moaned and bucked around on the couch as if he were being tortured, and the doctor knew that the kid couldn't hold out much longer. The youngster had already busted a nut just from kissing, and Livingston remembered being nineteen himself. It didn't take much at that age. He knew Rudy was already close to cumming a second time, and this was not how he wanted it.

He pulled his mouth slowly off Rudy's cock and licked the excess saliva from it lovingly. "I want you to fuck me," he said as he leaned down to kiss his patient on the mouth.

"What?" Rudy asked. His expression looked as if he'd been asked to walk a tightrope across the Grand Canyon. "I've never . . . I don't think I can . . ."

"Yes, you can," Livingston said as he got on all fours and turned himself around so that his ass was only inches from Rudy's face. "You said my ass was hot. So go for it. Lick it first and get it really wet, so that your cock will slide in easier."

Rudy leaned forward and stuck his tongue out tentatively. He'd never really given much thought to eating ass; it had really only been an insulting phrase that he and his friends threw around loosely. But once his tongue slid across the doctor's hard, smooth ass cheeks, ass eating became much more than a curse phrase. It became an obsession. His tongue had a mind and will of its own, and Rudy simply allowed the rest of his face to follow closely behind as the tongue licked every inch of the cool, marble-smooth cheeks and then slip boldly into the warm puckered hole nestled between them.

"Oh fuck, Rudy," the doc moaned loudly, and pushed his ass back deeper onto the snaking tongue. "That feels so hot."

Rudy tongue-fucked and nibbled on the doc's ass for several minutes and then couldn't wait any longer. He'd never fucked anyone before, but that didn't matter. Somehow his body knew what to do, and he moved along with his cock as it sidled up to the quivering ass in front of him. He spit a couple of globs of saliva onto the hole and rested his fat cock head at the entrance.

"Come on, Rudy," Livingston begged. "Stop teasing me. Shove it in!"

Rudy slammed his entire dick deep inside Livingston's ass in one swift and brutal thrust. The doc screamed out in pain and pressed a throw pillow against his mouth to muffle the noise. Rudy cursed at himself for hurting the doctor and being so awkward, but when he tried to pull out, the doc was adamant.

"Don't you even fucking think about it," he growled. "Fuck my ass hard."

His tongue must have been communicating with his cock, because from somewhere completely unknown to Rudy, it began sliding in and out of the clutching ass, slow and deep at first, and then with quick, stabbing jabs. When he buried the fat cock deep inside the doc and wiggled his hips from left to right slowly, Livingston moaned even louder and bucked backward onto him manically.

"Fuck me, baby," the doctor yelled. "Fuck my ass harder."

Rudy wrapped his arms around the doc's back and slid his cock deeper and faster into the warm, wet burrow. He grabbed Livingston by the hair and pulled his head back, then leaned in and kissed him passionately on the lips as he pumped his cock frantically into his ass.

"Oh God," Rudy yelled out suddenly. "I'm gonna cum again!"

"Pull out, baby," Livingston whispered as he caught his breath. "I want you to blast it all over my face."

Rudy pulled his cock out of Livingston's ass quickly and pushed the doc around so that he was lying flat on his back on the sofa. He leaned forward a couple of inches and aimed his cock right at the shrink's flushed and sweating face.

"Come on, Rudy," the doc said, "give it to me."

The cum flew from his cock like a torpedo and hit Livingston's face so hard that he recoiled as if he'd been slapped. Six or seven huge sprays of pungent seed covered every inch of his face and dripped down his neck and onto the couch.

"Shit, man, I'm cumming," the doctor moaned, and pulled Rudy down to kiss him.

Rudy felt the doc's hot load splash across his back and ass, and he shivered with the sensation it brought to his skin. He slid his tongue into the doc's mouth and kissed him slow and long and tenderly as the doctor spent himself all over his backside.

"I know you," the doctor whispered into Rudy's ear as they lay pressed against each other's naked body and struggled to catch their breath.

"I love you," Rudy murmured back right before he drifted off to sleep.

Dinnertime at the Baylor residence was not a Norman Rockwell portrait. When Senator Baylor was in Washington, the average unsuspecting onlooker might be fooled into believing it housed a normal, healthy, loving family. But on those weekends that the senator was home, not even the most heavily medicated neurotic would think there was anything close to resembling normal or healthy or loving about 2200 Westshire Lane or its inhabitants.

For the two days before the candidate came home, his house staff of twelve had run around frantically making sure that everything was perfect. The bedding in all six bedrooms had to have been freshly laundered and the beds made to army regulation, even though the senator was home only one weekend a month and there were only the three of them living in the house. The Mercedes, Cadillac Escalade, and the environmentally-friendly Lexus RX 400 hybrid all had to have been washed and fully detailed, even though he used the hybrid only when he was making a public appearance or press conference. Every plate and glass had to be sparkling clean, every rug tassel brushed out to an even length, and every photo positioned at the precise angle and layout that had been meticulously designed and ordered, even though the senator could not put a name with half of the "family" members in the photos.

But the house looked good. It was the perfect picture of the perfect future U.S. president.

"Goddamn it, Al, I don't care about the fucking polar ice caps or global warming. It's still plenty cold right here in Minnesota in the winter." Senator Baylor stormed into the dining room with his Bluetooth attached to his ear and a Manhattan in his hand. "Don't fucking tell me what I have to care about, Al. If I ever hear those words from your mouth again, you'll be sweeping floors at McDonald's. Is that clear? Senator Benjamin William Baylor is the only one who tells Senator Benjamin William Baylor what he has to care about. Make it go away, Al. Good night."

He finished his drink and waved impatiently at one of the kitchen staff to bring him another. His plate had been prepared and waiting for him at the table, but the maid took it away with his glass and brought him a fresh, hot one.

"Those goddammed liberals are killing me," he snapped as he shoveled a forkful of roast beef and rosemary potatoes into his mouth and then swallowed it with a swig of the Manhattan.

"I'm sorry, dear," Mrs. Baylor said. "But we're at the table now. Can't you please just . . ."

It only took one of his trademark raised eyebrows to silence her midsentence.

"How have you been doing, son?" the senator asked.

To Rudy, his voice sounded like the robot on the old syndicated show *Lost in Space.* Danger, Will Robinson, Danger. "Fine, sir. I've been good."

"Well I sure as hell hope so," the senator barked through a mouthful of mush. "That goddammed shrink is costing me a fucking fortune."

Mrs. Baylor cringed but said nothing.

"Is he helping you? I mean, after nine months you should be getting close to being cured, right? Are you getting any better?"

"Yes, sir, I am getting better," Rudy said quietly. "As a matter of fact, I think . . ."

"Senator Baylor," the old man yelled into the phone. He'd never really paid attention when his people explained to him that he didn't have to yell into the phone just because the microphone wasn't right in front of his mouth. Many of his staff wore earplugs when they called him. "Jesus Christ, Maury, couldn't this have waited until Monday?" he asked even as he threw his napkin to the table and walked out of the room. "I'm trying to have a nice dinner with my family."

Rudy and his mother sat quietly at the table, neither of them eating while his father was away from the table.

"He's trying, Rudy," his mother said as she leaned forward and patted his hand. "Really, he is. It's just hard, that's all."

Rudy looked into her eyes. He wanted to tell her to wake up and smell the coffee, to see that the senator never tried to do anything that didn't directly help him get closer to the White House, to see that they were both nothing more to him than a convenience for his position of power. But her lips were quivering and her eyes threatened to release the tears that were welled up in them, and so he nodded and patted her hands in return. "I know, Mom. I know."

"Who the hell do these people think they are?" Senator Baylor asked to no one as he sat back down at the table and emptied his drink. "Where do they get off telling me what to think and how to vote on issues? No one tells Senator Benjamin William Baylor what to do or think. No one." He wiped his plate with a dinner roll and then filled it again with another helping of beef and potatoes. "Where were we? The doctor, right?"

"Yes, sir," Rudy said. "Dan says I'm making real progress. He thinks . . ."

"What did you just say?" the senator asked quietly. His fork had stopped a couple of inches short of his mouth, and his eye twitched as he glared at his son over a mound of roast beef and gravy.

"I'm making progress?"

"What did you call Dr. Livingston?"

Rudy's eyes bulged with the realization of his slip, and Mrs. Baylor cupped her hand over her mouth.

"I called him Dan," Rudy said defiantly, and straightened his back and shoulders to look his father in the eyes.

"That fucking faggot!" Senator Baylor roared as he kicked his chair back from the table and stormed out of the dining room. "I'll kill that sick son of a bitch with my bare hands." He headed toward the closet where he kept his guns and his coat.

Rudy ran to catch up with his father, and when he did he swung him around and pinned him against the wall. The senator's face was red and sweating, and giant veins popped out across his neck and forehead.

"You're not going anywhere, Senator," Rudy said through

gritted teeth. "You're going to sit back down at the family table and finish your dinner, and you're going to listen to me."

"How dare you talk to me like that," his father growled, and raised his hand to slap Rudy. "Nobody talks to Senator Benjamin Will . . ."

"You lay a hand on me, old man, and it will be the biggest regret of your life."

"You cannot speak to me in that manner," Senator Benjamin William Baylor said, but he dropped his hand back to his side. "Nobody . . ."

"Shut up, you old fool," Rudy said, and shook his head. "You filthy, disgusting, pathetic hypocritical bastard. You stand up here and grandstand and say how nobody can tell you what to think or how to act or what to say, and yet that's exactly what you try to do to everyone else. We are not your property, Senator. You can't control us," he said, and looked over at his mother, who was still sitting at the table with her head down and moving her carrots around on her plate. "Well, you can't control me. I am my own man."

"You're a sick faggot," his father spit out. "And that quack of a doctor is even sicker. He's brainwashing you and molesting you. And I'm paying for it all." His face was now turning purple and he moved toward the closet again. "I'll have his license revoked."

Rudy slammed the closet door shut. "You won't do any such thing."

"You've lost your mind," the senator said in disbelief.

"No, I've found my heart and my soul. And my balls. I've finally learned to love me for who I am, and I've found the courage to stand up to you."

"That sick quack will never practice in this country as long as . . ."

"Who's Rocky Martinez, Senator?"

The old man stopped in his tracks, and all of the previous purple and red color drained from his face. His hands began to shake, and he leaned against the wall.

"I don't know what you're talking about."

"I think you do," Rudy said.

"You're crazy. You're a lunatic."

Rudy reached into his pocket and shoved a four-by-six photo in his father's face. "Jogging your memory any, Daddy Dearest?"

Senator Baylor grabbed the photo and ripped it into pieces, then threw them to the ground.

"There are more," Rudy said with a smile. "Lots more."

"You blackmailing, sick, son of a bitch faggot."

"I'm not blackmailing you, Daddy. I'm just stating a couple of facts. Fact number one: You will never see Dan again, nor will you threaten him in any manner. Fact number two: Dan and I are lovers, and I am moving in with him as soon as our little conversation is over. Fact number three . . ."

"Stop this," the old man said weakly. He looked defeated. "You cannot be serious."

"Oh, I'm dead serious, you sick hypocritical motherfucker. I'm outta here, and I never want to see you again. If you ever try to contact me or try to harm Dan in any way, then I swear to God, Rocky Martinez's name and pictures, along with you in some very compromising positions in his bed, will be posted all over the Internet and in every major newspaper in the country."

"You son of a . . ."

"I learned from the best, old man."

"What about the election?"

Rudy snorted and shook his head in disgust. "You're my father, and I won't betray you. As long as you stick to our little deal. But you sure as hell don't get my vote and I'll die in hell before I stand next to you at the podium."

"But I need my family with me."

"Your loving wife will be right by your side. You can rent yourself a son. I'm sure Rocky would be willing to stand by your side for the right price."

The senator flinched and wiped a dribble of spit from his mouth.

"I'm going upstairs to pack now," Rudy said. "Go back and finish your dinner. And tell Mother she looks pretty this evening."

"I can't believe you said that to him," Dan said as he kissed Rudy's lips and moved down to his neck.

"Well, I did. He won't bother either of us again."

"But how did he react? What do you think he was feeling?"

"Shut up and suck my dick, Doc," Rudy said with a smile, and spread his legs in the big bed.

Dan slid down the bed and kissed the head of Rudy's cock, then pulled it into his mouth and sucked it to full hardness. He'd always been mesmerized by the big dick and loved to suck on it for hours on end. Sometimes he even sucked Rudy off a couple of times before they ever actually fucked.

But over the past several months, Rudy had acquired a proclivity for taking Dan's cock up his ass, and the good doctor was not one to argue. As nice as his lover's cock was, his ass was equally beautiful. Perfectly round and smooth and hard as a basketball court. He could get lost in it for days. His cock was a couple of inches shorter than his young lover's, and nowhere near as thick, but Rudy loved it and thought it perfect.

"Come on, Doc," the young man begged. "Give it me. Shove your cock deep inside me and fuck my brains out."

Dan placed the head of his cock at the hole of Rudy's ass and slid in slowly. When he reached the hilt, he stopped and rested inside his lover, waiting for his signal to start moving. It didn't take long. Rudy lifted his ass off the mattress and wiggled it around, moving it from side to side and milking the doc's cock with it as he pulled it along with him.

"Oh my God, baby," Dan whispered. "That feels so good."

"Flip me onto my shoulders," Rudy said.

"Oh yeah, babe." This was his favorite position, and he knew Rudy was only asking to do it because he knew that. Without pulling his cock out of the tight ass, he pulled Rudy's body into the middle of the bed and raised his legs over his head, so that his ass was straight up in the air.

Rudy's cock now dangled only a couple of inches from his own face. "Come on, Doc," he begged. "Go deeper."

Dan fucked him harder and forced Rudy's legs down a couple more inches. Rudy stuck out his tongue and licked his own cock head, and when Dan moaned and pressed down even harder, he swallowed the first third of his shaft into his own mouth. They'd discovered this talent strictly by accident a few months ago, and it had quickly become their favorite. Rudy liked the taste and feel of his own cock, but it became a little painful to maintain the position for very long, so they could do it only for short periods.

That's all it took that night, though. Rudy was hornier than he could remember ever being, and he was ready to shoot his first load after only a couple of minutes.

"Oh man, babe," he warned as he let his cock slip from his mouth. "I'm gonna cum."

"Already?" Dan asked.

"Oh shiiiiiiiit!" The first couple of shots sprayed right down his throat, but then he began to gag a little and pointed his cock away from his face. A few spurts landed on his lips and cheeks, but the majority of it drenched the pillows on either side of his face.

Dan pulled out quickly and dropped onto the bed beside his lover. His body convulsed violently, and then his cock sprayed its load all over his upper body.

After a couple of minutes, when they'd both caught their breath and were beginning to drift into sleep, Dan turned to Rudy.

"How do you feel?" he asked.

"I feel loved and complete, Doc," Rudy said sleepily, and hugged his lover. "And my emotional reaction to that feeling is extreme happiness."

"Smartass," the shrink said, and hugged the future president's son.

"I love you, too."

The Immoral Majority

"Good evening, America," the mannequin-perfect host smiled as he walked onstage to thunderous applause. His Armani suit was meticulously tailored, and the spotlights reflected off his three-figure haircut. "I'm Brian Pederson, and welcome to *No False Idols*." The multicolored light show behind him exploded and waved around the huge audience. "Please join me in bringing America's Top Twelve Evangelists to the stage. Eleven of them will be safe, but one of them will be going home tonight."

The group of pastors from the mega New Covenant Community Church huddled around the television set and cheered as if they were in the live audience. "Praise God, who would ever have thought we'd be here?" Senior Pastor Richards said, and wiped a tear from his eye. "It wasn't even ten years ago that the number one show in this great country was this same program, but with the American public choosing something as meaningless as the next music superstar. Blessed be the Lord, we've seen the light and changed our sinful ways. In just three more months, America will vote into office the new chairman of the U.S. Evangelical Revolution Force."

The other twelve preachers clapped and whistled and slapped their leader on the back playfully. "And next year, when they're ready to elect the new chancellor, you're gonna run away with the title," Assistant Pastor Michaels said. "Hands down, there won't even be any competition."

"Oh, sure there will be," Pastor Richards said with a gleam in his eyes. "There are some fine, God-fearing ministers out there, and they're all as hungry for the title as I am. Besides, it wouldn't be any fun if there wasn't a little competition."

Everyone laughed and assured their boss that he had nothing to worry about, and then they quickly scattered to beat one another to one of the six restrooms on the ground floor as the show went to a commercial break.

"I think I'm gonna call it an evening," Aidan Pollard said as he stood up with a heavy sigh.

"Are you all right, son?" Richards asked.

"Yes, I'm fine."

"But the show has just started. We never miss an episode. We have to vote in a couple of hours. We're all taking a separate line from the church switchboard."

"Sorry, Stan, I'm gonna have to pass tonight. I've got a splitting headache. I'm gonna call it an early night."

"But . . ."

"I'll call from home, in bed."

"Promise?"

"Yes," Aidan said with a chuckle. "Jeez, you're like a little kid with this show."

"Hey, it's important business. It's critical that Brother Jones wins that title."

"Oh, there is no doubt whatsoever he will win. The coalition is unmovable in their phone networking. He's got it in the bag, you know that."

"We can't take anything for granted, son," the senior minister said. "Remember, it was only two years ago that we were certain Lewis Magnuson would run away with the title. We got lax in our voting, and then that Rodney kid snuck in and stole it from him. What a mess that turned out to be."

Aidan wanted desperately to say it wasn't that bad. In fact, it had been the best thing that could have possibly happened to the modern church. Heaven forbid a minister actually encourage his congregation to think for themselves and to question the swelling tide of self-righteous evangelism that had overpowered the United States like an unforgiving tsunami. The young Magnuson kid had planned his victory very well, feeding the people what they wanted to hear while he was competing for the title, and then pulled the classic bait and switch once he got into office. He preached that the current establishment of religious teaching and literally ruling the country was wrong and that it was not our place to judge others, but to nurture them in their spiritual development. For Aidan, Lewis Magnuson was a godsend. But the other 187 million members of the Evangelical Revolution Force didn't agree with him, and he was impeached from office in less than nine months, and six weeks later was found floating facedown in San Francisco Bay.

"Yeah, a disaster. We gotta be careful, you're right. Don't worry, I'll call from home. I just gotta take some aspirin and get to bed."

"All right, son. Take care of yourself. Don't forget, it's your rotation for confession on Sunday after church."

"Oh, I couldn't forget about confession," Aidan said. "It's my absolute favorite part of the job."

"You're a wonderful minister, Aidan," Richards said

proudly. "One of these days it will be you up there on that stage, and I have no doubt that you will win."

"Thanks, Stan. Enjoy the show."

"Oh, I will. Don't forget to vote!"

Aidan left the church and the other pastors, and walked slowly with his head down for the first block. But when he was certain he was out of sight from the eyes of his peers, whom he knew would be watching from the windows, he bolted into a full-on run. He didn't stop until he reached his apartment, and once there he slammed the door behind him and locked it quickly, then fell to the floor and cried.

He'd never been meant for the ministry, and he knew it. But when the Force exploded onto the scene twelve years ago and literally took over the country, he really didn't have a choice. Being involved with the ERF was the only way to make any money in the States anymore. Hundreds of thousands of gays and lesbians, Jews, Muslims, and any other group who disagreed with the Force were persecuted and forced to flee the country into Mexico, Canada, or Europe. Within two years of their "inauguration" on the political landscape, all sex outside of marriage and without the intent to procreate was proclaimed illegal. Their members fought Congress and Senate members who disagreed with them, and quickly replaced them in recall elections. The past two presidents were appointed by the chairman of the ERF.

Aidan was only twenty-six years old, and so he remembered a time when the religious right was very powerful but didn't yet govern the country and mandate their beliefs on every single citizen. He'd been really young, but recalled vividly his father forcing him to attend seminary and plan for a career in evangelism. It was the only way of making something of himself, and there was no room for discussion.

He stood up, wiped the tears from his eyes, and grabbed a bottle of water from the fridge before heading to bed. It was only 8:30, but he was physically and emotionally exhausted. Working at the church and living his lie 24/7 took a toll on him, and he didn't know how much longer he'd be able to hold out. He'd been checking out Canada for the past three months and had almost made up his mind to risk it all and go. It wasn't easy; the borders were very heavily patrolled with armed guards with orders to kill anyone crossing illegally. And it was nearly impossible to get a passport to travel anywhere anymore. Only members with strong credentials with the Force were given permission to leave the United States for any period of time, and then only under strict chaperone and while conducting ERF evangelical business. He was six months away from being able to apply for a visa to visit Canada on Force business. If he could just hold out a little longer and keep up his pretenses, he might stand a chance of escaping. But he wasn't sure he'd be able to last.

Aidan shucked his jacket and shirt and dropped them to the floor, then pulled his jeans and briefs off and crawled into bed. It was a warm May evening, and his windows were open, allowing a gentle breeze to whisk through the room and across his naked body. His cock responded, and in less than a minute was fully hard. He spread his legs wide on the bed and wrapped one fist around his long, thick cock and massaged his shaved balls with the other hand.

"Oh fuck," he moaned loudly as he stroked his cock and slid a finger between his balls and ass cheeks. He was so damned horny. He wanted to save his load for Sunday but knew he couldn't. It was four days away, and he was already about to explode. He had to cum now. It was okay, though. He'd have plenty more for Sunday, as long as he didn't get carried away and beat off more than once tonight.

He closed his eyes and tried to block out the visions of all the beautiful men he'd see on Sunday. If he gave in to the fantasy, he'd never be able to stop with one load. So he focused on his own cock, how hot and hard it felt in his hand, and how slick it got when the precum dripped out of his cock head and down his long, thick uncut rod. He squeezed it a little tighter and shivered as shock waves of tingling electricity shot up his torso and down his legs.

God, he hadn't been that horny in months. He could sure tell it was getting close to his rotation for confession. After twelve weeks, his cock got so hard that it ached every time he was naked or his mind drifted to any of the hot men he'd encounter at confession. Aidan lifted his legs slightly and slid one long finger inside his ass. He moaned as the hot walls of his ass clutched at the finger and squeezed it lovingly. "Fuck," he moaned as he wiggled the finger around the walls of his ass as deep in as he could go.

His thick cock throbbed and grew hotter in his hand. Large strings of slick, clear precum oozed from the tip and dripped down the long uncut shaft and between his legs. He was getting close so quickly. Damn it, he wished he could keep stroking his big dick for a while, but he knew he was about to lose it already.

Aidan lifted his legs higher and slid a second finger inside his ass, and moaned as his entire body shook with pleasure. "Oh God," he moaned. The first spray of cum flew from his cock and across his body, splashing against the wall behind him. The next couple hit his mouth and nose, and several more splashed across his chest and stomach. When he was completely spent, he withdrew his finger from his ass and waited for his body to stop quivering before getting up to wash up and brush his teeth.

He was now good to go until Sunday.

* * *

"Heaven has no room for sinners," Pastor Richards yelled into the microphone and smiled as he watched the crowd go into a frenzy. When he'd taken over the struggling church it averaged 1,500 attendees every week, with services being held every Sunday, Tuesday, Thursday, and Friday. Now, six years later, they held services twice a day seven days a week and averaged 100,000 parishioners a week. He was a shoo-in for the chancellor position with ERF next year, and his flock would hang on his every word.

"These are troubled times we live in, and they call for strong leadership. And not just from your pastor or your elected officials in Congress and the White House, but from you yourselves. Now, more than ever, you are being called to be pure in thought and in action. You are being called to shrug off the temptations and ways of the heathen world and to accept a higher mission. The ways of the flesh are wicked, and Satan with his army of demons are working overtime to win your souls. Will you let them triumph?"

"No!" the congregation screamed in response.

Aidan watched impatiently as his senior pastor worked the crowd into a frenzy and then released them into the world even more frustrated and confused than ever. But he wasn't complaining. It was with sermons just like this that the confessional became busiest, and sometimes the confession hour turned into a confession afternoon. He smiled as Pastor Richards dismissed the throng and admonished them to confess their sins and to promise to live a more righteous life.

"I think confession will be particularly busy this afternoon, Aidan," the lead minister said as he clapped the younger clergy on the back. "Want me to have Benjamin help you out today? You don't look like you're feeling 100 percent still."

"No," Aidan said a little quicker and with more anxiety than he intended. "I live for confession time. It's the only thing that gets me through life sometimes," he said, and was glad that his boss thought it was because he felt fed spiritually by the experience. "I'm sure it's exactly what I need to perk me up and make me feel better. You wouldn't want to take that away from me, would you?"

"Certainly not," Pastor Richards said proudly. "It's all yours, son. God bless you."

"And you too, Stan." He watched the elder clergy leave the church, and then he slipped into the wooden confessional box.

Ten minutes later the bells in the church tower began to ring, and Aidan's heart jumped in his rib cage. He kicked his shoes off and then slipped out of his slacks. His hard cock sprung to life once his pants were on the floor, and he took a deep breath as he heard the door in the confessional on the other side of the thin wall close shut.

"Forgive me, Father, for I have sinned."

Aidan recognized the deep baritone voice immediately, and a thick stream of precum oozed from his cock head. He slid the little wooden window to the left and reached inside. His hand found the hard cock right away, and he slid his fist up and down the length of it.

"Suck my dick, Father," the guy on the other side moaned softly.

Aidan pulled the cock closer and through the window, and wrapped his lips around the mushroom head. It was fat and bulbous and slick with precum, and Aidan lapped at it hungrily. The cock itself wasn't that big, but it didn't matter much. The guy was so horned up that he always came almost immediately. He loved having the head of his cock sucked, and it never took Aidan more than a couple of minutes to milk him dry.

Today was no exception, and before his knees had a chance to start hurting against the hard wooden floor, he was swallowing his first load of the afternoon. The guy pulled his shrinking cock back slowly. "Thank you, Father," he said softly.

"Go in peace, my son," Aidan said as he wiped his mouth. He glanced through the hole in the wall and out the door of the other stall when it opened. There was a line of maybe fifty men lined up against two of the walls waiting. The door didn't even close fully before the next guy stepped in.

"Forgive me, Father, for I have sinned."

Aidan's heart stopped for a second, and he fought to catch his breath. Tommy Barnes was his favorite of all. He was twenty-two years old and stood six foot three inches and weighed about two hundred pounds. He wasn't a bodybuilder but was extremely muscular, and his muscles flexed teasingly without Tommy even knowing it most of the time. His short blond hair, dark tan, and eyes the color of an empty Coke bottle presented a stunning picture and always took Aidan's breath away.

And then there was his cock. Ten inches long, sheathed in a thin layer of foreskin with veins the circumference of a pencil, with low-hanging shaved balls, it literally made the young priest's mouth water as if he'd bitten into a lemon, and it made him dizzy with desire. "Come on, Tommy," Aidan said. "Cut the crap. Stick it through."

"You want my big cock, Father?"

"Yes. Please give it to me."

The huge dick slid through the window between them slowly, and Aidan stuck out his tongue and lapped at the head before it was all the way on his side of the wall. He reached down and stroked his own cock as he opened his mouth wider and sucked the long shaft into his throat. When he had half of the cock in his mouth, he sucked harder on it and squeezed Tommy's shaved balls.

"Fuck yeah, dude," Tommy moaned loudly. He slid his cock

another couple of inches into Aidan's throat and rested it there for a moment, then began sliding in and out of the hot mouth slowly. "God, man," he whispered, "it's been so fucking long. I'm already close, dude."

"Not yet, Tommy," Aidan said as he cupped the young man's balls lovingly. "It's been way too long for me, too. So I want it to last a little this time."

"Can I fuck you, Aidan?"

"Hell yeah, you can fuck me," Aidan said, and stood up quickly. He leaned his ass against the hole in the wall and took a deep breath as Tommy's thick, uncut cock pressed against the twitching hole. "Come on, Tommy, stop teasing me. Fuck my ass."

Tommy shoved his big dick deep into his pastor's ass in one long and quick thrust and smiled to himself as he heard Aidan gasp on the other side of the wall and felt his hot ass clamp down on his giant cock.

"Come on," the next guy in line whispered as he knocked on Tommy's door. "Don't monopolize him. You've had your turn; there are lots of people in line here."

"We're almost done here," Tommy panted as he shoved his cock faster and harder into the moist ass. "You'll get your turn, just settle down." He slid his cock all the way out of Aidan's ass and then slammed it back in mercilessly.

"Oh Jesus, that feels so incredible, Tommy," Aidan moaned loudly.

"Father, be reasonable," the man outside said, now banging loudly on Aidan's door. "You're gonna get worn out, and there a lot more men out here waiting to confess."

"Don't worry, my son," Aidan squeaked out, "you'll get your turn, I promise."

"Damn right I will," the angry man yelled, and pulled the

door of Aidan's stall open roughly. He grabbed Aidan by the neck and pulled him out into the aisle of the church.

Aidan gasped loudly as Tommy's cock was ripped from his ass and pushed his hands out in front of him to catch his fall. Before he knew it, six or seven of his parishioners rushed him and turned him over roughly onto his stomach. They pinned his arms and legs to the floor.

"Come on, men," Aidan gasped through strained breath. "There's no need to get hostile. "We've got to maintain our comp . . ."

"Shut the fuck up," yelled the angry man who'd pulled him away from Tommy, and he spread Aidan's legs farther apart. "You guys hold his arms and legs. I'll fuck him first, and then we can all take a turn."

"Robert McCallister," Aidan said sternly, "get a grip. You know everyone will get a turn, but you've got to . . ."

"I don't gotta do nothing but fuck your sweet ass, Father," McCallister said, and slapped Aidan's ass hard to prove his point. The men to his side and behind him cheered him on, and he spit a large wad of saliva onto his dick head and shoved inside Aidan in one clumsy move.

The young minister yelled out in pain, and two of the men holding him down clamped their hands around his mouth to muffle his screams. McCallister slammed his cock in and out of Aidan's ass furiously, and the men around him began stroking their cocks and moaning. There were easily seventy men in the sanctuary now, each with their hard cock in their hands and moaning loudly as they stroked themselves first and then turned to one another.

"Hey!" Tommy yelled loudly, and banged on the door of the confessional from inside. "Don't hurt him, goddammit. Let me out of here!"

"Oh, we'll let you out of there, all right," one of the men in the mob said, and swung the door open violently and pulled Tommy out into the sanctuary.

Several men wrestled him to the ground and laid him so that he was facing his secret lover, their faces only inches from one another. The crowd around Aidan lifted him up by the waist so that he was on his hands and knees, and the group around Tommy did the same.

"Oh, shit man," McCallister yelled, "I'm gonna cum!" He pulled his cock out of Aidan's ass unceremoniously and sprayed his load all over the minister's smooth, muscular back.

The mob quickly pushed McCallister to the side, and another man slid in behind Aiden and slid his slick cock inside his smooth ass. It was Charles Montgomery. Aidan used to mow their lawn and babysit for him and his wife when he was in high school. He'd often fantasized about having Charles' fat cock buried deep inside him, but up to now he'd settled for just sucking the guy off a couple of times in confession. He relaxed his ass muscles and moaned loudly as his neighbor slid his big cock in and out of his ass.

"Oh FUCK!" Tommy yelled suddenly.

Aidan looked up just in time to see his friend being impaled from behind by one of the members of the church. He knew for a fact that the guy fucking Tommy didn't have a big dick at all; in fact, it was of the smallest he'd sucked in confession over the past two years. "Amateur," he groaned out to Tommy as Charles Montgomery's much bigger cock fucked him relentlessly. He winked at his lover.

"Shut up," Tommy laughed, and tried to steady himself from the clumsy assault from behind. "It fuckin' hurts. I don't know how you do this."

The crowd divided in two, with half of them lining up behind Aidan and the other behind Tommy. They took turns fucking the two young men relentlessly, several of them having the courtesy to whisper, "Forgive me, Father," as they slammed their cock into Aidan's ass. Each of the men were more excited than usual, which was an accomplishment in and of itself. It didn't take long for them to empty their loads into the hungry young asses.

It took a while for all of the men to get a turn at Aidan and Tommy, but the lovers weren't in a hurry. It'd be another three months before it was Aidan's turn at confession again, and so they relished every minute of the three-plus hours that the men assaulted their asses. At one point in the afternoon, about two-thirds of the way through the orgy, the two young men scooted closer together and kissed one another passionately on the lips as cock after cock after cock raped their increasingly tender holes.

There were only three men left waiting in line behind Tommy and two waiting their turn to fuck Aidan's now-red ass when the door to the sanctuary flew open.

"What in the name of Lucifer is going on here?"

Aidan panicked, and his entire body stiffened as Senior Pastor Stan Richards' voice boomed through the almost-empty cavernous chapel. *Oh shit,* he thought, and prayed for a quick and painless death without torture. He and Tommy were both frozen speechless in fear and watched in horror as the lead minister quickly advanced on the group. The men, however, were not paralyzed by their fear and scurried to grab whatever piece of clothing they could reach to cover themselves.

"Martin Bennett, Steven Sandoval, Arthur Watson, James Beatty, and William Reins, don't think for a moment that I didn't catch each and every one of your faces," Richards yelled when he was only a few feet from the group. "You cannot run from me, men. In my office, immediately."

The five remaining men darted away from their pastor and ran to the back of the sanctuary to his office.

Pastor Richards knelt down beside his assistant and cupped Aidan's chin in his big hands. "Oh my God, son," he said with tears in his eyes. "What have they done to you?"

"They didn't . . ."

"Shhh," the elder priest said, "don't say it out loud. I don't want to know the details. My God, it's horrible. The trust they betrayed as you were here offering God's gift of atonement. It's despicable. Oh my God," he said, suddenly noticing the other naked boy next to him. "Tommy, are you okay, son?"

"It was horrible, Pastor Richards," he said, and managed to spring a tear for effect. When the preacher bowed and shook his head, Tommy looked up at Aidan and winked with a smile, then snapped back into the victim character. "They overpowered us, sir. We simply couldn't fight them off. There were too many of them."

"Of course not, son," the minister said as he wiped his eyes. "This is not your fault. I know it's hard to believe that right now, but you must try. These animals succumbed to Satan's temptation of the flesh, and they will suffer swiftly and painfully the wrath of our Savior. Take comfort in that."

"I'll try, sir," Tommy said.

"You're a fine, brave boy, Tommy. God will reward you bravely for your torment at the hands of the heathens. Get dressed, please, and wait for me over by the door."

Tommy quickly gathered his clothes and climbed into them with very little finesse. He walked to the back of the room with only a cursory glance back at his forbidden lover, with no idea of their fate.

"Aidan, I am so very sorry," Pastor Richards said softly. "How can I ever make this up to you?"

Aidan Pollard looked into the eyes of his mentor and realized how horribly terrified the minister was. He could almost see the vision of Richards' evangelical career flashing behind the older man's defeated eyes.

"You can get me a visa to Canada."

"What? That's impossible."

"No, it's not. You've got more than enough clout with the Force to make it happen. Tell them I'm going on a spiritual retreat."

"But Aidan . . ."

"And we'll need a visa for Tommy, too."

A wave of enlightenment rushed over the senior pastor's face, and he turned a deep pink in color. "You're blackmailing me. I won't do it. You two boys are sick."

"Yes, we're blackmailing you. And yes, we're sick. Sick of your self-righteous and perverted values and hypocrisy. Don't think for a moment that I didn't know about your incognito visit to confession three months ago."

"You bastard!" the minister spat with disgust.

"We'll expect those visas by the end of the month," Aidan said as he stood and walked away. "I'm sure you can expedite the process. Come on, babe," he said to Tommy as he reached the door. "We've got some packing to do."

THE
DEEP
SOUTH

It's easy to conjure up an image of the Deep South. Tobacco plantations, rolling green hills, southern belles, and Colonel Sanders are just some of the common ones. But probably even more poignant are the traditions and established norms of behavior there. Southerners do things at their own speed, and by their own rules. Appalachian Granny Magic, voodoo, and other forms of magic have gone through various phases of acceptability and prominence and are still practiced today, though it's much more underground than it used to be.

Given the supernatural element in the definition of taboo at the beginning of this book, it seems strange that a land of such history and practices would consider much of anything taboo. But they do. No one needs to be reminded of the slavery era, or the way in which the majority white population treated the minority black population a little more than a hundred years ago. And though we've come a long way since then, anyone who believes that we're where we need to be in embracing and valuing cultures other than our own hasn't been paying attention enough. And especially in the South.

The first story in this section addresses the race issue and especially interracial relations. Though not illegal anymore, it is still frowned upon among most of the general public in the South, within both the African American and Caucasian communities. Again, this is not only considered taboo in the Deep South, it is indeed something that causes people to do a double take and struggle with their own belief systems all across the country. But since it was such a prominent issue in the South for such an important time in our history, I included it in this section.

Bondage is another taboo sex subject and brings back images of the same period in which slavery was so big in our culture. It was no laughing matter back then, when people were bound and restrained against their will and then abused. Today, though, bondage is an activity in which many men get turned on, and sometimes even pay good money to be tied up and deemed helpless.

Even the most intelligent of us would probably have to admit that we've seen at least part of a *Jerry Springer* show. How many times has he mediated a feud between two brothers or two sisters where one of the siblings "stole" the spouse of the other? More than I can count, I know (though, for the record, I am not admitting to actually watching that hideous show). Almost every single time, the people in the situation have a very strong and very recognizable southern accent. Coincidence?

I'll leave that for someone else to decide.

A Matter of Chance

Part Three
The Deep South

When he'd left San Francisco, his plans hadn't included a stop in Atlanta. It was several hundred miles out of his way and would add another full day to his trip. But Alan, the hot leather man who'd fucked him senseless in the sling and then his bed at Steamworks, had mentioned that "Hotlanta" was wrapping up in a couple of days. Chance had heard a lot about the circuit party and had always wanted to attend. But he'd never been able to justify the expense and taking time off work, and so he'd never been.

Now, in the middle of a cross-country trip and facing possibly the worst and most uncomfortable time of his life, he couldn't justify not attending the huge party. He needed it.

He knew his mother would call before he got to New York. She'd won her fight to get him to travel from one coast to the other. There was no way she'd let him go without keeping track of him and maintaining the control that she needed to survive. Not that his father ever put up much of a fight, but now that he was virtually a mute, his mother would be going crazy with her need of drama and control. With the fun and challenge of dominating her husband out of the picture, she'd need to find it elsewhere, and Chance was the only person left.

When his phone rang and his father's name appeared on the screen, he considered not answering it. His mother wouldn't be happy at all that he was already a day behind and had decided to go way out of his way for a night of fun. She'd be livid that this little Atlanta trip would make him at least a couple of days later than he'd first told her.

But he didn't care. The past few days had made Chance feel good again and had given him a sense of self-worth and confidence that he hadn't had in a very long time. Jeremy had wanted him to move in with him and to be his lover. Bud also wanted to run away and share his life with him, and even though Chance knew that it was a simple crush on probably the very first gay person the young McDonald had ever met, and had nothing to do with Chance himself, it made him feel good and sexy to be the object of someone's desire. Even Alan had made him feel special. He hadn't said in so many words that he was infatuated with Chance, but he made him feel that way, and there was no mistaking the look of lust and desire in his eyes as they made love.

And so, when the phone rang, he was emboldened, and he answered it.

"Where are you?" his mother asked, without saying hello or waiting for him to.

"Why, hello, Mother," Chance said as he rolled his eyes and tried not to clutch the steering wheel too tightly. "I'm doing just fine, thanks for asking. How are you?"

"Don't get smart with me. I'm just calling to . . ."

"To track me like a UPS package."

"You are so insolent. I don't know when or where you became this nasty person, but it's quite unattractive."

Chance remembered his daydream of his mother's hairy arms and mustache, and he tried not to laugh.

"I'm just wondering where you're at," his mother said, and Chance could perfectly picture her lips tightening. "You must be getting close by now. You're going to be here tomorrow."

"Yeah, well about that," Chance said, and noticed his knuckles were white. "It's gonna be another couple of days before I get there."

"What?" she screeched. "You can't do this to me. You promised me that you'd be . . ."

"I didn't promise you anything, Mother. I said I'd be there by tomorrow, but I never promised. I've had a couple of unexpected things come up, and I'll be there in another few days."

"A few days?" she said, and Chance heard her voice break. "But what if your father doesn't make it till then?"

"Stop being so melodramatic, Martha. Dad's not going to die. He had a stroke, but he isn't going to die. That would be too easy."

"You are despicable," his mother said, and this time she did cry. "I did not raise you to . . ."

"Yeah, Martha, I know. I know. And I'm sorry to have been so mean. But I'm not putting up with your bullshit anymore. I have a life to live, and I'm living it. I'll be there when I can."

"You can't talk to me like that."

"Yes, I can. I'm doing you a huge favor by coming all the way out there. I took valuable time off work and put my entire life on hold to come and help you. I don't know why I'm doing it, but I am. So don't try to make me feel guilty about not getting there at the exact moment it fits into your tidy little schedule."

"I'm going now," his mother said tersely. "Your father needs me."

"Good-bye, Mother."

*   *   *

WETbar was everything the gay guide said it would be and more. Chance was a little overwhelmed as he walked in the door and took in the scene around him. There were several bars, both upstairs and down, and a rooftop and ground-level patio to cool down and catch your breath. A large dance floor dominated the majority of the lower level, and a smaller rotating dance floor attracted the buffed and oiled boys who couldn't wait to shuck their shirts and flex their muscles for the admiring crowd a few feet below them.

Chance inched his way through the packed crowd and over to the largest of the bars, and ordered a Long Island Iced Tea. He'd barely taken his first swallow before he was grabbed by the arm and dragged out onto the dance floor. From his vantage point behind the guy pulling him, he could only see the back of his head and his naked, sweating back. But that was enough to get Chance's blood boiling, and his cock began to respond. The guy's hair was black and shaved very short. His back was strongly muscled and copper colored, shiny with the beads of sweat that covered it. It tapered down to a perfect V shape that disappeared into the waist of the guy's jeans.

"I love this song," the guy said as he turned around and smiled at Chance. "You have to dance with me."

Chance literally felt his heart drop into his stomach. The guy was beyond beautiful. He was obviously Latino, with the smoothest, most perfect brown skin Chance had ever seen. A thin line of black hair graced his upper lip, trying hard to look like a mustache. His lips were full and pink and begged to be kissed. His eyes were black and large and almond shaped, with thick lashes. A large, expansive chest was capped by tiny dark nipples, and a thick trail of black curly hair started at his navel and vanished beneath his jeans.

"I'm Rudy," the guy said as he pulled Chance closer to him and bounced up and down to the beat of the song.

"Okay," Chance said, and then blushed and shook his head. "I mean, okay I'll dance with you, not okay that your name is Rudy."

The hot Latino smiled, and Chance thought he'd lose the strength in his legs and fall to the floor. The sparkle in Rudy's smile matched that of his seductive eyes and brought Chance's cock to full attention. He pulled Chance to him by the back of the head and kissed him hard on the lips.

"Oh God," Chance moaned through the kiss, and returned it passionately.

"Are you ready to get sudsy?" a loud voice yelled over the sound system.

The crowd around them roared its approval and began jumping up and down with the beat of the music. Huge streams of foam fell from the ceiling and shot out from plastic tubes strategically placed in the center and around the parameter of the large dance floor. Within a couple of minutes the entire floor was covered in the white spume, and it quickly began to grow and climb up the legs of the dancers on the packed floor.

"Right on," Rudy said as he turned Chance around so that his back pressed against his own smooth chest. "I thought they'd never get started."

"What's goin' on?" Chance asked. He could feel Rudy's hard cock pressing against his ass, and shuddered as the Latino stud wrapped his arms around him and hugged him tightly.

"Foam party, man," Rudy said loudly. He pulled Chance up and closer to him, then leaned in and whispered into his ear, "You ready to get fucked?"

"What?" Chance said, surprised. But when Rudy pressed

his cock harder against his ass, he whimpered and wiggled his ass back onto the hard cock. "Where?"

"Right here."

"You've gotta be kidding me." Chance laughed nervously. He looked around him at the hundreds of gyrating men on the floor, and the thick white foam that was now thigh high.

"No, dude, I'm not kidding you at all," Rudy said, and kissed Chance on the ear. "In about five minutes the foam is gonna be floor to ceiling. No one will see us."

"I can't have sex on the middle of a crowded dance floor," Chance whispered.

"Yes, you can," Rudy said as he licked Chance's ear and reached down to cup his fully hard cock. "We won't be the only ones, trust me."

The dance floor got even more crowded, and as the lights dimmed and the foam grew thicker and higher, it became difficult to see even the guys right next to them, let alone anyone else on the floor. Chance struggled to keep his breath steady as Rudy reached around him and slowly unbuttoned his jeans and slipped his hand inside and squeezed his cock.

"See, baby." Rudy whispered into his ear and nibbled it playfully. "I told you nobody would see." He hooked his thumbs into the waistband of Chance's jeans and slid them slowly down Chance's legs. "You want me to fuck you, don't you?"

"Yes," Chance moaned, and ground his ass against Rudy's crotch. He reached behind him and fumbled with the Latin hottie's jeans until they fell to the floor. He gasped when he felt Rudy's hot and hard cock press against his naked ass. "Fuck me, baby."

Rudy bent him over at the waist and hugged him tighter to him. "You ready for my cock, man?"

"Yes," Chance said, barely audibly. He wiggled his ass again until he felt Rudy's thick cock slide between his ass cheeks and rub against them. The heat from the hard dick and the feel of it thickening between his ass as the blood flowed through it made him crazy with lust. "Come on, Rudy, shove it in my ass and fuck my brains out."

Rudy held his cock at the base and positioned the head right at the hole, then pushed forward.

"Oh FUCK!" Chance yelled, even as he slid his ass backward to take the entirety of Rudy's big cock deep inside him. He felt his face and body flush with heat as he slid back and forth on the big cock. He was completely covered in and surrounded by thick white foam. He knew there were hundreds of hot guys all around him, but he couldn't see any of them through the bubbly suds. "Fuck me harder," he said between gritted teeth as he ground down on his molars.

Rudy slid his cock in and out of Chance's ass slowly, and when he was buried deep inside the hot ass, he wriggled around inside, eliciting a deep moan from the hungry bottom. The guy next to him on the left leaned in and kissed him on the mouth and reached down to cup his balls and squeeze his shaft as it slid in and out of Chance's hole.

Chance could tell that something was going on behind him, and felt the presence of another person, but couldn't hear anything but whispers above the pounding bass and loud lyrics of the music all around him. When he felt a second pair of hands massage his ass, and then a couple of long, thick fingers slide inside his ass to join Rudy's cock, he gasped and tightened his ass instinctively.

After a couple of minutes of being finger and cock fucked, the fingers pulled out quickly. The guy moved along his left side, and a moment later he was standing in front of Chance. His cock was fully hard and bobbing in front of him. The guy was nowhere near as big as Rudy. He wasn't even as big as

Chance. But the cock looked hot all covered with foam any-way, and Chance was so drunk with desire that he couldn't be stopped.

Rudy was pounding him hard and fast now, and so Chance reached out with his hands and steadied himself by holding onto the new stranger's waist. He stuck out his tongue and licked at the guy's hard cock for a moment, and then sucked it deep into his mouth. It didn't stretch his jaw by any stretch of the imagination, or even make him gag. But it tasted and felt good in his mouth, and he sucked on it hungrily.

"Fuck, yeah," the guy in front of him moaned, and slid his dick in and out of Chance's mouth in perfect synch with Rudy's thrusts from behind.

Chance shuddered from the overwhelming sensations coursing through his body. He didn't sense his feet or legs at all, and felt like he was floating a couple of inches above the floor. His pores tingled and his head spun slowly. Every four or five seconds it felt like a fireworks show was exploding inside his ass as Rudy's long, thick cock found and slid across and past his prostate and deeper into his guts. Tiny pins of light glided across his line of sight, and a soft, high pitched buzz rang in his ears.

Loud, animalistic grunts and moans escaped his throat as the two men fucked him on either end. He felt the orgasm begin deep in his groin, and within seconds his body began to shake as the cum started its trek through his balls and up his shaft.

In a couple of seconds, four or five guys stepped from the curtain of foam and surrounded him. A couple of them had huge, thick cocks, and the others had decent-sized dicks, simi-lar to the dude fucking his face. They were all hard and red and looked to be close to shooting their loads.

"Oh shit, dude," the guy in his mouth said, "I'm gonna

blow!" He pulled his cock out of Chance's mouth and sprayed a huge load all over his face and across his shoulders.

The men surrounding him grunted in unison, and cum flew from their cocks and splashed all across his back and ass and arms.

"Fuck, man," Rudy yelled, "that's hot. I'm gonna shoot my load, papi."

Chance pulled his ass off Rudy's big dick and turned around to face him, falling to his knees on the floor in front of the Latino stud. The thick cock erupted like Old Faithful, splashing across his face with a force that caused him to jerk his head as it crashed into his nose and eyes. Chance opened his mouth and stuck out his tongue, catching as much of it as he could, swallowing it, even as more of the warm, thick fluid took the place of the stuff he just ate.

As quickly as the other men appeared through the white foam, they disappeared without a word. Chance sat on the floor trying to catch his breath and wiped the stray cum from his face.

"Dude, that was so fucking hot," Rudy said as he slumped to the floor and kissed Chance on the lips.

"Hell yeah, it was," Chance said after breaking the kiss.

"I'm starvin', man," he said, and punched Chance playfully on the arm. "Wanna grab a bite to eat with me? Maybe we can go another round later back at my hotel."

"Sounds good," Chance said. "I could use a couple of chorizo tacos."

Both men laughed, and stood to collect their clothes.

"But can we leave the foam behind?" Chance asked as he and Rudy walked out of the bar with their arms wrapped around one another's waist.

The sun was intense and brought a flush to his face and his naked chest and stomach. The humidity was dense and caused a thick layer of sweat to cover his body. He thought of putting the top up and turning on the A/C but just couldn't bring himself to do it. He'd bought the car so that he could enjoy the sun and fresh air. The sun and fresh air in San Francisco were much cooler and less severe, it was true. But he wasn't about to wimp out at the first sign of a warmer climate. Besides, a few really cute guys had passed him on the highway and honked and given him the thumbs-up, and he liked the attention.

Chance looked over at Rudy and smiled. The Latino boy was sleeping in the passenger seat, wearing nothing but a pair of cutoff denim shorts. The seat was reclined three-quarters of the way back, and he stretched his long smooth legs so that they rested on the top of the door and his feet hung out into the warm fresh air. His abs were defined and tight even as he slept, and his stomach rose and fell with each breath. His tiny nipples responded to the wind whispering against them, and the sight of them caused Chance's cock to match their hardness.

The two had had an amazing night of marathon sex the night before. The foam party at WETbar had been only the beginning. Before they finally fell asleep almost four hours later, they'd taken turns fucking one another six or seven times. When they couldn't go another round, they'd drifted into sleep drenched in cum and wrapped in each other's arms.

"You're staring at me again," Rudy said slowly and sleepily without opening his eyes.

Chance laughed. "Sorry. I can't help it. You're so cute when you're sleeping."

Rudy sat up and rubbed his eyes. "And what, I'm not cute when I'm awake?" He leaned over and kissed Chance on the lips.

"Of course you are."

"Where are we?" Rudy asked as he looked around at the scenery around him.

"We just crossed over into Florida about half an hour ago."

"Cool. We're about halfway there, then," Rudy said, and scooted over closer to Chance and kissed him on the neck. "You should've woke me up so I could drive. You must be getting tired."

"A little," Chance said, and reached down and squeezed Rudy's cock through his shorts. "But you looked so peaceful, I didn't want to wake you."

"That's sweet," Rudy said. "But there's a rest stop just a few miles up the road. Let's pull in and take a quick pit stop and grab a bite to eat. I can drive from there."

The rest stop was large and had a full restaurant. They downed burgers with fries and got a large soda to go, and were on their way in just over half an hour.

"Thanks again for giving me a ride, man," Rudy said as he pulled back onto Interstate 75 and resumed driving south toward Miami. "I'm afraid to death of flying, and I really wasn't looking forward to another sixteen-hour bus ride."

"Don't mention it," Chance said. "I'm not really looking forward to getting home and dealing with my mother, anyway. And if Carlos *is* as hot and amazing as you say he is, then I'm all about playing around a little before my final leg to Sing Sing."

Rudy laughed. "Yeah, I don't blame you. And Carlos *is* as hot and amazing as I say he is. I just called him while we were at the restaurant, and he's excited to meet you."

"How did you guys meet?"

"We met in the hospital."

"What?"

"When I came out to my family at age eighteen . . . well, let's just say they didn't take it very well. My parents totally freaked out. My father slapped me and told me never to say the word *gay* again in his house. My mother went ballistic and did the whole fainting and crying drama act. Her doctor prescribed Valium for her."

"Jesus Christ," Chance said.

"Yeah, they're a real bunch of winners, let me tell you. They made me talk to our priest, and even made me go to one of those freaky conversion groups. But it didn't work, of course, and just made the tension between us that much worse."

"I'm sorry. I thought my parents were bad, but they never made me do any of that shit."

"Yeah, well it wasn't easy. But the worst part was my older brother. He was twenty, and we shared a bedroom. When I came out, he became my worst nightmare. He teased me all the time and called me a faggot every chance he got."

"He was twenty and still living at home?" Chance said. "What a fucking loser."

"We're Latino, remember?" Rudy said, laughing. "That's normal. You don't leave home until you get married . . . and even then sometimes not."

"Just shoot me," Chance said.

"Yeah, sometimes it can be pretty miserable. Especially when you have a brother like Jaime and you have to share a room with him. After a couple months of just making fun of me verbally, he started hitting me. At first it was just rough-housing a little, but it got more serious as time went on. One night he came back from a date with his girlfriend, and he was drunk as shit and really pissed because his girlfriend wouldn't put out. He stumbled over to my bed and woke me up, then pulled his dick out and told me to suck it. I was quite a bit smaller back then, and I tried to fight him off, but he was a lot stronger. He hit me pretty hard a couple of times, and I finally gave in and sucked his cock. It didn't take him very long to cum at all, and if you ask me, I think he got off on it. But it really pissed him off, and after he came in my mouth, he lost it. He started beating the shit out of me. And I don't mean just brotherly messing around. He beat me unconscious."

"Fuck, Rudy, I had no idea," Chance said, and massaged Rudy's neck lightly. "Your parents didn't do anything to stop him?"

"Hardly. I can't prove it, but I think they may have known he was beating me up for a while before they stopped him. They never called an ambulance, and they didn't even take me to the hospital. My mother finally shook me awake, and I walked to the hospital alone. Carlos was the nurse who attended to me in the emergency room, and when I told him what happened, he called the police.

"He was so sweet and stayed with me the entire time and comforted me. He insisted I press charges against Jaime. He was so cute and nice, and I was really attracted to him. He's five years older than me but looks the same age as me. Even now he does, but back then he looked really young and hot, and I couldn't take my eyes off of him. So I did as he suggested and I pressed charges against Jaime."

"That must have gone over well with your parents."

"They were furious. They told me that I was not their son and to never come back home, not even for my clothes. Carlos gave me the keys to his apartment, put me in a cab, and paid the driver to take me to his place. And we've been together ever since."

"That's incredible, Rudy," Chance said, and hugged him tightly around the neck, careful not to block his view as he drove. "What happened to Jaime?"

"He got off with a slap on the wrist. Ten days in city jail and one year of probation. He still lives at home with my parents, and he has four kids by three different women."

"Can we say 'Jerry Springer'?" Chance said, and both men laughed.

Rudy jumped out of the car and ran up to the porch even before Chance had brought the car to a stop in the driveway. He jumped into Carlos' arms and kissed him as his boyfriend returned the passionate kiss and spun Rudy around. They kissed and hugged for a few minutes, and then Rudy pointed over to Chance still sitting behind the wheel of the car.

As the two boyfriends walked toward him, Chance felt elated and sad at the same time. Carlos was every bit as hot as Rudy had said he was. He was a couple of inches taller than his boyfriend and carried himself with an air of confidence. He wasn't as muscular as Rudy, but was toned and defined, and obviously strong, since he'd swung Rudy around the porch a few times with seemingly little effort. His hair was in tight corn-rows, and his green eyes sparkled even from a dozen yards away. As he walked hand in hand toward the car with Rudy, Chance saw how happy they were together, and he wished he had that kind of happiness.

"So you're the bitch you fucked my boyfriend, huh?" Carlos said as he walked over to the driver's side of the car.

His voice was much deeper and stronger than Chance expected, and he approached the car aggressively. It took him by surprise, and he slinked back into the seat reflexively.

"Stop it, babe." Rudy laughed and pushed Carlos playfully. "Chance doesn't know you well enough to know that you're kidding."

Carlos smiled and opened Chance's door. "I'm just messin' with you," he said, extending his hand and helping Chance out

of the car. "Rudy says you're really hot in bed. I'm looking forward to finding out myself. And I can't tell you how much I ap-
preciate you taking care of my baby and bringing him home
safely."

"It was nothing," Chance said. "I enjoyed it." He noted the
stern look on Carlos' face, and then added, "The company. I
enjoyed the company."

Carlos and Rudy both laughed. "You're really easy to fuck
with," Carlos said, and wrapped his arm around Chance's
shoulder and walked toward the house. "I can't wait to fuck
your ass."

They went to dinner at Quinn's seafood restaurant, and
Chance thought he'd skipped the rapture and just been jet-
expressed straight to heaven itself. He had a spiced Caribbean
snapper with grilled plantain, chayote, and black bean corn
salsa that literally gave him a hardon. The mojitos were strong,
and Carlos made sure they were never empty.

When they finished with dinner, they took a stroll along the
beach. It was dusk and there were several couples and groups
of people walking ankle high in the surf. Chance had never
seen so many beautiful and perfect people in his life. Everyone
was buffed and toned and worked out to the point that it
looked as if they were always posing. Their tans were deep
bronze and perfect, their hair coiffed with the trendiest cuts,
and their clothes were all high-name labels. He was sensitively
aware of how imperfect he was, and how much he did not fit in
with the South Beach crowd.

But Carlos and Rudy didn't seem to see that at all. They
both seemed genuinely into Chance, and made a point of
touching and kissing him every chance they got. After walking
for about half an hour, the crowds on the beach began thinning
out. Carlos took Rudy and Chance by the hand and led them
around a bend in the beach. They were in a secluded, little

private cove, with small shrubs providing protection from the noise and people several feet above them and a rocky cliff separating them from the row of hotels on the other side of the beach.

"Wow!" Chance said, breathlessly. "I've never seen . . ."

Carlos pulled Chance to him and kissed him on the lips as Rudy moved behind him and pulled his shirt off and started lowering his shorts. Carlos kissed him slow and deep, and helped Rudy undress him. He lowered Chance to the ground and gently laid him on the cool sand while Rudy lay beside him and nibbled on his neck.

The two boyfriends shed their clothes quickly and hugged Chance between them. Their hard cocks rubbed and pressed against him, and caused him to shudder despite the warm air around him. He moaned and rubbed his ass against Rudy's familiar thick cock, and reached down and stroked Carlos' cock. It was about as thick as Rudy's but much longer. He wrapped both fists around it, placing one on top of the other, and still had a couple of inches of cock towering over it.

"Holy shit!" Chance said.

"You like it?" Rudy asked as he kissed on Chance's earlobes.

"Uhhh, yeah."

"You wanna suck it?"

Chance moaned and pulled Carlos up to him so that he straddled his chest. He leaned forward and licked at the cock head for a moment, and then sucked the fat head into his mouth. It was hard, yet silky smooth, and as he sucked on it a thick stream of precum slid onto his tongue, eliciting a moan from him.

Rudy slid down Chance's body and spread his legs apart so that he could crawl between them. He sucked around the cock head for a few moments and then slowly slid his mouth down the shaft until the thick cock was buried in his throat. He kept the dick deep inside his throat, tightening his muscles around it.

"Oh my God," Chance moaned as he let Carlos' cock slip from his mouth. "That feels amazing, Rudy."

"You want me to fuck your ass, baby?" Carlos asked as he watched Chance slide his cock in and out of his boyfriend's mouth.

"Hell yeah, man."

Rudy stopped sucking Chance's cock and maneuvered him so that he was on all fours. He kissed Carlos as his boyfriend moved behind Chance and began caressing his ass. When Carlos knelt and spread Chance's ass and began licking it tenderly, Rudy moved to stand in front of his new friend and slid his cock slowly into Chance's ready mouth. "Suck my dick, baby," he said, and caressed Chance's head and the back of his neck lovingly.

Chance lapped at the big cock and swallowed it hungrily. He moaned loudly and pushed his ass backward onto Carlos' tongue, and steadied himself by holding onto Rudy's strong legs. He'd experimented with ecstasy a couple of times when he was younger, and the feeling he had at that moment reminded him of the sensations he experienced while under the influence of the powerful drug. He felt lightheaded, as if he were floating above the ground and even outside of his body. He swore he could taste and feel every pore on the skin of Rudy's cock as it slid in and out of his mouth. And his ass seemed to take on a life of its own, wrapping around Carlos' wet tongue and kissing and pulling it deeper into his hole.

"I wanna fuck you," Carlos said suddenly, and moved into position on his knees behind Chance. He slapped his big dick across Chance's ass a couple of times and then pushed forward until the head slipped inside the well-lubricated sphincter.

"Oh Christ!" Chance mumbled through a mouthful of

Rudy's cock. At the same time, he pushed his ass back so that it slid all the way down Carlos' long cock.

Carlos grabbed Chance by the waist and slammed his cock into his ass relentlessly. He slid it all the way out and then rammed it all the way back in until his balls bounced between Chance's legs. It didn't take long at all until all the thrusting and slamming knocked Chance off balance and onto the ground.

"Come over here, baby" Carlos said to Rudy as Chance picked himself off the ground. "I want you to fuck him with me."

"What?" Chance said, brushing sand from his knees. "I can't take both of you."

"Yes, you can," Carlos said, and sat on the beach, just a couple of feet from the surf as it washed across the sand. "Come over here and sit on my cock."

Chance looked back and forth from Carlos' long cock to Rudy's thick one. He was certain there was no way he could take them both inside him at the same time. Though he'd often fantasized about it, he'd never taken two cocks at once before. He figured it would have to hurt, there was no way it couldn't. But the more he looked at the two very different but equally hot cocks, the more he wanted to at least try. The ecstasy effect kicked in again, convincing him that he could do anything. He walked over to Carlos, kicking his legs closer together so that they almost touched, then turned around so that his back faced Carlos and straddled the tall Latino's legs.

He lowered himself slowly onto the long cock, taking a deep breath as the head pierced his hole and slid slowly but deliberately inside him. When the last inch of the big cock was buried deep in his ass, he sat unmoving, breathing slowly as he became accustomed to it again. After only about a minute, he began tightening his ass around the cock and then sliding up and down it, rising so that only the head remained inside him, and then slowly sliding back down the pole until he felt Carlos' big balls tickle his ass cheeks.

"Come on, baby," Carlos said as he pulled Chance backward so that he was lying against his chest and stomach. "Come over here and join me. I wanna feel your hot cock sliding against mine inside this boy's sweet ass."

Rudy jumped up and maneuvered between Carlos' legs. He pushed Chance all the way back so that Carlos could kiss him on the mouth, and his body was completely stretched backward and his ass was exposed. He spit a mouthful of saliva onto his cock and slid it slowly inside.

"FUCK!" Chance yelled, and tried to wiggle free from Carlos' strong arms. "I can't, I can't. Take it out."

"Come on, man," Rudy whispered. "You can take it. Just take a big breath and relax."

"Relax?" Chance said as he breathed in and out of his mouth quickly. He'd seen movies of pregnant women doing it while giving birth, and since this felt like he was delivering twins, he thought it might work. "It feels like I have a fucking baseball bat up my ass."

"I know, baby," Carlos said as he licked Chance's ear. "But just try to relax. It'll feel better in a minute."

"Promise?" Chance asked, still breathing heavily.

"Yes, I promise."

Chance closed his eyes and concentrated on breathing slowly and deeply. He couldn't imagine that the shooting pain stabbing through his ass and guts would pass anytime soon, let alone in a minute. But Carlos had promised, and so he gave it the good old college try. He had to keep his eyes closed, though, because he knew if he watched Rudy slide into him again and again, he'd never convince himself that it didn't hurt. Even with his eyes tightly closed, it was hard enough to make himself believe . . .

And then it happened. After about five minutes of excruciating pain that felt like he was a fish being gutted, the pain suddenly turned to pleasure. Deep inside him, Rudy's cock slid along Carlos' and pushed against his prostate, and it felt to Chance as if a switch had been turned on inside him.

"Oh yeah, man," Chance moaned loudly. "Fuck me."

Up to then, Carlos had been sitting perfectly still, with his cock buried deep inside Chance's ass, but keeping it still and allowing Rudy to do all of the moving. But once Chance relaxed and gave the word that he was more than ready to take both big dicks, Carlos started sliding his long cock slowly in and out of the hot ass, pulling out just as Rudy was slamming back in and then driving deep inside as Rudy retreated.

It was obvious to Chance that the boyfriends had sung this particular song before. They slid in and out of his ass with perfectly timed rhythm, and each seemed to know exactly where and how the other's cock would feel as it massaged his ass and prostate. The whole thing seemed effortless to Rudy and Carlos; they barely broke a sweat and they maintained a perfectly normal breathing pattern.

Chance, on the other hand, bounced up and down both big cocks frantically. Sweat poured from every pore on his body. He felt the heat rise from his skin as if he had been in a steam room or sauna for hours. He tried to moan . . . to cry out in ecstasy . . . to tell his new friends that he thought he was in heaven. But not a single sound escaped his throat. He simply rode up and down on the two cocks like a pogo stick and marveled at the force of the orgasm as it sprayed from his cock and flew in every direction.

"Holy fuck, baby," Rudy said. "He's shooting his load all over the place. I've never seen so much cum."

"Yeah?" Carlos said. Well, let's show him what real loads look like."

Both men pulled out of Chance's ass with lightning-like speed. Chance dropped to the cool sand as limp as a rag doll, unable to move a single muscle. Again he tried to speak, and again, nothing came out. Rudy and Carlos quickly moved into position on either side of him and stroked their cocks. Even in his semiconscious and completely exhausted state, he was acutely aware of how beautiful both men were, and how amazing their cocks were.

"Here I cum, baby," Rudy yelled. He arched his back and moaned as he blew his load all the way across Chance's body and onto Carlos' stomach and cock.

Chance opened his mouth to say how hot Rudy's load was, but was stopped short when Carlos quickly took his hand away from his cock just as the first spray flew from his cock and landed in Chance's mouth. He jerked his head as spray after spray of the warm, thick load landed on his eyes, nose, and mouth. He lapped it up as quickly as he could but couldn't believe his eyes as it kept coming and kept landing all over his face.

"Damn, dude," he said through a mouthful of warm cum, "aim that thing somewhere else."

Carlos turned and finished unloading himself across Chance's stomach. A couple of shots landed on Rudy's softening cock.

Chance finished swallowing the cum in his mouth and wiped the rest of the load from his face as the two boyfriends dropped to their sides and cuddled up next to him. He wrapped his arms around both of them and looked up at the stars above them. The waves were beginning to come farther inland, and splashed across his feet and knees. He thought that nothing was as perfect as this moment, and that nothing could ruin it.

"Catch your breath, baby," Rudy said sleepily as he cuddled closer to Chance. "Then we can go again . . . only this time I wanna take you and Carlos at the same time."

He was right.

The Back of the Bus

"I still don't know why you have to go all the way across the country to go to college, honey," Mrs. Bevins said as she cried into her wrinkled handkerchief.

"Mom, we've been over this a thousand times," Jon said. He was trying hard not to roll his eyes. "I'm not running away from home. I'm not leaving or deserting you. I'm not turning my back on my family. I'm just going to college."

"But *Philadelphia*?" the short and pudgy woman said in an accent that made Jeff Foxworthy sound like an elite socialite. "We got plenty a nice schools right here in Houston."

"Oh, yes, I can see that," he said with a chuckle, and hugged his mom tightly around the neck. "That last sentence there could very possibly win you a Pulitzer."

"Don't get sassy with me," his mother said, and swatted him playfully. "You know what I mean."

"Yes, I do. And I love you for it. But I need to do this, Mom. I need a little independence. And Philly is offering me a full scholarship. U of H was only bucking up with a ride."

"I know, I know," she said as she pretended to dig through

her purse. "See, you're smarter already. You're thinking so sensibly. There's no need to go to Philadelphia."

"Mother . . ."

"I'm kidding," she sniffled, and hugged him tighter. "Get on that damned bus before it takes off without you."

Jon kissed his mother on the cheek and slung his backpack over his shoulder as he boarded the Greyhound bus. There were only two other passengers on the bus, but it was the departing station, and he knew it would get more full as they drove east. He tossed his backpack in the overhead bin, took a seat two-thirds of the way to the back, and stretched across both seats in the row. He waved good-bye to his crying mother and rested his head against his window as he watched the landscape whiz past him from the window directly across the aisle. His eyes began to get heavy, and he was snoring softly before the bus even hit the Houston city limits sign.

It was dark and smoky in the club, and he needed some fresh air. Stepping out the back door into the alley, he was disappointed. It was just as dark if not darker outside, and though there was no smoke, the putrid stench from the Dumpster a few feet from the exit was worse and caused him to gag. He took a few steps away from the rotten odor.

"Hey dude, over here."

He looked around him quickly, ready to strike. This was not the best part of town by anyone's standards, and infamous for its muggings, rapes, and assaults. He didn't see anyone, but turned toward the car parked several feet ahead of him.

"Come suck my dick, man," he heard the voice coming from the car again.

"No, thanks," he said, and wrapped his fist around his set of keys, making them a makeshift weapon like he'd been taught in

high school self-defense class. "I'm on my way home and not looking for any trouble."

"I'm not trouble, man," the sexy voice said softly behind the bright orange spark of a lit cigarette. "I've been watching you all night in the club. I've been out here for half an hour waiting for you to walk by."

"Why," he asked.

The man in the car kicked the door open slowly and stretched his legs out in front of him on the street. The glow from the streetlight on the corner cast just enough light for Jon to make out the long, thick cock. The man stroked it slowly and slid his fingers across the sticky head.

Jon walked over to the car and dropped to his knees between the long legs of the stranger. He wrapped his fist around the thick cock and squeezed it playfully, and his mouth watered as the heat from the cock warmed his palm and spread through the rest of his body. He leaned forward and licked the salty precum from the head, savoring the slick texture and swallowing it hungrily.

"That's it, dude. I knew you wanted my big cock," the stranger said. "Suck it good."

Jon wrapped his lips around the head and sucked it gently into his mouth, tightening his lips around it as he pulled it all inside. He ran his tongue across the mushroom head and smiled as moans of lust escaped the guy's throat. Then he opened the back of his own throat and slid his head down the full length of the huge cock.

"Oh, fuck, man," the stranger moaned. "That's it, deepthroat my big dick."

Jon swallowed the entire cock, stopping only when his mouth reached pubic hair. He tightened his throat around the thick shaft and slid up and down slowly. The fat veins that ran the length of the fat cock tickled his lips as they slid over the vascular river. God, how he loved fat, veiny cocks like this one!

"Shit, dude," the still faceless stranger said breathlessly, "that's the best head I've ever had. I'm getting close."

Jon didn't want it to end yet and started to pull his mouth off the juicy cock. But the guy had other plans and locked his fingers behind Jon's head and applied just enough pressure to keep his mouth buried on the big cock, but not enough to hurt him. That was cool with Jon, too, and he responded by flicking his tongue playfully across the head as he deepthroated the massive cock again.

The man in the car lifted his hips a few inches in the air and began fucking Jon's mouth in earnest. He pulled the long cock out until just the head remained inside Jon's wet mouth, and then plunged it back deep inside his throat in long, deliberate strokes. He was leaking precum by the pint now, and Jon knew he wouldn't be able to hold out much longer.

He reached down and cupped the big hairy balls in his hands and squeezed gently as he increased the pressure from his mouth on the cock. The guy was fucking his face fast and hard now, and breathing heavily. Jon knew he was about to explode. He slipped one long finger under the man's balls and between his sweaty crack, and slid it a couple of inches inside the tight, warm hole.

"FUCK!" the man yelled.

A burst of salty-sweet cum splashed across his tongue and the back of his throat. There was so much of it and it came so fast, he gasped, and swallowed the first three shots. Then he pulled his head off the big dick and watched as the last five jets shot from the stranger's cock head and landed on his face.

"Dude, that was fucking incredible," the stranger said as he shook the last of his cum from his spent cock and stuffed it back in his jeans.

"Thanks," Jon said, licking what he could reach from his lips and wiping the rest with the back of his hand. "You live around here?"

"Nah, I'm from . . ."

* * *

"Natchitoches, Louisiana," the driver yelled loudly as the bus groaned and belched its way to a stop at the roadside diner and gas stop.

Jon jerked awake and reached out his hand to catch what he thought was a fall. How long had he been asleep? He rubbed his eyes and stretched his legs to get the cramps out. His cock was fully hard and throbbing halfway down his left thigh.

"Shit," he said quickly, and covered it with his hands.

He waited until all the other passengers were off the bus and then walked briskly to the restroom on the side of the white brick building. The small restroom was dimly lit and dirty and smelled overwhelmingly of Pine-Sol and urine. Jon gagged a little in his mouth, and almost turned around and ran out, but the throbbing hardon in his jeans demanded attention, and he knew it wouldn't go away on its own. He turned to lock the door, and wasn't surprised to see it had no lock.

"Great," he said, "welcome to Loseranna." He walked into the handicapped stall, pulled his jeans down to his ankles, and stretched his legs out. His cock sprung up against his belly immediately, and Jon was surprised by its heat. When he wrapped his fist around it, his whole body shook, and a tiny drop of precum oozed out the cock head.

"At least this won't take too long," he said with a laugh. He stroked his big dick a couple of times, staring at it as he did.

He had a beautiful cock, there was no doubt about it. Not that he needed it; as quarterback of his high school and junior college football teams, he was always the most popular guy in any room. A little over six feet tall, strongly built with bulging muscles, platinum blond hair that was always naturally stylish and with the perfect amount of "bed head" look, and sparkling indigo blue eyes, he was just about everyone's vision of perfection. Add to that his polished charm, and he couldn't be touched. Because he was raised to be polite and modest, he pretended not to notice the look of envy and resentment as his teammates glanced discretely at his flawless smooth and hard bubble butt and his thick eight-inch cock in the showers.

His mouth was already getting dry as his hand slid up and down the length of his fat cock, and his breath was getting more labored. He tightened his ass, which caused his cock to harden even more and sent shock waves across his body.

And then the door to the restroom opened.

Jon sat perfectly still and held his breath, hoping the newcomer would just piss really quick and leave. When the door in the next stall opened and then closed, he cursed under his breath and debated stuffing his cock back into his jeans and heading back to the bus. But he knew his hardon wouldn't give up, so he slowly began stroking it again.

The tap of a shoe on the floor to his right caught Jon's attention, and he looked over at the wall. How could he not have noticed the crudely cut hole just to the right of the toilet paper holder? It was about four inches in diameter and resembled something between a triangle and a square. He looked a little closer and saw the guy on the other side stroking his rapidly growing cock, and a second later, a moistened pair of thin lips appeared in the hole.

Jon stood up and squeezed between the toilet and the wall, and slid his cock through the hole. It was immediately wrapped in warmth and moisture, and the soft tongue on the other side definitely knew what it was doing. Jon's knees began to buckle in less than a minute, and he felt the orgasm boiling deep in his loins.

"Dude, that's hot," he whispered. "I'm getting close."

The guy on the other side increased his suction and wrapped his hand around the last half of Jon's cock that he couldn't get in his mouth. That's all it took for Jon, and he moaned loudly as his legs quivered violently and he felt the stream of fire shoot up from his belly, through his intestines, and up his shaft. He counted six significant jets of cum, and the guy on the other side registered two additional moans, which Jon guessed was the impact of the unseen guy's own load being spent onto the floor.

"Thanks, man," Jon said, and quickly left the restroom. He was famished and rushed inside to grab a burger and fries before the bus resumed its long trip to Philadelphia.

He'd never been a great traveler, and the twenty-four-hour road trip on the noisy bus was not really conducive to getting some good shut-eye. His catnap earlier had left him with aches and pains in every muscle of his body, and made any real REM sleep impossible. He drifted in and out of restless naps for several hours, and then gave up.

He was in the middle of reading the new Harry Potter book when the clumsy bus screeched to another stop.

"Roanoke, Virginia, folks," the driver announced. "This will be a short stop. Fifteen minutes. Please make sure you're back on the bus at 4:20 sharp."

He didn't need to pee or eat, but the cool Virginia morning air and a quick walk around the bus and truck stop to get the kinks out would do him some good. His long legs were not meant to be cooped up for twenty-four hours straight. He stumbled out of the bus and walked around for a few minutes, then returned to his seat well before the fifteen-minute time frame. The cool morning air might be good for him, but it was fucking cold, and he wasn't feeling it at all.

As the other passengers began filing onto the bus, Jon noticed a new addition to the group. The guy was African American and stood easily a few inches taller than Jon. His head was shaved close, and his large almond-shaped eyes drew Jon in immediately. He'd had a few black friends in school back home but had never been attracted to any of them. His parents, though they would never admit it, were more than a little racist, but Jon had never thought much about it. But now that he did stop to think about it, he realized that they had influenced him more than he'd thought. All of the guys he was attracted to were white.

Up to now. He couldn't take his eyes off this new passenger. His obviously gym-honed muscles strained to escape the confines of the thin white t-shirt and tight jeans he wore. His biceps flexed to cartoonish proportions as he placed his bag in the space above the seats, and when he turned around to find an unoccupied seat, the huge bulge in the front of his faded jeans caused Jon's eyes to bulge and his own cock to stir to life.

The newbie started to take an empty seat near the front, but then his eyes caught Jon's and they locked for a long moment. He stood back up and walked right up to Jon, never losing eye contact with him. When he was two seats in front of Jon, he smiled and raised one eyebrow, and then continued walking past him and to the back of the bus. He took the very last seat in the back row and sprawled across both seats, with his long legs dangling over the armrests.

Jon's heart pounded in his chest, and his cock was harder than he could remember it ever being. He could actually feel himself leaking precum, and he didn't usually have very much at all. He found it difficult to breathe. This guy's beauty literally took his breath away, and he couldn't stop turning around and staring at the guy. Apparently the feeling was mutual, because every time Jon looked back to steal a glance at the dude, he was staring right back at Jon and never dropped his gaze.

The newcomer glanced around briefly to make sure no one was looking and then motioned for Jon to come back and join him. They were the only two passengers in the last third of the bus and the only ones still awake, save for the old lady in the very front row, who was knitting a sweater and was almost completely deaf.

Jon jumped up and nearly tripped over himself trying to get back to the back row.

"Be careful." The sexy black man laughed as he moved his legs to make room, and Jon thought he'd melt then and there when he heard the deep sexy timbre of his voice.

"Sorry," Jon whispered awkwardly, and sidled into the seat next to his new friend. "I'm Jon."

"Trent," the guy said, and shook Jon's hand. He held it longer than necessary for a cordial handshake, and instead of releasing it, he pulled Jon in to kiss him on the lips.

Jon was trembling like he was standing in the middle of the Alaskan tundra in midwinter and cursed his lack of self-control. But Trent didn't seem to mind at all, and when he slid his warm, soft tongue into Jon's mouth, Jon sucked on it greedily and melted into his new friend's welcoming body. How he could ever have gotten through the past few years without falling head over heels for some of his black friends back home, he hadn't a clue. Visions of his parents seeing him wrapped in this embrace, kissing this beautiful man, and the look of pure panic, shock, and disgust flashed through his mind for a quick second.

And then it was gone. In its place was the smell, the feel, the taste of the most beautiful man Jon had ever laid eyes upon. He laid on top of Trent's torso and ground his hips into the newcomer's as he kissed him hard on the lips and ran his hands across Trent's smoothly shaved head. He fumbled with Trent's jean button and pulled them down to his knees roughly.

"Careful, man," Trent whispered as he looked up over the

seat to make sure no one was watching. "Slow down, and try to be a little quieter. We don't want the whole bus to know what we're doing back here."

"Sorry," Jon said with a shy grin, and then slid down Trent's body until he was on his knees in between his new friend's spread legs. He leaned forward and reached out with his tongue to lick the head of Trent's cock, and gasped when his tongue reached its target. "Fuck!" he whispered loudly. "How big is that thing?"

"Twelve and a half inches," Trent said. "I'm sorry. I know it's too big."

"Fuck that," Jon said, and sucked the fat head into his mouth. He sucked on it greedily and felt proud when he slid his mouth down the first third of the giant cock and felt Trent grab the seats for support and try to catch his breath. He took a deep breath and opened his throat as if he were yawning, and pushed his head forward, surprising even himself as inch after inch of thick uncut cock slid deeper and deeper into his hungry throat. About two-thirds of the way down, his mouth was stretched to its limit and his throat was filled with Trent's monster cock.

"That's so hot, dude," Trent moaned. "You're gonna make me cum."

"Not like this," Jon said as he quickly pulled his mouth from the cock. "I want you to fuck my ass."

"What?" Trent said. "You can't be serious. It's too big."

"Fuck me, Trent."

Trent sat up in the seat and pushed the armrest into the upright position against the back of the seat. He leaned forward and pushed Jon onto his back on the makeshift bed. He was every bit as fast and twice as quiet and nowhere near as clumsy in undressing the blond cowboy from Houston as Jon had been with him. When Jon was completely naked, Trent swallowed his cock and slid a long finger up his new friend's ass in one unceremonious move. Jon started to moan loudly, but Trent covered his mouth, and so he was left only to writhe under the strength of Trent's weight and heat and accept what was being done to him.

He didn't have a problem with that. He lifted his ass and slid it up and down Trent's finger, and then squeezed his ass muscles around it. When Trent maneuvered himself so that his giant cock was pressed against the quivering hole of Jon's ass, Jon pulled his legs into the air and taunted Trent with his hungry hole.

"Fuck me, Trent."

Trent spit a gob of saliva onto the puckered hole and pressed forward so that just the head of the huge cock slid inside.

Jon gasped, and covered his mouth with his own hand this time to keep from screaming out loud and waking the other passengers and possibly causing the bus to career off the road. He took a couple of deep breaths, and when he relaxed, Trent's foot-long cock slid deep inside him, not stopping until the big, low-hanging balls rested against his ass cheeks.

The huge cock slid against his prostate deep inside him and sent tiny bolts of lightning all through his body. He thought he'd have a hard time taking the baseball bat up his ass . . . that it'd hurt and rip him to shreds . . . that he'd beg the black sex god to take it out and possibly call him an ambulance.

And so when, instead, he arched his back up to allow even more of the big dick to slide deeper inside him . . . when he squeezed his ass muscles around the Coke-can-thick shaft, eliciting a moan of appreciation from his new fuck buddy . . . when he begged Trent to fuck him deeper and harder, to fuck his brains out, in fact . . . well, Jon was a little surprised. And more than a little proud of himself.

"Rape me, Trent," he whispered huskily as he thrust his ass deeper onto the chocolate cock inside him. "Slide that huge dick all the way up my ass and make me cry."

Trent was sweating now, and slamming his cock in and out of Jon's smooth, hard ass like a jackhammer. He withdrew the huge cock almost all the way out quickly and then slid it back inside the warm, wet tunnel as slowly as he could. He leaned down and kissed Jon passionately on the lips, sucking his warm tongue into his mouth and savoring its taste and feel.

"My God, you feel incredible," he said, breaking the kiss.

"Your cock is amazing, man," Jon panted. "I've never felt anything like this."

Trent slid all the way back inside Jon and laid on top of his torso, hugging him tightly and grinding the cock around the tight muscled walls of Jon's insatiable ass. The road was bumpy and the coach bounced up and down on bad shocks, driving Trent's cock deeper yet inside Jon's ass and eliciting low moans of approval from the platinum-haired stud.

"Fuck, man," Trent whispered in Jon's ear, "I'm not gonna last much longer, dude. I'm close."

"Me too," Jon said, and kissed him on the lips again.

That sent Trent over the edge. He returned the kiss fervently and quickly pulled his big dick out of Jon's protesting ass in one brutal retreat. He collapsed on top of the blond stud, still kissing him as his cock spurted out what seemed like a gallon of cum all over Jon's stomach and legs.

The two boys took a couple of minutes to catch their breath, and then Trent lay on his back, with his head against the window. He signaled for Jon to move closer to him. "Shoot your hot load all over my face, dude," he said, and his eyes sparkled.

Jon thought he'd never seen a more beautiful or sexy sight in his life, and his cock ached to let go with what he could tell was a gigantic load. He leaned forward on his knees, until his cock was only a couple of inches from Trent's face.

"I'm cumming, man," he grunted.

Trent opened his mouth, and Jon pointed his cock right at it. The first two shots missed their target, hitting Trent's nose and eyes instead. But the next three or four streams of warm cum landed in his mouth and on his tongue, and Trent lapped it up hungrily and swallowed every last drop.

"Wow," Jon said when he'd had a chance to catch his breath. "That was fucking amazing."

"Yeah, it was," Trent agreed. "You're one hot piece of ass."

"And you're an incredibly hot top, man."

The two boys got dressed and then fell asleep in each other's arms. They were awakened a couple of hours later, when the driver slammed the bus into park and announced they were in Gettysburg, their last stop before Philadelphia.

"So where you heading?" Trent asked as they stepped off the bus and stretched their legs. The sun was just rising and birds chirped loudly all around them.

"Philly. I'm attending school there this fall."

"No shit? Me, too."

"UPP?"

"Yeah," Trent laughed.

"That's crazy, man. What are you majoring in?"

"Political science. You?"

"Computer science. But I'm thinking of changing majors."

"Right on. To what?

"African American studies," Jon said, and laughed as the two boys walked arm-around-shoulder into the restaurant.

The High Price of Peace

"Will there be anything else, Mr. Garcia?"

"No, Marcia, that will be all for now." Anthony Garcia watched as his secretary turned and exited his office. Thirty years ago she must have been quite a knockout, he thought. Her olive skin was probably smooth and unwrinkled; her now dull gray hair was probably shiny and black. Her eyes probably sparkled and exuded life and energy. Her full, meticulously polished lips probably smiled and held mysterious secrets.

But all of that was probably thirty years ago, and it was really just speculation. He had no idea if Marcia Ross had ever smiled in her life. He had no idea if *anyone* had ever smiled, in fact. He'd never actually seen a smile. He'd seen pictures of smiles in old magazines, and there were a few of those old classic movies from the 1990s and early 2000s that hadn't been confiscated and could be found in some of the old underground black market movie theaters. People were smiling in those. But everyone knew those were only pictures and that the movies were fiction. He'd heard that actors had made hundreds of millions of dollars for making movies back in the old days, and he supposed for even a quarter of that salary, he might be able to conjure up a smile, too. He'd have to take some acting classes, of course, but he thought he might be able to train himself to smile.

Will this day ever end, he wondered, and looked at the clock on the wall by his office door. 3:47 P.M. Eventually it would, he knew, but not soon enough. Would this year ever end, he wondered, and glanced at the calendar on his desk. November 19, 2088. He supposed the year, too, would end, as it always seemed to do, and bring in another equally apathetic one. Would his life ever end? That one he wasn't as optimistic about, because Anthony Garcia was not one who was prone to wishful thinking. He hadn't been hand preened and appointed by the Counselor to be the Director of Global Communications Amalgamation by being prone to wishful thinking.

But still, with only an hour and thirteen minutes left of the last day of a typically noneventful work week, he couldn't help but wonder what life must have been like before the New Order went into effect. What would it have been like to experience crime and hunger and civil disobedience? What would it have been like to feel pain and love and joy and sorrow? What would it have been like to have a middle class? Had anyone ever really experienced fear?

"Your car will be waiting for you downstairs in half an hour, sir. So whenever, you're ready to leave."

"I'm ready," Anthony said.

"Pardon me?" Marcia Ross said. "But it's not yet 4:00. You've got over an hour left."

"That's fine," he said. "I've had a particularly productive week, and there's nothing else I can get done before I leave anyway."

"But your car is still at the wash, sir." She was probably confused, and maybe even a little concerned that her boss might be sick or maybe even worse. But no one had been sick in over twenty years, and crazy was no more. So there was no cause for concern, hadn't been any cause for concern in two decades. Therefore Marcia Ross showed no sign of anxiety or apprehension at all. No one ever did anymore.

"That's fine, I'll walk." He watched for her to flinch or to show any expression whatsoever to this quite unusual remark. He never walked anywhere. He was much too important. When she didn't respond at all, he said, "Aren't you going to ask me why I'm walking?"

"Of course not, sir," she said in an even tone and without looking into his eyes.

Of course not. There would be no reaction at all. Why would there be? There was no reason to be worried about walking; there was no crime in the world at all anymore. Even more important, it was inherently impossible for that particular reaction from Marcia. Genetically, she wasn't capable of it.

For the past sixty years, at the time of conception, every child was assigned a predetermined social class for the rest of his or her life. This social class was determined by a lottery, and parents had no opinion as to the assigned class of their child. Upon birth, the child was genetically injected to be cultivated into their class. Because there was no disease anymore, and no weapons or crime or violence of any kind . . . and to control the Earth's population, every baby was also injected with a predetermined expiration date. It was a controlled and blind administration of the series of injections, and no one knew their expiration dates or that of any of their family or friends. Some babies were determined to die within an hour, and others would live to be seventy-five. No one lived longer than that.

Inter- and intra-action guidelines within the classes were also predetermined and injected at birth. As an Elite, Anthony was greeted by a bow from Peasants when they passed him on the streets or in casual encounters. He acknowledged their respect and noted it on their Common Card, which allowed them to be rewarded an extra bag of food once they had collected enough acknowledgments. The Bourgeoise were not required to bow to anyone, but were land and property owners who leased housing to the Peasants, at a predetermined rate, of course. They were college educated but were not allowed to serve in government or high-ranking professions, and they sought counsel from the Elite.

Marcia was a Peasant and therefore had no opinion or reaction to Anthony's decision to walk home, or to anything. She simply exited the office and returned to her desk, where she resumed her work, and wished Anthony a good weekend as he left the office.

Anthony sat naked at his desk at home and alternated his stares from the computer monitor to the panoramic view from the wall-sized window of the metropolis that fanned out eighty stories below him.

<<You still there?>>
<<Yes, still here>> he typed back quickly.
<<Good, thought I'd lost you>>
<<Nope>>

He wasn't really in the mood for chatting at the moment but couldn't pull himself away from the computer, either. He paid a very high price for unlimited access to an unmonitored Internet site that could, if discovered, have him removed from office at GCA or, even worse, have his expiration date expedited.

But he didn't care. He couldn't help but think about what life would be like. Real life, where people had emotions, and individual and creative thought, and freedom to express themselves. Where they laughed and cried and smiled. He'd heard that such life had once existed, and he obsessed over what it would feel like to feel pain and fear. The thought brought his cock to full hardness instantly.

On this Internet network, one could indulge in every imaginable fantasy. People talked dirty to one another. They exchanged nude photos and treated one another disrespectfully. They lied and they performed sexual acts on cameras that broadcast all over the world. These were all things very strictly prohibited by global law and punishable by early expiration, which made it that much more exhilarating. This particular Internet company had some geniuses working for them, that was for sure, and probably some high-level New Order officials on their payroll as well. All the other sites that had attempted to provide this level of covert and secure service had been found out and shut down quickly, and their owners had been publicly expired. This was the only one that had time after time after time escaped the long arm of the law. But it could still all come tumbling down at any time, and that thrill was what brought Anthony, and thousands of others like him, to pay ridiculous amounts of money to be members and to indulge their every whim.

<<What are you looking for tonite?>>

<<I want to commit suicide. Wanna watch?>>

<<Very funny. There haven't been any weapons or drugs around for a quarter of a century>> There was a long pause, and then: <<How would you do it?>>

<<I live on the eightieth floor of the Sundyne Tower and have a magnificent balcony with a spectacular view. I could jump>>

<<Yeah, right>>

<<Don't believe me?>>
<<No>>
<<Watch>>

Anthony turned on his camera and secured the connection with the other guy. When he was sure they were online and he had an audience, he walked over to the balcony and slid the floor-to-ceiling glass door to one side, then walked out onto the balcony. He was completely naked, and the brisk wind was blowing hard that high up. It caused his cock to shrink, but he didn't care. He was going to jump anyway, and he knew his ass still looked incredible, and that was what the other guy could see from his vantage point behind the camera.

Anthony heard the arriving message tone on the computer and looked back.

<<Get hard and beat off for me. Then jump while you're shooting your load. That'd be hot>>

"You're a fucking pervert," he yelled back into the den area, loud enough to be heard on the computer's microphone. "You're sick." But his cock was responding to the suggestion, and even with the biting chill of the wind outside, it grew fully hard. Anthony reached down and stroked it for a couple of minutes. Maybe it wasn't such a bad idea, he thought. Imagine the headlines.

When he felt himself getting close, he moved closer to the wall of the balcony and looked down below him. The lights from the cars below looked like tiny ants. How long would it take him to reach the ground from this high up? He scooted a patio chair over to the ledge and stood on it. All he had to do was take one small leap forward, and it would all be over in about a minute. He should feel something, right? His heart should be racing and his palms sweating. He should be afraid.

But he didn't feel any of those things, and he wasn't afraid. So what was the point? If he can't feel that one piece of emotion in his last minute of life, then why bother rushing his death? He stepped down from the chair, and walked back inside.

<<I knew you couldn't do it>>

<<I thought it would be more exhilarating. I didn't feel any different out there naked on that ledge and about to jump to my death than I do when I'm presenting a financial report in front of my board of directors. That can't be right>>

<<I agree. I can help>>

<<How?>>

<<check out this site: www.fantasyescape.gxy It's grossly expensive, but worth every dollar. You won't be disappointed>>

<<What is it?>>

<<Can't tell you. Sworn to secrecy. But you'll love it, trust me>>

"Damn it!" Anthony screamed as the guy on the other end disconnected. He quickly typed in the Web address and in less than five minutes his cock was bouncing up and down like a pogo stick and he had his Black credit card in hand.

He'd been lying in bed, completely naked, for more than an hour. The guy at www.fantasyescape.gxy had told him that his order would arrive between thirty and ninety minutes, and he'd been hard from the moment he signed off the site and jumped into bed, as he'd been told to do. The guy had really asked a lot of questions and seemed very careful about making sure the order wasn't a sting operation. Anyone who had the kind of money it took to pay for his order had to be an Elite, and that was dangerous. He could be a trap, and he knew that. The guy was just being cautious, Anthony knew. But he was about to think that the guy had chickened out and decided not to send his order over.

And then he heard his front door open slowly. His cock twitched and throbbed a little painfully, and Anthony was surprised to feel his heart race. It pounded so hard that it hurt a little and skipped several beats, and he wondered if maybe his expiration date had ironically been tonight, the one night he was playing out his forbidden fantasy, and if his method of expiration was by heart attack. But as the noise increased in the living room, and he heard a man curse under his breath after hitting his knee against the marble coffee table, he realized he was feeling nervous and excitement.

He closed his eyes and pretended to be asleep, just as he'd been told to do. After about a minute he heard his bedroom door open slowly, and he could feel, rather than hear, someone approaching his bed. His heart was now threatening to leap out from his rib cage, and he struggled to keep his eyes closed. A small river of precum dripped from his throbbing cock and onto his belly as he sensed the intruder getting closer.

"Don't even think about screaming or fighting, punk, or you'll never see the sun rise again."

Suddenly there were hands all over his body, roughly pushing him onto his stomach. A knee planted in the small of his back kept him pinned to the mattress, while one hand grabbed him by the hair. Someone tied a blindfold around his eyes tightly and then pulled his arms straight above him.

"I'm not going to gag you, because you're gonna need that faggot mouth of yours," the same rough voice said as Anthony felt a thick rope tied around both wrists and then secured to the headboard. "But I swear to God, if you scream or make any noise other than what I tell you to make, I'll cut out your tongue."

Anthony sighed. Nice try, he thought, but everyone knew that there were literally no weapons left on earth. His hardon started to fade with the amateurish actor's attempt at scaring him. He'd paid extremely good money to feel the one thing he'd never experienced . . . fear. Although the scene had started out promising, making an idle threat that could never be carried out was a little anticlimatic.

"Don't even make the mistake of thinking I'm not serious, bitch," the voice said.

Anthony felt something sharp and cold press against his ass cheek, and a second later, felt it slide across his ass. It stung with pain, and he felt a trickle of blood slide down his meaty cheek.

"Ow! What the fuck?" Anthony said.

Suddenly the knife was at his throat. "Are you ignorant or what? I said, you don't make a sound unless I tell you to. The next time I won't be so gentle, and it won't be your sweet ass I cut. Do you understand me?"

Anthony nodded his head and felt his cock harden again as his heart picked up its earlier erratic rhythm. Where did the intruder get that sharp a knife, and what the hell had Anthony gotten himself into? A knife, for crying out loud. Even the most hardened criminal more than twenty years ago hadn't been able to get his hands on anything this sharp or dangerous. Who was this man, and what did he plan on doing with Anthony?

His cock throbbed beneath him, and a high-pitched ringing filled his head, beginning behind his eyes, then spreading across his skull and down his neck. Memories of his childhood flashed before his eyes, behind the blindfold, and he couldn't stop thinking about the more than ten million dollars worth of art and collectibles he had in his penthouse. Or of what the

Counselor might think of him when they discovered his slashed and dismembered naked body drenched in blood the next day.

"Suck my cock, punk," the man said roughly, and pulled his head to the side.

Anthony opened his mouth and gagged as the man thrust his big cock deep inside his mouth in one brutal stab. He felt the tears begin to fall down his cheek as he struggled to keep from choking and to accommodate the big cock now fucking his mouth. Suddenly, from behind him, a second pair of hands grabbed his feet and spread his legs wide, then tied his ankles tightly to the foot of the bed. He was now spread-eagled on the bed, on his stomach. He'd never been more exposed or vulnerable in his life, and the euphoria of being completely out of control of everything was beginning to make him dizzy.

As he sucked the big cock in his mouth, he felt a pair of strong hands spread his ass cheeks apart and then a hot, wet tongue licking between the crack of his ass. He tightened up with automatic reflex and coughed around the cock in his mouth. But the tongue on his ass knew what it was doing, and in a couple of minutes, Anthony relaxed and began squirming on the bed and struggled to lift his ass higher for the talented tongue to have better access.

A sharp slap landed on his ass, and the sting was immediate. "Lie still, faggot," a second voice said, this one was softer and gentler than the first, and the words sounded foreign coming from the voice. He was either a rookie at this or very young. But either way, Anthony didn't care. He could die right then and there with the guy's tongue buried deep in his ass and be perfectly content.

The man behind him shifted on the bed, and a couple seconds later, Anthony felt a hard, warm cock slide between his ass crack. It was so long that it spanned the entire length of his crevice, and he could tell it still extended at least another couple of inches beyond the small of his back. Damn, how he wished he could see it. It felt so perfect!

With no warning at all, the cock slipped inside his ass. Anthony gasped and felt his jaw tighten as the pain ripped through his unsuspecting ass and bowels.

"Fuck!" the guy fucking his mouth yelled, and slapped Anthony across the face. "That hurts, bitch. You bite me again, and I swear to God I'll cut your throat."

Anthony relaxed and tried to take a few deep breaths, which wasn't easy with his mouth still stuffed with the big cock. The guy behind him began sliding his cock in and out of his ass slowly at first, and then picked up a faster rhythm. His cock felt so incredible that Anthony thought he'd cream right there, without touching himself.

"Goddamn, his ass is sweet and tight, dude," the guy behind him said.

"Yeah?" his friend in front said. "Wanna switch places for a little bit?"

"No man, I'm getting close already. I wanna fuckin' explode deep inside his ass, man."

The friction of both men fucking Anthony from either end, and the sound of their voices as they talked about him as if he weren't there, was driving him crazy. He ached to roll over and rip the blindfold off and make mad, passionate love with both of them. But they had him tied tightly to the bedposts, and he barely had room to move more than an inch with any of his arms or legs. When he tried to move more than that, the rope scraped against his wrists and ankles and stung him.

"That works for me, buddy," the guy in front said. "I'm

close, too. I'm about to shoot my load down his throat any minute now."

Anthony moaned and tightened his ass muscles around the long, thick cock inside him, careful not to bite down or scrape with his teeth the cock in his mouth. His load rolled around in his balls for a moment, and then shot up his shaft and out the head of his cock before he could prepare for it.

"Oh fuck, man," the guy fucking his ass yelled. "I'm blowin' it, dude!" He thrust his huge cock deep inside Anthony one last time and left it buried all the way to his balls. His entire body convulsed as he emptied his load inside the bound and blindfolded victim, and Anthony could feel his cock grow thicker with each pulse of his intruder's orgasm. After eight or nine contractions, Anthony felt a thick stream of cum leak out of his ass and down his balls. The big cock was still buried inside him.

"Here I cum, man," the first guy grunted. His load was powerful and thick, and it poured down Anthony's throat faster than he could swallow it. A mouthful of it dripped from his lips and down his chin.

Both men kept their cocks inside him for a few moments and caught their breath before pulling out. Neither said a word as they got dressed.

"That was really hot, guys," Anthony said. "Everything I expected. Thanks. Why don't you untie me now so I can see your faces."

"Yeah, right," the rougher guy snorted.

Anthony heard them rustling through his drawers for a moment and then their footsteps faded down the wooden hallway. "Hey," he yelled, "wait a minute. Come back here. You can't leave me tied up like this."

He heard the front door shut, and then the house was perfectly quiet.

"Fuck!" he yelled. He struggled against the ropes for a couple of minutes, then gave up when he felt them dig into his skin and draw blood.

He took a deep breath, and then in a very controlled voice, said, "Computer Access," loudly into the black air beyond the blindfold.

"Access sequence, please," the female voice activation system answered.

"639ZTN52."

"Proceed."

"Call Kyle Witford," he said in a defeated tone.

The soft sound of a dialing sequence could be heard from the built-in speaker system wired throughout the house.

"Hello," a sleepy voice answered after three rings.

"Kyle, it's Anthony."

"Anthony? Are you okay? It's after midnight."

"I know, I'm sorry. I'm fine, but I need a big favor, and I must ask for your utmost discretion."

"Of course."

"I need you to come over to my place. Don't bother ringing me, I can't answer the telecam. Just enter in my code—it opens the main door in the lobby, it's the access code for the elevator to my penthouse, and it's the same code for my front door."

"What? Are you sure you're okay?"

"I'm fine, Kyle. Do you have a pen to write down my access code?"

"Yes, I have a pen. What is it?"

"2276490328."

"Got it. I'll be there in about twenty minutes."

"Complete discretion, right?"

"Sure, sure. You know me."

"Good. Just come right in when you get here. I'll be in the bedroom."

Kyle disconnected the call, leaving Anthony alone in the dark room. He couldn't help but wonder what Kyle would think when he walked into the bedroom and found him blindfolded and tied to the bed with dried cum all over his mouth and ass.

His cock began to harden again as he pictured the look on his best friend's face.

The Night Before

Cruz sprawled naked across the bed and spread his long legs over the comforter. He couldn't stop staring at his sister's fiancé's beautiful face. In the picture Charrell had sent, her soon-to-be husband was fully clothed, of course, with a suit and tie, and embracing Charrell lovingly from behind. His shaved head gleamed from the photographer's lights, and his lavender eyes sparkled just as brightly. His brown skin couldn't hide the shy dimples, and his slightly raised eyebrow hinted at a bit of mischief that caused Cruz's cock to swell to its full ten inches.

He wrapped his fist around his shaft and slid his hand up and down the length of his big cock several times, trying to block out his older sister in the photo and focus on Tyson's sexy face and the thought of his hard, naked body underneath all the clothes in the picture. It wasn't that hard. He hadn't been able to think about anything else since he received the picture from Charrell three days ago. He'd never met Tyson, but his big sister couldn't stop talking about him, and he sounded like a great guy. But Cruz had had no idea that he'd be so fucking hot!

He spit into his fist and stroked his cock, squeezing harder and cupping his big shaved balls in the other hand. When he reached the thick base, he slipped a long finger between his ass cheeks and teased his hole. He moaned loudly as goose bumps shot up his entire body and his legs shook with anticipation. It was an aerobic exercise just stroking his huge cock, but much more fun than going to the gym. His tiny nipples hardened as his abs flexed to show each of the lines in his eight-pack.

He looked back down at the picture and imagined his face and his body in Charrell's place. They looked like twins, even though she was a year and a half older. Their father was full-blood Puerto Rican and had blessed his two children with strong and defined bone structure, healthy muscular bodies, and baby blue eyes. And he'd gifted Cruz with the legendary ten-inch and wrist-thick Camacho cock. Their mother was half white and half African American, and stunningly beautiful. Both kids inherited her tempestous dimples, bright white and perfect smile, and baby-soft skin. And Charrell had been blessed with a carbon copy of her mother's pornstar-sized and perky breasts.

Cruz was sure Tyson was a fan of his sister's cleavage, but right now, in this moment, with his hand fisting his throbbing cock furiously, Tyson was all about grinding his cock against Cruz's marble-hard bubble butt. His ass cheeks clenched tightly with just the thought of his future brother-in-law's cock sliding against them, and he wriggled around lustfully on the bed as his finger slid in another couple of inches.

"Come on, Tyson," he moaned to the picture as he beat his cock faster and harder and fucked his ass with his long fingers. "Fuck my ass. Shove it all the way deep inside me."

He could feel the load building from behind his stomach and quickly moving through his intestines and through his belly button. He locked his long legs and released his cock, watching it throb against his belly and way over his navel. He opened his mouth in anticipation.

The load burst from his purple cock head like a bullet, and the first couple of shots flew over his head, as Cruz heard them crash against the stucco wall. The next several spurts landed across his eyes, nose, and cheeks, and a couple flew directly into his mouth. He swallowed them hungrily as the last of his load oozed from his cock and dribbled onto his stomach and down his sides.

He wiped his hands on the comforter, brought the picture to his lips and kissed it, then laid it on the pillow next to him and fell asleep.

"Ladies and gentlemen, we'll be landing in Huntsville, Alabama, in just a few minutes. In preparation for landing, please bring your seat backs to their full and upright position and make sure your tray tables are locked onto the seat back in front of you."

Cruz let out a sigh of relief as he stretched his legs and locked his seat back into place. The six-hour flight to Huntsville had been torturous. He'd never been keen on flying anyway, but being seated between a ninety-year-old granny with uncontrollable gas and a four-hundred pound redneck who thought he had to scream into the plane phone in order to be heard by the six people he'd called and described every detail of the flight to just clenched the deal for him.

He vowed never to fly again. He wouldn't have taken this flight if it hadn't been for the prospect of seeing and spending some time with Tyson. Of course, Charrell thought he was making the huge sacrifice for her sake, and that was fine by him.

He deboarded the plane and hurried through the SkyJet

tunnel as quickly as possible. Charrell had told him that Tyson would meet him at the gate, because the bachelor party was starting less than an hour after he was scheduled to arrive. He'd endured six hours of toxic ninety-year-old gas and loud hillbilly banter, and he couldn't wait a minute longer to finally see his sister's man.

"Cruz, over here!"

He looked to his right and stopped in his tracks. He found it hard to breathe. The photo did no justice to Tyson at all, and had left Cruz ill-prepared for his overwhelming beauty. Cruz stood six foot one, and Tyson was easily three or four inches taller than him. In the photo, his suit and tie camouflaged all of the bulging muscles riddled with thick veins and the tree trunk legs. Now he was just wearing an old pair of worn jeans and a plain white t-shirt that strained to accommodate all of his rippling brawn. Charrell had told Cruz that he was a bouncer at one of the hottest clubs in town, but he hadn't expected Hulk Hogan.

"Dude, I thought you'd never land, man," Tyson said, and wrapped a strong arm around his shoulder. When Cruz shuddered, he said, "You all right, bro?"

"Yeah," Cruz squeaked out in a high-pitched voice. He cleared his throat and tried again. "Yeah, I'm fine. It was just freezing on the plane," he said, and prayed to Jehovah that Tyson didn't notice the raging hardon that was quickly growing down the inside of his left thigh. "I'm just glad to be off the plane and away from the manufactured air."

"Right on," Tyson said, and flashed a smile that melted Cruz's heart and caused his legs to quiver. "Let's get outta here. It won't look good if I'm late for my own bachelor party."

The twenty-minute drive was excruciating and felt like an hour. Cruz couldn't stop glancing over and staring at the huge bulge in Tyson's crotch, and he was sure the stud had noticed.

His heart was beating a thousand times a minute and felt like a gong being beaten with each thud. As much as he'd longed and dreamed about meeting Tyson and spending some time alone with him, he was never so happy to arrive at his destination and be lost in the crowd.

"The man of the hour has arrived," someone yelled as they walked into the door of the banquet hall.

Tyson was ripped from the doorway and dragged deeper into the room, leaving Cruz thankfully alone for a few minutes. Jesus, he needed to clear his head. How could Tyson be having this effect on him? Yeah, he'd thought the guy was cute, and he'd beat off to his picture about half a dozen times in the past three days. But he wasn't prepared at all to be this nervous and excited by his sister's fiancé.

Even from across the room, with close to a hundred men in the room, Tyson stood out like a banana in a basket of apples. His friends were very polite and social and gracious. After being introduced to only a couple of them, Cruz found himself being passed around and drawn into a number of conversations. They seemed like good people.

Every time he glanced over at Tyson, his brother-in-law was staring back at him. That gleam in his eyes and the perpetual smile on his full pink lips drove Cruz up the wall and caused his cock to play jump rope in his jeans. He had to untuck his shirt about an hour into the party just to hide the very obvious hardon. But that didn't stop him from flirting with the stud. He licked his lips, sucked cherries into his mouth and made a production of chewing them, and after more than a few drinks, he even winked at the man with whom his sister would spend eternity.

"So you're Charrell's baby bro, huh?"

"What?" Cruz yelped, and dropped his hands to cover his bulge. "Oh yeah," he said to the stranger.

"She's a good girl, man. I don't know what she sees in Ty."

"He seems all right to me," Cruz said.

"Oh, he's a great guy," the drunk stranger said, and then belched. "I'm just a little jealous, that's all. Wish it was me."

Cruz watched as the man walked away, shaking his head. When he turned back around, he saw Tyson standing next to the restroom door, looking at him. Was Tyson staring at him again or was it the nine drinks he'd had? When the guest of honor raised an eyebrow and nodded slightly toward the restroom, Cruz's heart pounded in his chest, and he walked toward the restroom.

He waited just outside the bathroom for a couple of minutes, then took a deep breath and walked in. Tyson was standing at the urinal and didn't look up to see who'd just entered the restroom. Cruz walked over to the urinal next to his soon-to-be brother-in-law and slowly pulled his cock out of his jeans and let it hang heavily over the top of his zipper. When he moved his hand away, he saw Tyson look over at his cock from the corner of his eye.

His cock began to throb to life instantly as he felt Tyson's gaze on his manhood. When it was fully hard and stood out almost a foot in front of him, he turned around and faced Tyson, and leaned against the wall of the stall next to him.

"Suck my dick, bro," he said in a strange, deep voice. Where the hell did that come from?

Tyson let his own pants fall to the ground and dropped to his knees. He lunged forward, a little off balance, and reached out to steady himself on Cruz's strong legs. He licked at the big dick awkwardly for a moment, and then sucked a couple of inches of the thick pole into his mouth. He was a clumsy cocksucker and scraped the sensitive skin as his teeth raked across it.

"Ouch, man, that hurts," Cruz said, and pulled Tyson's head from his crotch. "Here, lemme show you how to do it."

He lifted Tyson up by the arms and knelt between his legs. His sister's fiancé's cock was enormous . . . at least a couple of inches longer than Cruz's and as thick as his wrist. He leaned forward slowly and kissed the mushroom head that was by now stretched tight and turning a dark purple. He licked around the piss slit and then slid his tongue inside it

"Oh fuck," Tyson moaned, and pulled Cruz's head closer to his sweaty pubes.

Cruz opened the back of his throat and slid his mouth down the long, thick rod as far as he could go. He was a pretty damned good cocksucker, by many accounts, and had never run across a dick he couldn't swallow. Until now. He only got about two-thirds of the massive cock down his throat before he began to gag.

Tyson moaned even louder and ground his hips deeper into his little brother-in-law's mouth. Cruz reached down and stroked his own cock as he slid his mouth up and down the length of the giant cock and flicked his tongue over the head.

"Dude, you suck cock better than your sister," Tyson said hoarsely.

Cruz pulled his mouth off Tyson's cock and smiled. "Of course I do," he said smugly. "I know what it feels like and how to make it feel better."

"Fuck yeah, you do. What else do you do better?"

Cruz knew he shouldn't go there. He told himself not to. And yet he found himself standing up and leaning with his arms pressed against the stall siding, and his ass sticking up in the air, begging to be fucked.

"Are you sure, little brother?" Tyson asked, even as he spit a large gob onto the head of his cock and rubbed it in.

"Hell yeah, I'm sure," Cruz said, and wiggled his ass temptingly at Tyson. "I wanna feel your big cock all the way inside me, man. Let you know what a *real* fuck feels like." There it was again . . . that deep, cocky voice that said things he'd never imagine saying out loud to his brother-in-law.

Tyson moaned loudly and wrapped his fist around his cock as he lunged forward. Cruz thought the guy might tumble to the floor, but he caught his balance just as his hot, hard cock slid against the crack of his ass.

"Oh fuck, yeah," Cruz moaned, and tightened his ass cheeks.

"I wanna fuck your ass, man," Tyson whispered.

"Then shut the fuck up and do it," Cruz said roughly. "Slide your cock inside me and fuck my brains out."

Tyson grabbed his cock and guided it toward the puckering hole in front of him. He spit on the head again and slid it inside Cruz's hungry hole just enough for the head to slip inside.

"Oh SHIT," Cruz cried out, and clutched the wall tightly as Tyson slid another couple of inches inside him. He could feel his ass spasming around the thick cock and sucking it deeper inside him. Tyson's deep, growling moans let him know how much his ass was appreciated.

After a couple of slow but forceful jabs forward and deeper into Cruz's ass, Tyson wrapped his arms around Cruz's waist and back and slammed his giant cock deep inside him. He didn't stop until his pubes tickled the soft, tender skin of Cruz's ass cheeks.

"That's it, man," Cruz growled. "Fuck my ass hard."

Tyson grabbed him by the waist and began thrusting his thick cock in and out of the clutching ass. Slowly at first, and then with more force and speed. After a couple of minutes of fucking furiously, he slowed down.

Cruz was on autopilot now and was unstoppable. He fisted his fat cock as he slid his ass back and forth onto the big cock buried inside his ass. Each stab drove in deeper than the last and slid against his prostate and deep into his intestines, sending shock waves of ecstasy up through every nerve in his body.

Tyson pulled him down onto the floor and onto his back in one surprisingly graceful move, never pulling his cock out of his quivering ass. He pulled the long cock out slowly until just the head remained inside, and then slammed it back in all the way to the base, eliciting a moan of approval from Cruz. He pulled his brother-in-law's legs up and rested them on his shoulders as he pounded his ass relentlessly.

"That's it, man," Cruz whispered as he slid his hand up and down his cock. "I'm gonna cum!"

Tyson sped up his thrusts, making sure each one hit the spot deep inside Cruz that caused him to gasp and moan. "Yeah, baby. Shoot that load all over yourself."

"Ungh," Cruz whimpered, and thrust his ass up to take even more of the huge dick inside him. A couple of deep thrusts later, he covered his mouth with his hand and yelled into it as he blasted his load all over his chest and stomach. His body convulsed as he emptied himself.

"Fuck, man," Tyson growled. "I'm cumming!"

He pulled his cock out in one fast move that felt to Cruz like his guts were being ripped out with the big dick. He barely got it all the way out before the first spray of cum splashed across Cruz's balls and raw ass. The next few spurts flew across his body and landed on his face, and Cruz lapped up as much of it as he could.

Tyson collapsed on top of Cruz's sticky body and struggled to catch his breath. Cruz felt his brother-in-law's heartbeat pounding against his own and smiled as Tyson's python cock throbbed still hard against the inside of his legs.

"Dude, that was fucking hot!" Tyson said when he was able to speak again. "Maybe I'm marrying the wrong Camacho."

"Yeah, right." Cruz laughed as he pushed the muscled stud off him and stood up to clean himself off. "You wouldn't be able to handle me on a regular basis."

"Yeah, okay." Tyson laughed. "Whatever, dude."

"But anytime you're up for a little extracurricular activity, you know where to find me."

"Oh yes, I do," Tyson said. "Perched right on top of my throbbing cock."

"Brains and a hot body," Cruz said. "That's hot."

"Come on, little brother," Tyson said, and wrapped his arms around Cruz's shoulders after tucking his shirt back into his pants. "We'd better get outta here before someone gets suspicious."

They exited the restroom with Tyson leading the way. Cruz pinched his ass just as they walked into the big main room and laughed as Tyson swatted him away and scurried off to mingle with his guests.

THE
EAST
COAST

When one thinks of the East Coast, he can't help but think of chic sophistication. New York, Boston, Washington, DC . . . the cities are where movers and shakers congregate. The money here is old money, and it speaks volumes and gets things done. Nothing in this region of the United States is done half-assed or normally. It's all or nothing.

The taboos described in this section of the book are narcissism, rape or nonconsensual sex, and necrophilia. One is little more than a twist on vanity, and the other two are highly illegal and would land you in jail. That might only add to the lure of the taboo for some. But typical of the East Coast mentality, these three stories have a bit of a twist to them.

As I mentioned earlier, few things are black and white, right or wrong. There are a lot of gray areas in just about everything, and taboos are no different. Even when dealing with topics as disturbing, emotional, and uncomfortable as rape and sex with the dead, there are unique circumstances to consider.

Are these things ever acceptable? Read for yourself and see if you leave with the same thoughts and ideas on these subjects as you had when you started the stories.

A Matter of Chance

Part Four
There's No Place Like Home

Chance rolled into New York City with more dread than he'd felt for as long as he could remember. He'd experienced dread a lot growing up, and he'd even relived some of those times on the drive back home the last few days. But even as strong as the memories were, they were still nothing but memories, and for that he was thankful. This new sensation, the tightening in his stomach, the overwhelming sadness, and the urge to run as far away as possible was fresh and new and very real.

He parked the Sky and walked around Central Park, trying to clear his head and to gather the nerve to go home. It was a little after eleven in the morning, and the park was already bustling with joggers, kids on playgrounds, seniors feeding ducks in the ponds, and businessmen and women enjoying an early lunch. He'd forgotten how beautiful and serene the park could be, and yet how uniquely New York City it was, too.

He grabbed a couple of hot dogs from a street vendor and walked over to his favorite place in the entire park. The Angel of the Waters fountain was a magnificent eight-foot bronze statue of a beautiful female angel blessing the large blue stone fountain below and was famous around the world. Chance had always found peace there, and it was the place he went when he needed to center himself.

It was going to be an unusually warm and sunny day. Already it was nearing sixty degrees, and a light breeze brought a much-welcomed moment of relief from the intense sun. Several joggers ran past him at various paces, and Chance watched with varying levels of interest as they came into and then left his line of sight. He sat on the rim of the big fountain, opened his hot dog wrappers, and stretched his legs out to eat more comfortably.

He'd always been a big people watcher. When he was younger, in elementary and junior high school, he used to sit and watch the other kids in his classes and wonder what their lives were like at home. Did they have nice and loving and supportive parents, or did they live a nightmare like himself? In high school and college he loved watching TV and movies and imagined being rich and famous. Whenever he had to travel, he always arrived at the airport a couple of hours earlier than he needed to, just so he could watch the other passengers board and de-board their flights, and he couldn't help but fantasize about what their lives were like . . . what they did for a living; who their significant other was; what business they had in their destination or arrival city; and always, when the guys were cute, if they'd be up for a rendezvous in the airport restroom. He couldn't help it, he'd always had a very active imagination. And nothing satisfied him more than forgetting his own life and fantasizing about someone else's . . . creating fun and exciting lives for them, and sometimes being a part of that life himself.

The old man walking by was a prime example of someone

waiting to be watched and begging for an imaginary life to be created for him. Chance figured him to be in his mid- to late nineties. The little hair that he had left was snow white and thin to the point of frailty. He wore thick, black Buddy Holly glasses low on his nose, and struggled to keep them from falling off. His gait was slow and deliberate, as he was hunched over and watched his feet intently. He held a nylon leash in one hand, and at the end of it was a tiny gray poodle. The dog walked as slowly and deliberately as his owner, and Chance guessed he was maybe as old.

His life story went like this: When the old man was a young man in his midtwenties, he was drafted into the air force and flew dangerous missions during WWII. He had a beautiful young girlfriend waiting for him back home, and she volunteered to work in the local metal factory to help her country and make up for all the lost labor as the result of so many American men being sent overseas to fight for our rights as a free and democratic country. On a rare R&R visit back home, the man and his pretty girlfriend conceive their first of four kids—a boy, of course. They don't know that yet, and when he returns to Europe after two weeks, he does not know that he will miss the birth of his firstborn by three months. They get married two weeks after he returns and buy their first and only home a few months later. He becomes middle management for the local bank and she stays home and raises four stellar kids . . . two boys and two girls. The kids all go off to Ivy League colleges and become very successful. The beautiful girlfriend who became the beautiful wife and mother dies of cancer at the age of 65, leaving the old man to grow even another twenty-five years older and feeling only half of himself because she's gone. The grown-up kids send money and a card every year for Christmas and his birthday, and they think he doesn't know that they have been talking about putting him in a home for the past three years. He talks only to his dog and often thinks that Pepper is his dead wife. He takes his daily walk in Central Park because he doesn't know anything else to do, and because he and Girtie used to walk there every morning.

Or at least that was his life according to Chance.

He swallowed the last of his second hot dog, wiped his hands on his shorts, and opened the can of grape soda. He downed half of it in one swallow, then belched loudly.

Jogging toward him was a guy with a really nice build and big well-developed legs. He was wearing red jogging shorts and a yellow tank top, which showed off his lean but muscular chest. Chance imagined him to be a gym teacher for a local high school. He was married but had no kids, and his wife wasn't happy about that. He found himself going out for a few drinks after work and had recently missed a few dinners at home because he'd stayed a little later for a couple more Seven and Sevens. The last couple of trips to the Boar's Head had resulted in him getting blown in the restroom by another of the regulars. He was miserable at work and he was miserable at home. He was thinking about quitting his job and leaving his wife. He was . . .

"Dylan," Chance yelled out as the guy jogged past him. He didn't know where the outburst came from, and when the guy stopped just a couple of steps behind him and turned around to look at him, Chance felt his heart drop in his stomach.

"Chance?" The guy looked Chance up and down, and looked as if he was struggling with whether to stick out his hand for a shake or run up and hug him.

"Oh my God, what are the chances of us running into each other here?" Chance asked.

Dylan walked over to Chance and held his hand out. "Nice to see you again, Chance," he said tentatively.

"What's with the formality?" Chance asked, and pulled

Dylan in close to him and hugged him tightly. "Christ, man, it's been . . . what . . . seven years?"

"Eight," Dylan said. "Eight long years."

"Wow. Where did all that time go?"

Dylan scratched his head and shifted from one foot to the other as he glanced back and forth between the statue of the angel and the old man with the gray poodle a few yards away.

Chance couldn't take his eyes off of Dylan. When they'd dated eight years ago he had been a cute boy, nineteen years old and right out of four years of high school football practices and games. His body was hard and muscular, and he had the boyish good looks and the smile of a budding model. He'd swept Chance off his feet immediately, and their awkward making out sessions early on quickly turned into the lovemaking of two men intimately knowledgeable and comfortable with one another's bodies. But now the cute high school jock had turned into an incredibly hot and masculine man. He'd grown a few inches since the last time Chance had seen him and filled out his muscles much more proportionately. He was still built like a brick shithouse, but now he looked like a young man who knew how to use those muscles rather than a boy who had them only for show. His chin was strong and clefted, and covered with a thin layer of dark stubble. His cheeks were flushed from jogging, and his eyes sparkled even as he obviously avoided looking directly into Chance's.

"So, what are you doing in New York, Chance?" Dylan asked. "And how's your wife and son?"

"Oh, my dad had a stro . . ." He stopped in mid-sentence. "What? What the hell are you talking about?"

"He must be . . . what . . . six, six and a half years old now?"

"Dylan, it's me . . . Chance. Do you not remember fucking my brains out? Why in the world would you think I'm married and have kids?"

228 / Sean Wolfe

"You're not?" Dylan asked, and crossed his arms uncomfortably.

"No. Why would you think that?"

"Your mom told me that. When you just left so suddenly, I called your house every day for a couple of months. No one ever answered the phone. One night, about six months after you left, I got drunk and went to your house. It was like three in the morning, and I banged on the door until your mother came down and talked to me. She told me that you'd been seeing a girl out in Chicago for a couple of years and that you'd finally decided that you were done experimenting with the whole gay thing and that you'd moved to Chicago to marry your girlfriend. I told her I didn't believe her and that I wanted to talk with you. She escorted me to my car and told me that you were expecting a kid and that you'd asked me not to try and contact you."

"And you believed her? Don't you remember how we kissed and made love?"

"Yes, of course I remember. But she was really convincing. And about six months later she saw me in the grocery store and she showed me a picture of your baby. Well, of *a* baby, anyway. She was really proud."

"Oh, I'm sure she would be, if I ever really did get married and have a kid. But Dylan, come on. I was totally into you. You were my entire life back then. How could you believe even for a minute that I was straight and married with a kid?"

"She was convincing, Chance," Dylan said, and sat down on the rim of the fountain. "And since you never called or got in touch with me, well, it was easy to believe, I guess. I just wanted you to be happy and didn't want to be a problem for you."

"I did try and get in touch with you. My parents sent me

away to live with my aunt and uncle in Palo Alto. It took me a couple of months to get away from them, but when I finally left and moved to San Francisco, I wrote you a letter. I told you I couldn't come back to New York but asked you to come out and join me in San Francisco."

Dylan dropped his head into his hands. "I moved not long after you left. I got a small apartment closer to school. I never got your letter, Chance. I thought you didn't care about me, and then when your mom said you were married and expecting a kid, I just didn't want to be a complication in your life. So I let you go."

"That fucking bitch," Chance yelled, and kicked the stone fountain.

"Chance, don't . . ."

"No, I'm sorry, Dylan, but she has fucked up my life one too many times. I'm not going to let her do it anymore. I loved you, Dylan. You were the one good thing in my life, and I loved you. And she fucked that up for me."

"Did she?"

Chance stopped kicking the fountain and looked at Dylan.

"Are you in a relationship now?" Dylan asked.

"No."

Dylan stood up and walked over to Chance and pulled him into his strong arms and kissed him lovingly on the lips.

The drive to Chance's parents' house was almost totally silent. Dylan cuddled next to Chance as he drove, and he kept leaning in and kissing him on the lips and neck as Chance struggled to keep his hands on the wheel and his eyes on the road.

Chance couldn't remember ever feeling as elated as he was right then. His heart wouldn't slow down to a normal rate, and he couldn't stop smiling. It felt as if he'd burst into tears at any moment, and a part of him wished he would, because it was the only way he'd be able to release some of the intense emotions he felt. In his wildest dreams he wouldn't have dared to believe he'd see Dylan again after all these years. He hadn't even thought of his old boyfriend in at least a couple of years. And yet the moment he laid eyes on Dylan, all of the old feelings and sensations returned, and it felt as if they'd never been apart.

"Well, there it is," Chance said as he pulled the car to a stop at the curb. "Elphaba's dungeon."

"Take a deep breath, babe," Dylan said, and leaned in to kiss Chance on the mouth. "It's all over now. Don't let her get to you."

"Too late," Chance said as he opened the door and stepped out of the Sky. He opened the door for Dylan and walked arm in arm up to the front door. "You ready?"

Dylan smiled and squeezed Chance's hand, then reached over and rang the doorbell.

Chance heard footsteps descending the stairs on the other side of the door. "He's here, Arthur," he heard his mother yell from what he guessed to be about halfway down the stairs. "He's finally here. Three days late, I might add, but at least he finally got his sorry ass here."

Despite the rudeness of his mother, Chance smiled. He knew what her reaction would be when she opened the door, and it took all he had not to giggle out loud just thinking about it.

"Well, it's about time," his mother said as she swung the door open dramatically. "We thought maybe you'd gotten . . ."

And there it was. The exact expression he knew would appear on her face. He broke into laughter as he watched the corners of her mouth draw back almost to her earlobes and the creases in her forehead crawl closer together until they merged in the middle of her eyebrows. Her eyes squinted and he swore he could see smoke rising from her ears. "There it is, babe," he said, and hugged Dylan tighter. "God, I wish I had a camera right now."

"What the hell is he doing here?" his mother said tersely, and pulled on the screen door, as if she could pull it any closer than it was.

"Hello, Cruella," Chance said, and smiled. "Nice to see you, too. How's Dad?"

She crossed her arms across her breasts and her face hardened even more. "Don't be such a smartass. I asked you a question. What's he doing here?"

"Oh, you remember Dylan? Well, it seems as if he and his wife have recently separated, too, just like me and my wife. We ran into each other down at the titty bar in the Bronx, commiserating our misfortune, and decided we could support one another."

"You're a hateful man, Chance McAllister. You're despicable."

Chance leaned in until his face was an inch from the screen and his hands rested on both sides of the door. "Despicable, Mother? Hateful? Do you wanna show me the picture of my 'son'? Do you have pictures of my wedding and honeymoon all nice and pretty in a photo album, too? Do you really wanna talk about hateful and despicable?"

Mrs. McAllister looked beyond her son and at Dylan. Her eyes glared through the screen. "I did it for your own good," she said, turning back to face her son.

"What would you know about what is good for me, Mommie Dearest? You don't know me well enough to know what is good for me, and you never have. You've never once asked me what I wanted or what I thought. And on the few times when I asserted myself to let you know who I am and what I wanted or needed, you never once supported me."

Her mouth began to quiver as she crossed and uncrossed her arms. "Don't be so mean, Chance. Say good-bye to your friend and come inside. Your father needs you."

Chance's fists tightened on the sides of the door, and he felt Dylan's hand tug lightly at his waistband. He took a deep breath. "You're even more ignorant than I thought," he said softly. "I'm not coming in. I'm not going to help you or Dad. I only came by so I could tell you face to face that I'm done with you. You lost. I didn't really know that you'd lost until I ran into Dylan again this morning, but you did. Because as hard as you tried to get me to believe it, I know that I am not nothing. I'm not worthless, and I'm not despicable. The one good thing about this trip is that I found myself, Mother. I know who I am now, and I'm a really good person with a lot to offer. People like me and they find me attractive and they think I'm a pretty stellar guy. And most of all, despite all of your meddling and conniving, I've reconnected with the love of my life. And I'm not letting him go this time."

Chance wrapped his arms around Dylan and pulled him in close for a kiss.

His mother slammed the door but stayed behind it on the other side. "That's sick, Chance. Stop it right this minute and get in here. Your father needs you."

"Go to hell, Martha," Chance said, and walked off the porch and down the sidewalk with Dylan at his side.

"Where are you going?" his mother yelled out the living room window. "You can't leave us here alone, Chance. You have to come in and help me."

Chance helped Dylan into the car and then walked around to the driver's side. He started the car and revved the engine.

"What if he dies, Chance? What will you do then?" his mother yelled to be heard over the loud car.

He threw the car into drive, spun the tires on the hot pavement, and sped away from his mother's screeching yells.

"It's a little small," Dylan said as he opened the front door and waved Chance into the living room, "but it's home, and it's all mine."

Chance grabbed Dylan by the neck and kissed him hard on the lips as he fumbled around the living room and made his way down the hall and into the bedroom. He pushed Dylan backward onto the bed and quickly stripped his clothes. Then he lay down on top of Dylan and kissed him tenderly on the lips as he struggled to disrobe him.

"God, I've missed you," Dylan whispered as he helped Chance get him out of his clothes. "I can't tell you how many times I've thought about you over the years."

"I missed you, too, baby," Chance said.

When Dylan's clothes were lying on the floor, Chance slid down his lover's body and caressed him. He wrapped his hands around Dylan's cock and squeezed it lovingly, watching as it grew longer and thicker in his hands. Just looking at it gave him butterflies in his stomach. It wasn't that it was so huge . . . it was about the same size as his own, maybe a little over seven inches and fairly thick. He'd certainly had much bigger, and even just on this trip. But still it made him smile and took his breath away.

He licked around the head for a few minutes and then sucked it into his mouth. It was hot and hard and tasted sweet. As he sucked on it slowly, Dylan squirmed around on the bed and clutched at the comforter. Chance smiled inwardly and lowered his mouth farther on the pole, taking more of the cock into his mouth. When the head hit the back of his throat, he took a deep breath through his nose and swallowed the entire cock deep into his throat.

"Oh God, baby," Dylan moaned, and lifted his hips to drive his cock deeper into Chance's throat. "That feels so good, man. Keep sucking me."

Chance wrapped his lips tighter around Dylan's cock and slid his mouth up and down the rod. He reached under the cock and massaged the big shaved balls in one hand as he pinched Dylan's nipple with the other. It elicited another moan from his boyfriend, and Chance wanted nothing more than to keep sucking Dylan's cock and making him moan and feeling like he was right at that moment forever. He couldn't imagine anything better than the feel of his lover's cock in his mouth and knowing that it felt good to Dylan and made him moan with lust.

He released Dylan's balls and let his hand slip between his lover's ass cheeks. They had a light layer of hair on them and were as hard as bowling balls, even though the skin was soft. Chance considered himself versatile but usually preferred getting fucked over fucking. But when his hand slid between Dylan's cheeks and his fingers tickled the asshole, something clicked inside him. When Dylan moaned and squirmed around on the bed, Chance knew that he wanted to fuck him more than anything.

He lifted Dylan's legs, pressing his knees against his chest and raising his ass into the air. The cheeks were lightly hairy, but the hole itself and the area right around it was smooth. The sphincter twitched and puckered reflexively, and Chance's cock responded instantly. It had already been fully hard, but when he looked at Dylan's ass and saw it begging to be fucked, it throbbed harder and a long string of precum dripped out of the head and onto the comforter.

"Come on, babe, eat my ass," Dylan moaned and lifted his ass another couple of inches.

Chance knelt on his knees between Dylan's ass and licked around the hole for a moment, then stuck his tongue inside.

"Oh fuck!" Dylan said between gritted teeth as he clutched the comforter even tighter.

Chance attacked his lover's ass, licking and kissing and sucking on it until Dylan begged him to fuck him. He let several drops of saliva drip from his mouth and pool around the hole, and then brought his cock to the ass.

"Fuck me, baby," Dylan pleaded. "Shove your cock up my ass."

He pressed his cock head against the hole, and rubbed it around the entrance for a moment, smiling as he watched his boy squirm and wiggle around beneath him. Then he pressed forward slowly until it popped inside. His cock head was instantly enveloped in wet heat. He took a deep breath and counted to ten as he felt the ass muscles wrap around his cock and suck it deeper inside.

"Oh God, Dylan," Chance said in a deep growl. "You feel so good, baby. Your ass is so hot."

Dylan smiled, and then pulled him down by the back of the head and kissed him passionately on the mouth, pulling Chance's cock deeper inside his ass at the same time. He lifted his ass to take every last inch of Chance's cock inside him and squeezed his ass muscles around the cock.

Chance slid his cock in and out of Dylan's ass slowly at first, and then with more and more speed. As much as he wanted this to last forever, he knew he wouldn't be able to hold out much longer. Dylan's ass was sucking his cock deep inside him and milking him with every thrust. He wanted to take it slow and tenderly, but his cock and his hips seemed to have a mind of their own and insisted on slamming into the hot ass. He struggled with controlling himself and his thrusts, and hoped it didn't come off as some spastic or convulsive movement.

"Come here, babe," Dylan whispered. "Kiss me while you slide your cock into my ass."

Chance leaned forward and kissed Dylan on the lips as he slowed down and forced himself not to cum too quickly. He sucked on his lover's tongue and slid his slowly into Dylan's warm mouth. He loved the way Dylan sucked on just the tip of his tongue for a moment and then pulled the rest of his tongue deeper into his mouth. He began moving his cock in and out of Dylan's ass at the same tempo that his tongue was sucked into the hot mouth, and soon developed a synched rhythm. Dylan sucked his tongue slowly into his mouth at the same moment Chance pulled his cock out of the hungry ass, and then as he slid back inside, Dylan would slowly let go of his tongue.

After a few minutes, Dylan began breathing harder, and his ass began thrusting faster to meet his strokes. He moaned as he kissed Chance, and his body took on a life of its own.

Chance knew his lover was getting close, and his own orgasm boiled in his groin and shot up into his cock without warning.

"I'm cumming," he said as he stopped kissing Dylan. He tried to pull himself off Dylan's quivering body, but his boyfriend was having none of it.

Dylan pulled him back down for another kiss with one hand and grabbed his ass in the other hand and shoved him deeper inside his ass. He sucked on Chance's tongue even as Chance moaned loudly and shuddered and released his load deep inside Dylan's ass. His own cock was squeezed between his own stomach and Chance's, and when he felt his lover's cock thicken and shoot its load inside him, his cock sprayed its load all over both stomachs and chests.

The two lovers continued kissing as they caught their

breath, and then Chance collapsed on top of Dylan and hugged him close.

"I love you," Dylan whispered into Chance's ear.

"I love you, too."

"I don't want to live without you again. I can't."

"You think this apartment is big enough for the two of us?"

Dylan leaned on one elbow and stared into Chance's eyes. "Would you really move back here with me?"

"In a heartbeat, babe," Chance said, and kissed him again.

"What about your job? Your apartment in San Francisco?"

"Fuck my job," Chance said. "It's a dead end road. I've been passed over for a promotion three times in the past six months. It's obvious there's no future there for me. And I'm on a month-to-month lease on my apartment. I'm not emotionally attached to it."

"Are you sure?" Dylan asked. "Please say yes."

Chance laughed. "Yes, I'm sure. My future is here, with you."

"What about your mom and dad?"

"New York is a large city. We can avoid them. Besides, I can easily see us never leaving this bedroom."

Dylan laughed and rolled Chance onto his stomach. "My turn. Your ass is mine."

"You better believe it is," Chance said, and leaned back to kiss his lover.

Self-Service

"What about that dude over there?" Marquis yelled into Jared's ear over the loud bass beat of the music and pointed toward the back of the dance floor.

"Too tall and lanky," Jared yelled back after barely a glance in the direction his friend was pointing. He chewed on the last piece of ice from his drink and continued scouring the large room with little interest.

"It's been three months since you've seen anyone, Jared," Marquis said as he motioned for another round of drinks. "By this point I'd think you'd be happy with anything with a heartbeat."

"Well, that's where you'd be wrong," Jared said. "Some of us have standards and are a little more picky than . . . others."

"Okay, then, you go on with your picky standard-ass self, then," Marquis said as he paid for the drinks. "But just remember, it was you that called me up a couple nights ago, crying about not having a man. I'm not asking you to settle, for crying out loud. But at least give some of these guys a chance to show you that they can live up to your high expectations."

"But they're ugly!"

"That man leaning against the railing over by the dance floor is not ugly."

"Oh, him," Jared said with little interest. "He's got that mole thingy right under his nose."

"That's sexy as hell, man," his best friend said. "Enrique Iglesias had that same make and model. So does Cindy Crawford. People pay to have that put on them."

Jared snorted and turned his back to his friend.

"What about that cute blond boy over there playing pool?"

"His ass is hanging out of his jeans, Marquis. He looks like a total slut. Were you not paying attention when I mentioned I have high standards?"

"Yes, I was. But I was paying even more attention on Wednesday evening when you were crying your eyes out on my shoulders and telling me how miserable you are being alone."

"I would hardly say I was crying my eyes out."

"Oh, you were. I taped it. Want to watch it?"

Jared laughed and hugged his friend.

"I love you, Marquis. Why can't you be just a little cuter and a little taller and a little smarter so we could be boyfriends?"

"Bitch, I am cute enough and tall enough and smart enough for ninety-eight percent of the population in this city. In fact, I'm *too* cute and *too* tall and *too* smart to be hanging around with the likes of your sorry ass. Good thing I love you, too. Now, what about that hottie over by the patio? You can't possibly find anything wrong that fine specimen."

Jared looked at the young man standing alone. He had to admit, the guy was pretty damned hot. He was a couple of inches taller than Jared, with shoulder-length light brown hair with blond streaks through it. He wore one medium-sized silver hoop earring and a simple cross around his neck. His white t-shirt clung to his muscular chest and highlighted a set of washboard abs. He had a tiny waist, and his legs were long and muscular, and stretched the denim material of his jeans. The hint of stubble on his face parted to reveal a beautiful white smile as someone walked past him and whispered something into his ear.

"He's got small feet," Jared said, and took a long swig of his vodka with Red Bull.

"That's it!" Marquis yelled loud enough to make Jared jump. "I give up. I'm not going down this road with you. There are too many bumps and curves on that road, and I get motion sickness easily. You're on your own."

"Marquis, wait," Jared said, and grabbed his arm to keep him from walking away. "Don't be upset with me."

"I'm not upset with you, baby. I'm sad *for* you and disappointed *in* you. I don't know when it happened, but somewhere down the road you created this long list of unrealistic and unreachable 'standards' for finding a new man. And baby, I'm telling you, no one is ever going to meet them all. So you're gonna have to either be a little more forgiving with that list or just learn to live with the fact that you're going to be alone for the rest of your life. And since I don't see you as the especially forgiving type . . . you'd better get used to the idea of fucking yourself. We all know how much you love yourself, so that shouldn't be too difficult. You're the only one who's ever going to measure up to your 'picky' standards."

Jared watched with his jaw dropped as his friend downed the last of his drink and then walked away without kissing him on the cheeks as he always did. "Marquis, wait," he said only half-heartedly, and wasn't surprised when his friend continued walking away and eventually out the front door.

It seemed colder and lonelier in his apartment that night. Jared knew that was impossible; his goldfish were still swimming in the aquarium and the stuffed lion on his bed still seemed happy to see him walk into the room, as they had been doing for the past four years. Nothing had changed, yet it seemed colder and lonelier.

After making a ham and cheese sandwich and a cup of milk, he sat at the desk in his bedroom and signed on to his favorite chat site. As always, he was greeted with an onslaught of pop-up ads. He cursed himself for not purchasing the heavy duty software to prevent the annoying ads and started deleting them one at a time. But the last one on his screen refused to disappear.

"Goddamn it," he said through a mouthful of ham and cheese, and hit the Delete button several more times. Still the window wouldn't disappear.

Searching for Mr. Perfect?
Everyone's Idea of Perfection Is Different . . .
. . . But Your Perfect Man Is Waiting for You NOW.
Money Back Satisfaction Guaranteed.
Click Here to Find Him!

"Wouldn't that be nice," Jared said to himself. He tried again to get rid of the window, but it refused to budge.

By now his interest was piqued, and so he clicked on the button.

Welcome to Paradise!
Your Perfect Man Awaits You.
What's Your Deepest, Darkest Fantasy?
Wanna Be Fucked by Your Favorite Movie Star?
Ever Wondered What It Would Feel Like
to Make Love to JFK?

Have the Hots for Your Brother but Are Afraid
to Approach Him About It?
We Can Make Your Dream a Reality.
Guaranteed!

Jared realized he wasn't chewing his food and that his cock was as hard as a rock. The perfect guy. Did he even exist? At twenty-six years of age, he'd never found a single guy that he'd been able to be intimate and romantic with for more than a couple of months. They bored him after a while. Every single one of them. He'd often tried to fantasize about a celebrity while he was with someone else, but even that didn't work. He had plenty of sex and never had a problem cumming. But he always, without exception, exaggerated the intensity of the orgasm for the benefit of his partner.

The only time he ever felt completely satisfied with sex was when he masturbated. He loved looking at his naked body, and especially his long, thick cock. When he ran his hands over his chest and stomach, it took his breath away and caused chills to cover every inch of his skin. When he wrapped his hand around his cock, he shuddered with excitement, and his body got hot. His orgasms exploded way past his head and covered his entire torso. And afterward, he slept more soundly and dreamed more peacefully than he could ever remember.

The perfect man. According to the ad, all he had to do was type in the exact features he was looking for in a guy, and within minutes, Mr. Right would be knocking on his door. For first-time visitors to the site, the cost would be $50. After that, a two-hour visit would be $200. They were so absolutely positive that you will come back and that they would make their money on subsequent visits that they could make the money back guarantee first-time offer of $50. What did he have to lose?

Jared leaned back in his chair, staring at the screen and stroking his cock through his jeans. It hardened instantly and sent shivers through his body. He had to get off.

Marquis's words rang through his head again: *"You'd better get used to the idea of fucking yourself. We all know how much you love yourself, so that shouldn't be too difficult. You're the only one who's ever going to measure up to your 'picky' standards."*

Jared stood up and walked over to the dresser, where he'd left his wallet. Was he really entertaining the idea of paying this site in a vain effort to find Mr. Perfect? There was no doubt.

He looked in the mirror and felt his cock stir again. His black hair was buzzed almost to the scalp around the ears and in the back but was longer and perfectly spiked on top. He'd been told on more than one occasion that his blue-gray eyes seemed to peek into your soul. They were framed with long, curly black lashes. His Columbian heritage graced him with smooth, copper skin, and his deep dimples and bright white smile had landed him several modeling contracts. He was by far the hottest guy he knew, and all of his friends told him the same thing. His favorite sex was setting the mirror at the end of the bed and watching himself beat off, or shoving his favorite dildo up his ass as he stroked his thick, uncut cock.

He rushed back to the desk and quickly entered in his credit card information. A new window popped up and asked him to describe his ideal man.

Height: 6' 2"
Weight: 180
Body Type: Muscular
Race: Latino/White
Hair: Black
Eyes: Blue/Gray

Cock Size: 8 x 6
Cut or Uncut: Uncut

It was a long and exhaustive form to complete, but Jared didn't care. He'd always wanted to know what it would feel like to be fucked by himself. His partners always seemed to really enjoy it and get off on it, and he'd often pictured himself in their place, being kissed by his own soft lips and pounded with his thick cock. It had been the impetus for more than one of his legendary orgasms.

It took Jared more than twenty minutes to fill out the form, but he didn't mind. He was glad the questions were as thorough as they were. He wanted this to be perfect and was meticulous in his description detail, right down to noting the tiny brown mole just on the inside of his right knee. It was almost perfectly heart shaped, and Jared was proud of it. It pissed him off that not one of the scores of guys he'd been with had ever even mentioned it, and even after having been pointed out, most of them shrugged it off indifferently.

A message came up on the screen.

Thank you for your order. Delivery will take place in less than one hour. If you are not 100% satisfied with our product, please click on the link below for a full and immediate refund applied to your credit card. You have eight hours from the time posted on this e-mail to claim your refund . . . though we're extremely confident that you won't be requesting one. Thanks again . . . and HAVE FUN!

Jared walked into his bedroom and stripped off his clothes. He was already fully hard just thinking about the possibility. Would it live up to his expectations? He stepped into the shower and took his time soaking and caressing every inch of soft skin on his body. His cock throbbed painfully, even under the cool water, and Jared knew he'd have to relieve it. If he didn't, and the guy he'd ordered really did live up to his expectations, then he'd blow his load in just a couple of minutes, and he didn't want that.

He wrapped his fist around his cock and squeezed it lovingly. His knees trembled visibly as waves of pleasure rocked his body. He pulled on the foreskin, stretching it out a couple of inches past the head, and ran his finger along the inside of it, causing it to rub against his hard cock head.

"Oh God!" he moaned, and leaned against the wall as he stroked his cock slowly and tenderly. He spread his legs a little wider and lifted one foot to rest on the side of the tub. Then he scooped up a couple fingers worth of suds and slid them across his asshole. This elicited another deep moan, and Jared slid first one finger and then a second deep inside his twitching hole. He wiggled his fingers around inside himself for a moment, steadying himself on the walls as he began fucking himself with his fingers.

"Fuck!" he yelled. Three giant shots of cum sprang from his cock and splashed against the wall a couple of feet in front of him. Several more exited his shaft with slightly less turbo, and then the last few simply oozed out and slid down his still hard and throbbing cock.

Jared took a moment to catch his breath and then rinsed the sticky orgasm from his smooth and hardened body. He finished drying off and was just stepping out of the shower when he heard a knock on the living room door.

"Shit," he whispered. He'd only been in the shower for less than ten minutes. There was no way it could be his trick already. It was probably Mrs. James, his next-door neighbor. At least three times a week she came over and asked to borrow something or another . . . eggs, milk, sugar . . . it didn't matter.

Jared was certain the middle-aged divorcee was just looking for excuses to see him half naked and wet. She seemed always to catch him either in the middle of a sweaty workout or just getting out of the shower. "Just a minute, Mrs. James," he yelled out into the living room as he draped the thick towel around his waist and wondered what she was asking to borrow that night.

He opened the door and took a deep breath. He'd expected a decent-looking guy, someone who had all the right basics . . . black spiked hair, slate blue eyes, approximately his own height and weight. But the guy standing in his doorway was an *exact* copy of him. It was as if he were looking in a mirror.

The guy took a couple steps forward and entered his apartment, wrapping his hand around the back of Jared's neck and kissing him passionately on the lips as he pushed him backward into the apartment and shut the door behind him. He pulled Jared close to him and slid his tongue gently into his mouth, licking his bottom lip and then sliding back inside so that Jared could suck on it.

Jared pulled the stud's warm tongue deep into his mouth and recognized the taste immediately. It was his own favorite mint gum. He returned the kiss and wrapped one arm around the guy's waist and the other around his neck. He could feel the stranger's cock hardening against his leg and felt his heart racing in anticipation. Without removing his arms from the Internet hunk's waist and neck, he kicked off his towel and pressed his naked body against his clone.

"God, I love you," the guy whispered into Jared's ear as he broke the kiss and nudged him backward into the bedroom. In one move he pushed Jared onto the bed and spread his legs with his own.

Jared shuddered and moaned as he watched himself kneel between his legs. A moment later his cock was enveloped in wet warmth, and he felt himself being sucked into the hot mouth. His cock throbbed and thickened as the guy swallowed more and more of him into his throat. He clutched the blankets on either side of him as his cock head rubbed against the back of the dude's throat, and then slid easily past it.

"Fuck me!" Jared whimpered.

"Oh, I'm going to," he said, as he licked his way up the inside of Jared's thighs and around his balls. "I'm gonna fuck your brains out. I'm gonna suck that big cock of yours until you blow your hot load down my throat, and then when you don't get soft, I'm gonna slide my thick cock deep inside your ass and fuck your sweet butt until you beg me to stop."

It was his exact voice saying these nasty things to Jared, and it was turning him on more than he'd ever been turned on before. The guy still had his clothes on, but Jared knew without a doubt what was resting beneath them, and he wanted it. He needed to feel his own cock fucking him breathless, as he'd fucked so many guys before. He needed to beg for more of his cock deeper inside him, as he'd heard them all beg for more. And he knew he was going to get it.

"Oh God, I love you," Jared said to himself, and pulled him closer to kiss him on the lips as he scooted to the middle of the king-sized bed.

"I love you, too," he said, and maneuvered himself so that he straddled Jared's chest. He ripped his clothes off clumsily and threw them to the floor, and then moved closer to Jared's face. Now he was only a couple of inches from Jared's hungry mouth, and his cock was straining against his underwear.

"Come on, man," Jared begged. "Give it to me. Let me suck your dick."

"You want my cock?" he teased, and squeezed it through the thin material of his briefs.

"Yes."

"Beg for it," he said, and smiled coyly.

"Please let me have your cock, man," Jared pleaded. "I need to taste your cock."

He pulled the band of his shorts down, and his thick uncut cock bounded out of its restraints and landed on Jared's lips.

Jared licked at the head frantically, straining his neck up so that he could get more of the big cock head into his mouth. It was hot and sweet and hard and soft all at the same time, and Jared loved the taste and feel of it in his mouth.

"You like sucking my cock, baby?" he asked.

"Yeah, I love it," Jared said, and sucked half of the giant cock into his mouth.

"Oh fuck, yeah," he moaned, and slid the big cock deeper into Jared's throat. When the mushroom head slipped past the tonsils, he held Jared by the back of the head and slid all the way inside his mouth and throat in one final thrust.

Jared recognized the move at once. It was his favorite way to really conquer a guy and throw him over the edge. He had a great cock, and everyone loved sucking it. When he grabbed them by the head and forced them to swallow his thick cock, they always went wild. Exactly as he was going wild right this minute, with his own cock sliding in and out of his throat.

"Man, I love you so much," he said to Jared as he fucked his face with more and more intensity.

Jared wanted to say that he loved him too, but the thickening cock in his mouth and the increasing speed at which it was sliding in and out of his mouth prevented him from talking. He could tell he was getting close. His cock always got thicker and thicker for the last minute or so building up to a load.

"Yeah, baby," he said. "That's it, swallow my fat cock. I'm getting close, babe."

Jared's heart was beating erratically, and he knew that in a couple of seconds he would taste his own load. Not exactly for the first time, but for the first time in which he'd been able to deepthroat himself.

"Oh God, here it comes, Jared!"

A second later, Jared felt four blasts of warm, sweet cum splash against the back of his throat. He swallowed them hungrily, and kept sucking. Three or four more spurts landed on his tongue and the inside of his cheeks, and he let the feel and taste lie in his mouth for a moment before gulping them down.

Jared's own cock throbbed painfully, and even though he wasn't touching it at all, he knew he was about to blow a load. He couldn't breathe because of the fat cock buried in his throat, and as he began to panic a little, he felt the first jet of jizz shoot up his shaft and land all over his chest and stomach.

"Oh, dude," he said as he pulled his cock slowly out of Jared's mouth, "you just shot your load all over my naked ass."

"I'm sorry," Jared panted as he tried to catch his breath. "I had no idea . . ."

"You're gonna pay for that, man," he said, and grabbed Jared roughly by the wrist. From out of nowhere he clamped a wrist cuff around Jared's wrist and tied it to the headboard, and then did the same with his other hand.

By now Jared wasn't the least bit surprised that he knew of his proclivity for bondage. This was not a stranger, nor was it a trusted confidant with whom he shared his deepest secret fantasies. This was Jared fucking himself and playing out his every desire and fantasy with him.

"Look at all of that cum on your stomach, man," he said to Jared as he slid down Jared's naked and quivering body. He licked some of the cum into his mouth and smiled as he drank it. "You want me to fuck you, baby?"

"Yes," Jared gasped. "Please fuck me."

He slipped between Jared's legs and spread them farther apart, and then slid his cock around the pool of cum in and around Jared's navel until his cock was covered in the thinning slimy fluid.

"Take a deep breath, baby, because I'm not goin' in easy," he said in a voice that Jared had perfected three or four years ago and had used to break innumerable hearts.

Jared did as he was told and took a deep breath, just as he felt the thick cock brush against his hot asshole. "Fuck me, babe," Jared said through gritted teeth.

"You want my big dick?" he asked.

"FUCK ME!"

He slammed his cock deep inside Jared in one brutal thrust, until his pelvic bone rested against the fleshy part of Jared's ass cheeks, and then he ground the big dick around inside Jared's ass several times.

"Yeah, dude," he said, "you love taking that big dick up your ass, don't you?"

"Yes," Jared whimpered as he wriggled around the fat cock sliding in and out of his ass.

"You're a fucking pig, aren't you?"

"Yes," Jared moaned, and lifted his ass to take even more of his thick cock deeper inside him.

"Take my cock, you punk-ass bitch," he grunted as he slammed his cock in and out of Jared's ass.

Jared's head was spinning, and he felt as if he were having an out-of-body experience. Everything was so fucking heightened right now. His skin was on fire, and every time the cock inside him slid across the walls of his clutching ass, his nerves exploded like a New Year's Day fireworks display. Jared smelled him, and his scent entered Jared's nose and then diffused throughout every cell in his body, burning itself onto his very soul.

Jared looked up into his face, and into his eyes. He wasn't surprised that he was staring right into Jared's eyes as well and that when their eyes met, it felt as if the gates to heaven had been unlocked and thrown wide open.

"God, I love you," he whispered to Jared, and leaned down to kiss him lovingly on the lips.

Jared returned the kiss, and because his hands were still bound, he was unable to wipe the tears that rolled down his cheeks.

"You're crying," he said as he broke the kiss and slid his cock deeper into Jared's ass. When Jared nodded and bit his lower lip, he leaned down and licked the salty tears from Jared's face. "You're so beautiful."

"Fuck me harder, baby," Jared whispered. "I'm getting so close."

He pulled his cock all the way out of Jared's ass and then slid it all the way back in until he rested against Jared's ass cheeks. "I'm close, too, baby," he said after a few thrusts deep into Jared's soul. "I'm gonna shoot my load deep inside you."

"Give me your load, dude," Jared said, and squeezed his ass tighter around the big cock inside him as he slid up and down it feverishly.

"Ungh!" he groaned, and buried himself as deep as he could go inside Jared, then stayed perfectly still as he spent himself.

Jared could feel each one of his contractions when his cock thickened with each burst of the orgasm. As he unloaded into Jared, Jared felt the heat and the slick force of each spurt of jizz. He felt himself filled with not only cum, but with spirit and life and love.

As the last of his load released itself into Jared, he took Jared's cock into his mouth and sucked it gently. That was all it took, and Jared groaned and tightened his body as he shot his load into his mouth. He swallowed it and then leaned down and kissed Jared on the lips.

Jared sucked on his tongue and relished the taste of his own cum being sucked off of his tongue. "Baby, that was amazing," Jared said after breaking the kiss.

"I know," he said, and unbuckled the wrist cuffs and untied Jared. "I have to admit, that was the best fuck I've ever had."

"Me, too," Jared said. "It's like you . . ."

". . . complete you?"

Jared laughed. "Yes. I know that sounds like a corny movie, but . . ."

"No, it doesn't. It sounds right."

"I love you so much."

"I love you, too."

"So am I really gonna have to shell out $200 a pop every time I wanna feel you inside me or when I wanna fuck your sweet ass?"

He laughed. "Them's the rules. Either that or you're gonna have to learn to love and want someone else. Someone you don't have to pay for. Someone . . . less."

Jared looked over at him and bit the corner of his bottom lip. "Damn. I guess I better start looking for a second job."

The Pendulum

Dr. Nathaniel Jordan stood backstage and took a couple of deep breaths. It wasn't like him; he'd done hundreds of interviews and had performed dozens of times on local and national television. He didn't get nervous. He was the immaculate professional. No one ever saw him sweat or shake. Nothing scared him or made him nervous. Dr. Nathaniel Jordan was cool, calm, and collected.

But this was no ordinary gig and no ordinary television show. This was the *Olga Show*, and it had a viewing audience of scores of millions. He was already somewhat well known, but far from famous; he'd appeared on all of the big late-night talk shows and hosted his own local cable special. But Olga's fans were rabid in the fanatical support of her and had even started a petition for her to run for president. An appearance on her show would make him a household name. A superstar. And he was nervous.

"You're in for a real treat, ladies and gentleman," Olga said excitedly from onstage on the other side of the curtain. "Please give a huge Olga welcome for Dr. Jooooooordaaaaan," she boomed in that famous drawn-out introduction that had made her the brunt of many a comedian's jokes and numerous skits on *Saturday Night Live*.

Nathaniel took another deep breath and parted the curtains with his hands as he walked onstage with a smile on his face.

Olga took both of his hands in hers and kissed him warmly on the cheeks as she hugged him tightly. It was obvious she was a fan, and for that Nathaniel was thankful.

"Good afternoon, Dr. Jordan," Olga said cheerily as she waved for Nathaniel to take a seat on the sofa next to her.

"Please, call me Nathaniel. We're old friends, right?"

Olga smiled and nodded enthusiastically. "All right, Nathaniel. And you're right, we are old friends. Why don't you tell the audience how we met."

"Well, the truth is, and very few people know this, but Olga and I were lesbian lovers in a previous life, around the same time as Cleopatra."

The audience was stunned and eerily silent for a moment. But once Olga laughed and slapped his knee playfully, they roared in laughter and clapped loudly. If Olga said it was okay, then it was okay with them, and if Olga thought it was funny, then they would laugh.

"You're so mischievous," Olga giggled, and hugged him again. "The truth is, we met in an elevator at the Luxor in Las Vegas."

"She was smitten with my good looks," Nathaniel said with a smile, and batted his eyelashes.

The audience roared its approval, once again taking their cue from their idol.

"Well, that's partly true," Olga said, and cupped his face in her chubby hands. "I mean, how could I not be. Look at this gorgeous face! But the real truth is that we started talking and Dr. Jordan . . . Nathaniel . . . told me he was performing a show that night in the grand ballroom, and he invited me to the show as his special guest."

"Mama didn't raise no dummy," Nathaniel quipped. "This is *Olga*. When word got around she'd be in the audience, the show sold out in ten minutes."

"Stop it," Olga said with a giggle and a blush. "He was just so charming and fun, and I was intrigued by the thought of seeing a hypnotist show. I'd heard some rumblings from some of the other guests in the hotel about it, and I was curious. So I went, and to say I was blown away would be an understatement."

They bantered back and forth for the first quarter of the show. When they came back from the first commercial break, Olga asked the audience if they were ready to be amazed, and they erupted in applause and whistles.

Nathaniel walked out into the audience and randomly chose three nondescript people to "volunteer" with him. Well, he normally chose three nondescript people . . . that afternoon he chose a nondescript middle-aged man; a nondescript forty-something frumpy housewife; and a beautiful young man with smooth olive skin, midnight black hair, and light brown almond-shaped eyes. From the moment Nathaniel laid eyes on the kid he was breathless, and he struggled to slow his heartbeat down to somewhat normal.

He sat the three audience members on a straightback chair on stage, with the hot Arab guy in the middle. He instructed all of them to stare into his eyes and think of nothing but him. All three looked directly into his eyes, and he could see the concentration they were committed to. But after a few seconds, he lost focus of the two audience members on either end and was solely in tune with the hot guy. His heart sped up and he felt his cock hardening in his jeans with each beat of his heart. Thank God his back was to the cameras.

"You and you," he pointed to the housewife and the middle-aged man, "you are fast asleep and cuddling with your favorite teddy bear. Now." As he snapped his fingers, both audience members closed their eyes and clutched an invisible teddy bear to their chests. The audience roared its laughter.

"You," he pointed to the Arab boy. "You see me, don't you?"

"Yes," the young man said in a deep voice that brought Nathaniel's cock to full hardness.

His eyes were distant and unfocused for a few minutes, and then they bore into Nathaniel's and took his breath away. Nathaniel wanted the boy more than he'd ever wanted another man in his life. *Concentrate, Nate, concentrate.*

"What is your name?" the doctor asked.

"Kareem."

Sweet Jesus, his voice was beautiful. And his face was angelic, with his light brown eyes with thick black lashes and his pink, full lips. What must his chest look like under that tight t-shirt? And how hot must his strong legs be? Would his cock be thick and uncut or long and thin?

"And what do you do, Kareem?"

"I'm a student at Berkeley."

"Kareem, what is the one thing you've always wished you could do? Think of a superpower . . . what power would you choose?"

"I'd like to fly," he said softly and in a slow and steady tone that drove Nathaniel up the fucking wall.

Nathaniel turned and looked at the audience. "Watch closely," he told them, and then returned his gaze to Kareem. "Kareem, do you see me?"

"Yes, sir."

Sweet Mother of God.

"Do you believe me when I tell you that you can do whatever you wish to do?"

"Yes, sir."

"Good. Kareem, you will now close your eyes, but you will still see me." When the boy did as he was told, Nathaniel continued. "Kareem, do you still see me?"

"Yes, sir."

"Are you ready to fly?" Nathaniel asked, as he waved his hand frantically behind him for the audience to pay attention.

"Yes, sir."

Nathaniel made a production of slowly raising both hands at his sides, and on the second time around, the audience gasped as Kareem, still in the seated position, raised about six inches from his chair and floated there in thin air. A few people screeched and clasped their hands to their mouth, others just gawked with their mouths wide open, and a couple covered their eyes with their hands and looked away. Olga's eyes popped wide open and she bounced around on the stage, verbally disclaiming what her eyes were witnessing. But when she finally calmed down and began clapping, her audience shook the rafters with their own appreciation.

Kareem floated above his seat for a few moments, and then as Nathaniel moved his hands and arms around him, Kareem began floating in the direction of his movements. Nathaniel's eyes never left Kareem's, and he guided the young man until he was hovering directly over his seat, and then slowly lowered him so that he was seated.

The audience gasped again, and several members wiped nervous tears from their eyes. A few had to get up and leave the room.

"No way," Olga screamed. "I did not just see that happen before my very eyes. You didn't do that one in Vegas. How did you do that?"

Nathaniel put a finger to his lips and quieted the audience, and then clapped his hands together three times in front of Kareem's face. Kareem blinked his eyes open a couple of times and then looked around him.

"Fuck!" he screamed.

"Okay, we'll have to bleep that one out," Olga said as the audience broke into laughter.

"How did you do that, man?" Kareem asked as he patted himself down and looked all around him on every side. "I was just up there onstage. How did I get here?"

"You flew," Nathaniel said. "I asked you which superpower you'd like to have, and you said you'd like to fly. So I hypnotized you and you flew from your chair there on the stage, right back to your seat."

"Shut *UP!*"

"No, I'm serious, Kareem. You flew, didn't he, audience?"

The audience whistled and stood on its feet as it clapped.

"I don't believe it," Kareem said, still feeling around his body.

Nathaniel laughed. "I often get that response, but watch the tape. You'll see I didn't use any tricks . . . not wires or cables or anything. We just connected our energies, and I helped you believe that you could fly . . . and you did!"

"That's fucking *awesome*, dude!" Kareem said with a wide smile that caused Nathaniel's heart to skip a beat.

"Oooops, there's another bleep," Olga said nervously. "Maybe we should go to a commercial before I lose all my sponsors."

The next couple of weeks were more chaotic than Nathaniel could have imagined. Literally thousands of e-mails and hundreds of phone calls overwhelmed his simple little communication system in his small office in the Bronx. After only three days it became very obvious that he'd need to hire an office manager, something he'd not had to do in the past eight years of being in business for himself. But just answering all of the mail coming in would be more than he could handle, let alone scheduling all of the resulting appointments, filing all of the paperwork, following up with the customers, and then handling the books.

He walked into his office and threw his jacket on the chair by the window, then hit the Message button on his phone. There were thirty-six, just since he'd cleared the machine before leaving the previous evening. He wrote down all the names and phone numbers, and added them to the other couple hundred that were waiting to be answered by his soon-to-be-hired office manager. The second thing on his to-do list today, after checking these messages, was to call a few of the people who'd responded to his ad and bring them in for an interview. He hoped to have a manager hired by the end of the week.

"Hi, Dr. Jordan, I don't know if you remember me or not, but my name is Kareem," the voice on message sixteen said, causing Nathaniel to drop the pen and gasp out loud. His cock stirred instantly. "I was in the audience the day you appeared on the *Olga Show*, and you hypnotized me. I can't stop thinking about the whole experience, and I was wondering if you were taking private appointments. I know this is short notice, but I'm actually in New York now and will be here through this weekend. Anyway, I'd love to hear from you . . . I mean, if you would have a chance to see me . . . you know, for a session, or whatever you'd call it. My cell number is 415-555-3279. I hope you call."

Nathaniel ended the messages and dialed the number. His hands were shaking, and his heart pounded so hard in his rib cage that it hurt.

"Hello," the familiar deep voice with the slightest hint of an Arab accent answered.

"Hello, may I speak with Kareem, please." Nathaniel did his best to sound professional and disconnected to the emotions that overwhelmed him.

"Dr. Jordan?"

"Yes, this is Dr. Nathaniel Jordan." Was it just his imagination, or did Kareem sound really happy to hear from him?

"Great! Wow, I didn't expect to hear back from you so soon."

Shit, did he sound desperate or overly excited? "Well, I can't say that I'm always this prompt at returning calls. But the past couple of weeks have been a little overwhelming, and if I don't get back to people right away, then the messages just get buried and I'd never get to them." He looked over at the enormous stack of unanswered messages from the past couple of weeks, and cringed.

"Right on," Kareem said. "So, I was wondering if you might be able to squeeze me in for a session this week. I know you must be really busy and all, especially after such an amazing show with Olga. But I'm only here for a few days before heading back to San Francisco, and I was just hoping . . ."

"I could meet you in an hour," Nathaniel blurted out.

"Really? I figured . . ."

"I actually had a client cancel just a few minutes ago. If you're available, I could meet with you at noon."

"Very cool. Yeah, I am definitely available."

Nathaniel's cock was throbbing, and he felt a string of pre-cum slide down the inside of his right leg. "Good. Do you know where my office is?"

"Yeah, I walked by there yesterday but you were already gone."

He knew he should be concerned and maybe a little cautious. Stalkers and fanatics were nothing to take lightly. But he actually felt happy that Kareem had taken the time to track him down.

"Good, well then, I'll see you in about an hour."

"I can't wait. I'll see you in a little bit."

"Just sit back and relax," Nathaniel said, acutely aware of the way Kareem's tight faded jeans hugged his big legs and round ass. When Kareem did sit, Nathaniel couldn't take his eyes off the huge bulge that settled into the boy's lap. "This is all about having fun and experimenting. It's not a therapy session. So . . . you want to find out about what happened to you in a past life, who you were?"

"Nah," Kareem said as he settled into the sofa and rearranged the significant bulge in his crotch. "I'd rather know about the future. Who I'll be then, and what will happen to me."

"We can do that. But remember, this is all purely entertainment. I'm not a psychic or anything like that. What you will experience here is all a result of your subconscious, and nothing else. It's just fun, okay?"

"Very cool," Kareem said, again cupping his crotch as he settled deeper into the sofa. "Let's have some fun, then."

"Are you familiar with the pendulum?" Nathaniel asked as he set a large wooden-based one with a long metal rod with a circular mass at the bottom in between him and Kareem on the glass tabletop.

"Not really. I mean, I know what one is," Kareem said awkwardly.

"Well, this is really easy. Just stare at the swinging arm and focus on the round disc at the bottom of the rod. I'll chat with you a little as you watch it swing back and forth, and then when I count to five you will be hypnotized. Then we can take a look at what your future has in store for you, according to your subconscious energy, like you asked to do. Any questions?"

"No, I'm cool."

"All right then, watch the swinging arm. Don't allow anything to distract you or look away from it. Notice how slowly it swings, and how long it takes to make a full swing. With every swing of the arm, it's taking longer and longer to make a full swing. Do you notice that?"

"Yes," Kareem said groggily, and Nathaniel noticed that his eyelids were dropping the slightest bit.

"Now, close your eyes, and when I count to five you will be hypnotized. You will be completely free of any inhibitions and any concerns linked with right now, with today, with yesterday, and with tomorrow. You will be completely safe and completely aware of everything that is happening. With your eyes closed, your mind will see very clearly what your life has in store for you. With every tick of the pendulum you will hear and feel and taste your future. You will be in the future. Are you ready?"

"Yes, sir."

"On the count of five. One . . . two . . . three . . . four . . . five."

Kareem's head dropped.

"What do you see?" Nathaniel asked.

"I'm in a big room. It's hot. Very hot," Kareem said slowly and melodically.

"Do you recognize the room?"

"No."

"Can you describe it to me?"

"It's white, with stone benches and a couple of hidden alcoves in the back. There's some kind of mist all around me. It's so hot in here," Kareem said, and wiped a couple of beads of sweat from his face.

The room Kareem was describing was more than vaguely familiar to Nathaniel. He visited the Coliseum Spa at least a couple of times a month, and his favorite room was the steam room that Kareem was describing. A large lump formed in his throat, and he found it hard to swallow. Was it possible that he was subconsciously visualizing Kareem in the steam room and that Kareem was picking up on it? He'd certainly never had *that* particular experience with hypnosis before, but he knew enough about the craft to know that almost anything was possible. He shook his head a couple of times to clear his mind, and hopefully to erase any image there that Kareem could be in tune to. For him to be forcing an image or an experience into his client's head for his own pleasure would be extremely unethical.

"What else do you see in the room, Kareem?" *Where the hell did* that *come from*, Nathaniel thought. The last thing he wanted was for Kareem to continue seeing that room and describing it in detail. The hardon in his pants would be difficult enough to ignore without a specific description of his favorite sex place.

"There are a couple of guys sitting around on the benches. They're naked, except for a white towel."

"Kareem, I don't think this is a good place for you," Nathaniel said, sitting forward in his seat so that his elbows rested on his knees. "I think you should leave this room."

"No," Kareem said. "It's all right. You're there, too."

"What?"

"You're in the very back," he said, turning his face up to Nathaniel but keeping his eyes closed. "You're motioning for me to come to you."

Nathaniel's heart raced in his chest, and he struggled to catch his breath. He sat back in his chair and shook his head a couple more times, trying once again to clear his mind of any picture of himself and Kareem naked in the bathhouse steam room. But the funny thing was, he wasn't aware of any such picture to begin with. Just how subconscious must it be?

"You're naked, Dr. Jordan."

"Kareem, really, I don't think this . . ."

"God, what a beautiful, big cock you have, Dr. Jordan."

"Kareem . . ."

"You want me to do what?"

Nathaniel opened his mouth to start counting to five, so that he could bring Kareem out of the trance, but no sound came out. His eyes widened as he watched his client fall to his knees on the floor and crawl over to his chair.

"Kareem . . ."

"Yes, sir."

"Suck my cock," Nathaniel said. His eyes bulged with shock even as he spread his legs wider to accommodate Kareem between them.

Kareem's eyes were still closed, but he reached out and unbuckled Nathaniel's belt and pulled his pants down with little effort. He reached between the doctor's legs and cupped his balls inside his boxers, causing Nathaniel's shorts to tent out several inches in front of him. He leaned forward and licked the head of the hard cock through the sheer material of the boxers, and when Nathaniel moaned loudly, Kareem wrapped his lips around the fat head and sucked it into his mouth.

Nathaniel shook his head again, trying in vain to clear his head. He opened his mouth to count to five again, in an attempt to end this madness and to bring Kareem out of the trance. "Oh Jesus, Kareem, that's so hot. Suck my dick, baby." Shit! That is so not what he'd intended to say.

Kareem ripped the shorts from Nathaniel's waist and threw them to the side. He wrapped one fist around Nathaniel's thick cock and licked it from base to head, and then back down again, taking some extra care to lick and suck on the doctor's big, shaved balls. He slowly slid one finger inside Nathaniel's ass, and when it elicited a deep moan from the doctor, he swallowed the big dick in one slow and deliberate move.

"Oh God, Karcem, suck my cock, man!"

Kareem continued to finger fuck the doctor as he slid his mouth up and down the length of the thick and veiny cock. With his free hand he squeezed the dick as he bobbed up and down on it.

"Fuck, baby," Nathaniel moaned. "I'm gonna cum."

Kareem tightened his mouth around the big cock and sucked on it hungrily. He was an expert cocksucker and never once gagged as the thick pole slid past his tonsils and into his throat.

The hot, tight mouth was more than Nathaniel was able to stand. He clutched the arms of his chair and tightened his body. He let out one pathetic moan as he felt his orgasm shoot through his cock. Six, seven, eight shots, and still it kept coming. Kareem swallowed every one of them, and kept sucking until there wasn't the tiniest drop of cum left.

What the fuck just happened, Nathaniel wondered. Kareem sat back on his legs and licked the remaining cum from his lips. His eyes were still closed.

"Kareem, get up and go back to the sofa, please."

"Yes, sir." He stood up and walked over to the sofa a few feet away, and then sat down.

Nathaniel stood up shakily and walked into the restroom. He splashed a couple of handfuls of cold water onto his face and straightened his mussed hair. Then he pulled up his pants and tucked his shirt back into them. When he was confident he could walk evenly and that the flushed red had left his face, he walked back into the office and sat back in his chair.

Kareem sat perfectly still on the sofa, with his hands resting calmly on his knees. His eyes were still closed.

"Kareem, are you ready to come back now?"

"Yes, sir."

"Listen to the tick of the pendulum. Feel it bringing you closer and closer to the present. On the count of five you will return here. One . . . two . . . three . . . four . . . five."

Kareem opened his eyes and blinked a couple of times. "What happened?"

"Do you remember anything at all, Kareem?"

"No, nothing. Did you put me under already?"

"Yes."

"Well? What happened? What does my future look like?"

"You are very talented, Kareem, and you're going to be very successful. But I can't tell you more than that. Knowing too much of the future could jeopardize it. Your destiny could be altered. So let's just suffice it to say that you will be very happy, and you'll make your future partner extremely happy, too."

"Really, Dr. Jordan?"

"Yes, Kareem. I promise."

"Right on!" Kareem said excitedly, and stood up. He reached into his pocket. "How much do I owe you?"

"Forget it," Nathaniel said. "This session is on me. For being such a good sport on the *Olga Show.*"

"Serious?"

Nathaniel laughed. "Serious."

"Thanks, Doc. Hopefully I'll see you around."

"Have a safe trip home, Kareem," Nathaniel said as he walked his client to the door and closed it behind him.

* * *

Nathaniel Jordan actually drove all the way home and got undressed and climbed into bed before he realized he had not intended to be home and in bed. He tossed and turned for a few minutes, and then reached for a sleeping pill. As he brought it to his mouth, his hand flung away and threw the pill against the far wall.

As if in a trance, Nathaniel got out of bed, quietly got dressed, and walked out to his car. Forty minutes later he put the car into park, stepped out, walked across the parking lot, and entered the Coliseum Spa. He paid the attendant, walked quickly to his room, stripped off his clothes, wrapped the skimpy white towel around his waist, then locked his door and walked slowly to the steam room.

It was dark inside, and a plume of steam rushed out and into the hallway as soon as he opened the door. Normally there were several soft and low-wattage lights placed sporadically around the room. But today it was almost completely black inside the big room. Nathaniel heard low moans of lust all around him, and his cock began to thicken beneath the towel.

In the very back of the room there was a low, soft light. Nathaniel knew that there was a single small bench lining the back wall, and he could see the shadow of a man sitting in the middle of it, alone. Even from his distance of about fifteen feet away, and in the midst of a blast of fresh steam, Nathaniel could see the huge cock protruding from the middle of the man's crotch.

"Come here," the deep voice called out.

From the sounds of the moans all around him, Nathaniel could tell that there were at least a dozen men in the steam room. Yet, he somehow knew the order was for him. He took a couple of steps forward, and with every step, his cock grew harder, until it eventually tented out several inches in front of him.

"On your knees, Dr. Jordan."

He recognized the voice this time. "Kareem?"

"Of course. Were you expecting someone else?"

"No."

"Good. So get on your knees and suck my cock." He spread his legs wider and scooted to the edge of the bench.

Nathaniel hooked his thumb beneath the waist of the towel and dropped it to the floor. His own cock was bobbing up and down as he knelt between Kareem's legs. He reached out with one hand and grabbed the thick cock throbbing in front of him. It was at least ten or eleven inches long, and so thick that he couldn't wrap his fist around it.

"Don't just fist it, man," Kareem said, and pulled Nathaniel's head forward. "Suck it, dude."

Nathaniel stuck out his tongue and licked at the salty head. It was slick and hot, and he couldn't get enough of it. He wrapped his lips around it and sucked it deep into his mouth, and flicked his tongue around it several times.

"Fuck, that's hot, Doc."

Just the sound of Kareem's voice made his heart race and his cock throb. He opened the back of his throat and leaned forward. He didn't think he'd be able to get even half of the big dick down his throat, and so when the fat head pressed against his tonsils and then past them and deeper into his throat, he felt his eyes bulge. He continued swallowing the cock, not stopping until he smelled the musky sweat from Kareem's balls and pubic hair.

"God, Doc, I'm gonna blow my load if you keep that up."

Nathaniel wanted nothing more than to taste the sweet and salty load that he was sure would be shot from the huge cock. He wrapped his lips and throat tighter around the pole and sucked harder on it.

"No, dude," Kareem moaned. "Not like this. Stand up."

As much as he wanted to suck Kareem to completion, he knew what standing up would bring, and he wanted that even more. He gave the thick Arabian cock one last swallow and tugged on Kareem's balls as he slid his mouth up the long rod. Then he stood up and leaned against the wall, pushing his ass out toward Kareem's bouncing cock.

"You want my big dick buried deep up that sweet ass of yours, don't you, Dr. Jordan?"

"Yes," was all Nathaniel was able to mutter.

"Lift your leg up and rest it on the bench," Kareem ordered.

Nathaniel lifted his right leg and planted his foot on the stone bench. He felt Kareem's big hands grab a cheek each, and he shuddered as the thick, strong fingers massaged his ass and slipped between his crack. His legs shook visibly, and he struggled to control his breathing as one finger, and then another, slipped inside his puckered hole.

"Oh God, Kareem," he moaned loudly. "I need you to fuck me."

Kareem dropped to his knees and pressed his face against Nathaniel's ass, forcing him against the wall. A second later Nathaniel felt the Arab's hot, wet tongue lick around his sphincter for a moment, and then slide confidently inside.

"Ungh," the doctor moaned louder, and bit down hard on his arm.

Kareem licked and kissed and bit at the twitching ass for a few moments, stopping only when he felt that Nathaniel was about to blow his load all over the wall.

"You ready for my big cock, Dr. Jordan?"

"Yes," Nathan pleaded, "give it to me, please."

Kareem stood up and pressed his giant cock against Nathan's ass crack. "Take a deep breath, Doc."

Nathaniel did, and then gasped as he felt first the fat head and then the rest of the big dick slide deep inside him in one slow and deliberate move. He'd taken a few cocks that were so big that they took his breath away, but none of them had made him feel like this. He was completely filled up, but it didn't hurt. Instead he felt as if he'd found a part of himself that he'd been searching for for years. Every atom in his body tingled and threatened to burst as Kareem slid in and out of him.

"Fuck me harder, Kareem," he yelled as he reached back and pulled the young man onto him harder and deeper. He felt and heard the other men in the room gather around them, and soon he and Kareem were surrounded. Certainly this could not be a good thing. He was famous. These men could very easily recognize him, and if they were so inclined, they could destroy his career. If any of them had a camera phone, it could all be over. But he didn't care. At that moment, the only thing Nathaniel Jordan cared about was feeling Kareem's huge cock sliding in and out of his clutching ass. "Shove that big cock deeper inside my ass and fuck my brains out!"

Kareem grabbed Nathaniel's arms and pulled them behind his back, holding his wrists together with one hand as he held him from the shoulder with his other, and pounded into him relentlessly.

Nathaniel slammed into the wall violently, and then was pulled back onto the cock inside him, and then thrown back into the wall, over and over again, until he became dizzy. The entire room began to spin around him, and the men around them became blurry as Kareem increased the speed and intensity of his fucking.

"I'm going to cum, baby," Kareem screamed. A second later, he ripped his cock from Nathaniel's ass with no further warning.

Nathaniel whimpered as spray after spray of Kareem's hot, thick cum splashed across his back and ass. It dripped down his crack, dribbling across the raw and sore hole, and Nathaniel moaned as he tightened his hole, trying to suck the cum inside him. He still had his back to Kareem, and so he couldn't see the man or his cock or cum. But it felt as if the Arab stud had emptied a couple of gallons of spooge onto his sweaty back.

"Sweet Mother of God," Nathaniel cried out. "I'm gonna shoot."

"Turn around, baby," Kareem said as he dropped to his knees. "I want your cum all over my face.

Nathaniel turned around and leaned backward onto the wall. Without even touching himself, his cock shot forth eight or nine spurts of jizz. He gasped to catch his breath as he watched his load cover Kareem's sweet, beautiful face. His knees gave out as the last couple of shots flew from his cock, and he slumped to the floor.

Kareem scooted over on the floor and leaned against the wall with Nathaniel. He wrapped his arms around Nathaniel's shoulders and kissed him as the men around them closed in on both sides and in front of them. Before they could prepare themselves for it, cum was flying from every cock in every direction and splattered across both of their faces. They both lapped at the cum on their faces and wiped it from their chests and stomachs.

"Holy *fuck*, that was hot, Doc." Kareem said as the men turned and walked out of the steam room, leaving him and Nathaniel alone.

"Hell yeah, it was," Nathaniel said, leaning in to kiss Kareem on the lips. "But I have to confess something."

"What's that?" Kareem asked as he laid his head on Nathaniel's shoulder.

"I'm not really a doctor. It's just part of an entertainment title. I have a doctorate in education, and so I can legally use the title, but I'm not a medical or psychiatric doctor."

"I know."

"You do?"

"Yes," Kareem said, and kissed Nathaniel on the chin. "I did my homework. And now I have something to confess, too."

"Oh?"

"I'm not really a student at Berkeley."

"You're not?"

"No."

"What are you, then?"

"I'm an actor and a professional hypnotist. The entire time we were in your office and you were supposedly hypnotizing me, I was really the one who was hypnotizing you."

"You mean . . . that's why I couldn't . . ."

"That's correct. I've wanted you for the past six months, ever since I saw you on the *Tonight Show*. I just knew I had to have you. So when I heard you were going to appear on the *Olga Show*, I arranged to be there."

"So it was you who made yourself fly across the room?"

"Yes, I've done it many times. It's simply a matter of manipulating energy. You were right about that. But I suspect you'd never actually achieved that particular stunt before, and were probably a little taken aback by it. You probably were prepared to hypnotize the entire audience and make them believe they had seen me fly, right? It's the oldest trick in the book."

"Yeah. But why go to all that trouble? Why not just run into me and meet me?

"I wasn't sure you'd like me, and I wanted to at least make an impression."

"Well, that you did."

"But now I want to know what you really think about me. Without the hypnosis and manipulation."

"Are you sure I'm not still under your spell?"

"Yes." Kareem laughed. "And it's not a spell. Just a little

help moving things along. But now you're all alone with yourself and your thoughts. So?"

"Hmmm, let's see," Nathaniel said. "I think I'm madly in love with you and can't stand the thought of a single day without you in it."

"Serious?" Kareem asked excitedly.

"Serious. Hey, maybe we could be an act together. Professionally, I mean, as well as personally."

"I'd love that."

"But I'm a little afraid about the guys that were in here with us. What if they recognize either of us? They could make a mess and cause some real problems."

"I doubt that," Kareem said mischievously. "I hypnotized them all right before you got here. Just in case you didn't go under or fall for the hypnosis, they were prepared to pin you down and force you to submit to me."

"Kareem!" Nathaniel said, and slapped him playfully on the arm.

"Well, I had to be sure. I had to have you. And to calm your worries, all of those men saw you as a fat, balding, middle-aged white man, and they saw me as a skinny, hairy, and gray-haired middle-aged African American man. They'll never know the truth about either of us."

"Wow, you're good."

"Thank you, you're not too bad yourself."

"Wanna go again?" Nathaniel asked.

"Yeah, I think the sling room is empty. Let's go."

Gone but Not Forgotten

"God, I love you so much, baby," Roman whispered into Mitch's ear as he nibbled it lovingly. He tickled the outside of the ear with his tongue, and then slipped it slowly inside.

Mitch squirmed and wiggled around the bed, pretending to struggle and get away from his lover, when in actuality he wanted nothing more than to stay there, wrapped in Roman's embrace with his hot and talented tongue making love to his ear for eternity. "I love you, too, cariño," Mitch said, and struggled to keep the tears inside his eyes.

Roman moaned loudly and grinded his cock against Mitch's naked leg. "You know it drives me crazy when you call me that," he said, and moved his mouth from Mitch's ear to his mouth, kissing him lovingly. "Even though you sound as white as a slice of Wonder Bread, it is still so fucking cute. And just the fact that you learned a little of my language shows me just how much you care about me."

"Care about you?" Mitch said, and pulled Roman on top of him. "That's a slight understatement. I couldn't live without you. I couldn't breathe or eat or sleep . . ."

"Or make love," Roman said with a grin.

"Or make love," Mitch agreed, and reached down and squeezed his lover's hard cock. Just the feel and the heat of the thick, uncut cock sent shivers up and down his body. From the first time he'd laid eyes on it ten years ago, he knew he'd never need or want another for as long as he lived. And in the decade that they'd spent together, he never had. Not once had he felt the need, much less the desire, to look at another man with longing. Roman was all he ever needed, and he felt lucky to have found him.

"I want you so bad," Roman whispered into his ear.

"Badly," Mitch corrected. "You want me so badly."

Roman laughed. "Okay, well if we're really speaking correctly, then let me say what I really mean. I want to slide my cock deep inside your ass and fuck you until our bodies meld together as one, and then even more until we sink deep into the mattress and disappear altogether into the energy of the universe."

Though Mitch would never admit it out loud, hearing his lover speak like this turned him on almost as much as the sex. Roman had never suffered from the typical Latino macho façade that most Mexican men prided themselves on. On their first date, he'd held Mitch's hand on the street and at dinner. He'd kissed him in public and caressed his arm and leg at every opportunity, regardless of where they were and who was watching. And not a single day passed in ten years that Roman did not tell Mitch how much he loved and desired him. And not just once a day, but multiple times.

He pulled Roman's face to his own and kissed him lovingly, savoring the taste and feel of his lover's tongue as it danced with his. Their naked bodies pressed against one another, and as Roman slid his cock up and down the length of Mitch's, a thick drip of precum slid from the head. Mitch moaned and lifted his body up to press even harder against Roman's and to smear the warm precum all over his cock.

"You want me to fuck you, baby?" Roman asked.

"I need you to fuck me, cariño."

Roman kissed him again and then slid his body down the length of his lover's. He bit and licked at Mitch's neck, and grinned when it elicited a moan and squirm. Mitch had always loved the way he made love to his body with his mouth, and Roman prided himself on his oral talents. He continued down Mitch's body, biting the tiny nipples until they hardened, and then licking his way past the rib cage and to the thick, black treasure trail that started at his lover's navel and disappeared in the bush at the top of his groin. He licked and sucked on the hair, and he watched Mitch's stomach twitch as he flicked at it with his tongue.

Mitch's cock was fully hard and stretched a couple of inches past his belly button. Roman closed his eyes to keep himself from attacking it immediately, because as much as he loved sucking the big dick, he also enjoyed licking every inch of his lover's body and seeing him squirm around the bed as he did so. He was a legs man, and Mitch's long and muscled thighs and calves and his feet had always excited Roman. He could spend hours licking and kissing and caressing them, and he always saved them for the last part of foreplay because after worshipping them with his mouth and tongue, his cock was as hard as it could get, and primed for fucking Mitch until both men could not hold back another moment and exploded onto one another.

Roman lifted Mitch's legs into the air, pulling his smooth ass up with it. He leaned down and kissed the puckered hole. When Mitch moaned his approval, he flicked his tongue around it several times and then slid it as far inside the spasming tunnel as he could get it.

"Oh God, baby, that feels so good," Mitch gasped as he raised his ass higher into the air so that it could take more of his lover's tongue.

Roman tongue-fucked him a few moments longer, then spread the smooth ass cheeks apart and slid a finger deep inside. He knew this drove Mitch crazy with desire, and he grinned when his partner moaned even louder and pulled a pillow to his face to muffle the screams of lust. When Mitch began thrusting his ass up and down on his finger, Roman took his cue and slid a second finger inside the warm burrow.

"What do you want, baby?" Roman asked. "Tell me."

"I want you to fuck me," Mitch said as he threw the pillow across the room.

"Your face is so red and your body is so hot, amor."

"It's because I need you inside me so bad," Mitch panted.

"So badly." Roman laughed. "You need me inside you so badly."

"Shut up and fuck me," Mitch said, pulling Roman's mouth to his own and kissing him. "Slide your big cock deep inside me and fuck my ass until I'm unconscious."

Roman moved between Mitch's legs and rested his thick cock between the ass cheeks. He was always amazed at how hot his lover's body got during sex and the amount of control Mitch had over his ass muscles. They flexed and squeezed his cock, pulling it closer and closer to the twitching hole.

He worked up a good amount of saliva in his mouth and let it drop down onto his cock head and between Mitch's ass. Then he slid the bulbous head around it for a few seconds before sliding the fat head inside.

"Oh God," Mitch gasped as he clutched the blankets on either side of him.

"You okay, babe?"

"I will be once you shove the rest of that cock inside me," Mitch said, and lifted his ass again, sliding another couple of inches onto Roman's dick.

As his cock slid farther and farther inside the tight, hot hole,

Roman held onto Mitch's legs and looked into his face. He tried to count to fifty, or think of something extremely unpleasant . . . anything to keep from cumming too quickly. But it was hard to do that when he was looking into his lover's beautiful face. Mitch's creamy skin, blond hair, and deep blue eyes had always overwhelmed him and taken his breath away. It was such a contrast to his own copper-colored smooth skin, black hair, and dark brown eyes. And never so evident as times like this, when they were making love and one of them had his cock buried inside the other, so that their opposite looking bodies became one.

"I love you so much, baby," Roman said, leaning down and kissing Mitch on the lips as he slid the last inch of his cock inside his lover's hole.

"God, I love you, too, cariño," Mitch said, grunting as he moved his ass up and down the entire length of Roman's big dick.

Just then the phone rang. Mitch's eyes bulged and began to tear up before he could stop them. "No, no, no . . ."

"I'm so sorry, baby," Roman said as he leaned down and kissed Mitch again, lingering this time and holding his face in his hands.

"I won't answer it."

"It doesn't matter. The truth won't go away simply because you don't answer the phone." Already his cock was out of Mitch's ass and was quickly deflating.

"No, this can't happen again," Mitch cried as he watched his lover dissipate before his eyes.

"I love you so much, baby."

"I love you, too, cariño."

And with that, Roman was gone, and Mitch was left with the familiar tingle inside his ass and deep in his guts. He reached over and answered the phone.

"Hello?" He wiped the tears from his eyes and smeared his

fingers across the precum that was still slick across his hard cock and stomach. "Yes, of course I'm alone. It's one in the morning. Who would I be with?"

"You really should have come with us last night, Mitch," Julian said as he shoved a forkful of salad into his mouth. "The club was packed, and not with the normal skanky crowd. There were a lot of hot guys there."

"I was busy."

"Oh, I'm sorry. Did I forget there was a *Jeopardy* marathon on, or maybe it was the guaranteed million dollar winner on *Deal or No Deal?*"

"Don't be such a bitch," Mitch said, and looked around the patio as he sipped on his iced tea. It was always the same, tired crowd every Sunday at brunch. He'd been friends with three-quarters of the people sitting around him a couple of years ago. But now he made them uncomfortable and most of them didn't speak with him anymore. Instead, they kept their eyes on their plates when they noticed him and avoided conversation at all costs. Only Julian was still there by his side, and so he treaded lightly. "It's gonna give you even more wrinkles than you already have."

"What?" Julian screeched, and touched his face. "I have wrinkles?"

"Sweetie, you're thirty-five. Of course you have wrinkles."

"Thirty-four."

"You'll be thirty-five in two weeks. Close enough."

"You're mean," Julian said, and dropped his fork as he looked at himself in the reflection of the knife. "It's very unattractive."

"I'm sorry. I just thought you'd want to know. You're the only friend I have left, and I want you to know that I love and care about you."

"Ahhh, that's so sweet," Julian said, and leaned over to hug him. "I love you, too. But I'm very worried about you."

"Worried? Why?"

"Because you never go out anymore. You're always depressed, and all you talk about is Roman. It's not healthy."

"I don't go out anymore because I get exhausted watching all the young twinks bounce around on meth and spill their drinks all over me. And I am not depressed. I'm just quiet. And I don't only talk about Roman. In fact, I haven't spoken about him in almost six months."

"Because no one is around to listen."

"You're around. When was the last time you heard me mention Roman?"

"Okay, so you're being more careful so the men in the white coats don't come looking for you. But it's still not good, honey. You never leave the house unless I drag you out to dinner or brunch, and even then it's like pulling teeth. You're not making any new friends, and you've driven all your old ones away."

"If my friends can't be there for me in my time of need, then they weren't my friends to begin with, and I don't need them."

"See, that's what I'm talking about. That's not a healthy response to someone losing his friends. Roman died two years ago, Mitch. I know you loved him, but you have to move on. When you don't, it freaks your friends out and they tend to leave."

"We've been together for ten years, Julian. I can't just forget about him."

"No, sweetie. You haven't been together for ten years. You *were* together for eight years. He died two years ago. You're supposed to stop counting when that happens."

Mitch bit his lip as he remembered the touch, the sound, the smell of Roman making love to him earlier that morning. He knew Julian would try to negate Roman's presence, and so he

284 / Sean Wolfe

hadn't even showered before coming to brunch. His lover's precum was still dried onto his leg and cock and stomach. But he knew there was no sense in pulling up his shirt and showing the evidence. Short of a DNA test, Julian would probably insist that the sticky stuff was Mitch's own, and insisting on the test would most likely result in his best friend calling in those men in the white coats that he'd mentioned a moment ago.

"I still love him, Julian. I don't stop counting just because he's not physically here anymore. I still love him."

"I know you do, honey," Julian said, and blew Mitch a kiss. "And I'm not asking you to stop loving him. It'd be useless for me to ask that anyway, but I wouldn't ever do that. But you seriously have to accept the fact that he's gone and he'll never be back. And you have to move on and meet new guys and open yourself up to love again."

"That's ridiculous. I'm still in love with Roman. What part of that don't you get?" Mitch raised his voice, and then lowered it as he looked around and saw half of the patio staring at him. "I don't just love him. I'm still *in love* with him, Julian. Could you open yourself up to the prospect of love with someone else if you were already in love?"

"I wouldn't fall in love with a ghost."

Mitch flinched. "I didn't fall in love with a ghost and you know it. That's not fair. I fell in love with a man. I fell in love with Roman."

"I know, and it was seriously the most beautiful love story I have ever seen," Julian said. "And I'm not just saying that, I mean it. You two were more in love than anyone I know. But he's dead, Mitch. He's been dead for two years. You simply cannot remain in love with Roman. You can continue to love him until the day you die, but to stay in love with him is just plain wrong. It's crazy. You have to open yourself up to the possibility of loving like that again. With someone who is alive and breathing and can love you back."

"This conversation is over," Mitch said, and stood up to leave.

"No, it's not," Julian said, and grabbed Mitch by the wrist. "Because if you walk away from me and leave, then our friendship is over. I'm worried about you, Mitch, and if I can't express that to you without you getting up and leaving, then being your friend means nothing to you."

Mitch looked down at his friend and saw that he was serious.

"Your friendship means everything to me, Julian," he said as he sat back down, and smoothed out an imaginary wrinkle in his shirt. "You know that."

"I don't mean to hurt you, babe."

"I know."

"But I'm afraid for you. It's normal to grieve and to miss what you had with Roman. But it's not normal for you to become reclusive and never leave your house, and to speak about Roman as if he were still alive and right here with you."

Mitch sipped at his tea and said nothing.

"Come with me to Charged tonight. Let's have some fun, and if, by chance, you meet some hot guy, then do me a favor and at least give it a chance. A chance to fail or succeed, but an honest chance. Deal?"

"Deal," Mitch said, and prayed to God that the tears he felt behind his eyes wouldn't fall.

The cover charge was steeper, the dance floor more crowded, and the music several decibels louder than Mitch remembered. Of course, the club had changed owners and names, as they often did in that community. The music seemed foreign to him; he didn't recognize the beat or the voice. And the kids bouncing all around him wore strange clothes and accessories, and they were pierced and tattooed in places he'd never imagined were made to see a needle.

But he'd promised Julian that he'd try, and so he smiled and held onto his friend's beltloops as they made their way through the crowded dance floor and over to the bar. They weren't at the bar a full minute before someone came up and tapped Julian on the shoulder.

"Hey, stud, I thought you'd never get here," he said to Julian, and kissed him on the cheek.

The guy was about Mitch's height, a little over six feet tall, and was powerfully muscled. It was obvious he spent more than a few hours at the local gym. He was definitely Latino, and if Mitch were to guess, he'd venture to say he was from Brazil or Venezuela. Short, curly black hair and light hazel eyes that bore into your soul when he looked into yours. His smile was wide and bright white, and the slightest trace of a dimple threatened to break through with each one.

"Rogelio, this is my friend, Mitch," Julian said, as he turned and smiled.

"Nice to meet you, Mitch," Rogelio said, and held on to Mitch's hand several seconds longer than customary for a first meeting.

"You, too," Mitch said. He found the guy amazingly beautiful and tried his best to smile and return the warmth in the handshake. But after several seconds, he began to feel uncomfortable.

"If you boys will excuse me, I have to use the little girls' room," Julian said, and turned and quickly walked away from the bar.

"Would you care to dance?" Rogelio asked.

"Neither one of you are great actors, you know." Mitch laughed.

"What do you mean?"

"You didn't even wait until we ordered our drink before you approached us, and your eyes barely left mine the entire time."

"You're very cute."

"And you're oh so very kind," Mitch said, and grabbed Rogelio by the hand and led him to the dance floor. "A liar, but very kind. And Julian said he needed to use the restroom, but he walked away in the opposite direction of the bathrooms."

"Oh."

"It's obvious Julian set you up to meet me. You're exactly my type, down to the semi-hairy chest and the dimples and your beautiful smile."

"Look, Julian did tell me he had a friend and that he'd like me to stop by and meet you. But he did say there was no pressure. The truth is, I find you very attractive, and from the moment I set eyes on you I wanted to meet you. And to dance with you."

"Then shut up and dance," Mitch said, and pulled him closer to his side.

The lights were out, but the candle on the nightstand and the moonlight shining through the bedroom window cast enough light for Mitch to see that Rogelio's body was every bit as beautiful as his face. He lay completely dressed on the bed and shivered uncontrollably as he watched the hot Latino slowly strip. His heart pounded uncontrollably in his chest as Rogelio tossed his shirt to the floor and stepped out of his pants and underwear. He gasped loudly and tightened his body as the boy from Rio crawled next to him and hugged him tightly.

"Relax, baby," Rogelio whispered as he unbuttoned Mitch's shirt.

"I'm sorry," Mitch said softly. "It's just been a while."

"I know. But I won't hurt you, I promise. I just want to see your incredible body and make love to you."

Rogelio took his time undressing Mitch, and kissed every part of his body as the clothes came off and revealed them. When Mitch was completely naked, Rogelio worked his way back up to his head and kissed him on the mouth. He reached down and cupped Mitch's balls in one hand and slipped his tongue inside his mouth.

"I'm not sure I'm ready for this," Mitch said as he broke the kiss and tried to sit up on his elbows.

"Of course you aren't," Rogelio whispered into his ear. "But isn't that the whole point?"

"Yeah," Mitch relented. "Yeah, I guess it is." He lay back down.

Rogelio reached down and stroked Mitch's cock until it was fully hard, and then slid down and licked it for a moment before sucking the entire length into his mouth. When Mitch finally relaxed a little and moaned, Rogelio deepthroated it over and over again, and he could tell that Mitch was getting close.

"Not yet, man," he said as he released the cock from his mouth. He slid up to the head of the bed and straddled Mitch's chest. "Suck my dick now. I want this to last a little while."

Mitch stuck out his tongue and licked the head. Rogelio's cock was long and thick and uncut, and Mitch knew what to do with it. He licked around the head for a minute, savoring the taste of the precum, and then leaned forward so that he could swallow the rest of the big cock easier.

Rogelio slid his cock in and out of Mitch's mouth for several minutes, taking his time and making sure Mitch was able to take his huge cock without choking. After a few minutes, when he saw that Mitch was relaxed and getting into it a little more, he lay down beside him and rolled Mitch over onto his side. He spooned up next to him and slid his cock against Mitch's ass.

"God, your ass is so hot, baby," he whispered into Mitch's ear.

Mitch screamed loudly and pushed himself off the bed.

"What's wrong?" Rogelio said, startled. He jumped out of bed and tried to come around to Mitch's side.

"Get out!" Mitch screamed.

"What? You've got to be kidding me. What did I do?"

"How did you do that?" Mitch said, panicked as he grabbed his clothes from the floor.

"How did I do what?" Rogelio asked.

"You said, 'I love you so much, baby' and it was in Roman's voice!"

"No, I didn't. I said your ass is so hot."

"Get out!"

"Baby, I swear to God . . ."

"Don't call me baby, either. Just go, please."

"Okay," Rogelio said. "All right, I'll go. Maybe this was a bad idea. Maybe it was just too soon. But I don't think it was wrong, and I really like you, Mitch. I'll go, but can we maybe try it again some other time? I promise we'll take it as slow as you need to."

"I don't know," Mitch said as he sat down naked on the bed. "I can't think about it right now. I'm sorry."

"No worries, man," Rogelio said as he slipped on his jeans. "I'll call you in a couple of days, okay?"

"Sure."

Mitch watched him walk out of the bedroom and waited until he heard the front door shut. Then he lay down on the bed, held his pillow close to his chest, and cried. He thought he'd been all cried out, but after more than half an hour, he realized he was wrong.

"Why the hell did you leave me, cariño?" he cried loudly. "You know I can't live without you. I can't get through this alone. You know that." He pounded his fist on the bed and threw the alarm clock across the room. "You selfish son of a bitch. Why didn't you wear your seat belt, asshole? I need you, Roman. I just can't live without you by my side."

When he couldn't cry another tear, he drifted into sleep.

He wasn't sure how long he'd been asleep when he felt the mattress sag next to him. A couple of seconds later he smelled CK1, Roman's favorite cologne, and felt his strong arms wrap around his own arms and shoulders.

"Hey, baby." Roman *whispered into his ear and licked it softly.*

"Oh God, cariño," Mitch *said, and turned around to kiss his lover softly on the lips.* "I'm so sorry. I don't know what I was doing. And I didn't mean what I said."

"Shhh," Roman *whispered, and kissed him back.* "It's okay. You were lonely. It's difficult. It's not your fault."

"I thought I could move on, but I can't."

"And you don't have to. I'm right here, baby, and I will never leave you."

"Promise?"

Roman *laughed.* "Yes, baby, I promise."

"Make love to me, cariño."

Mitch's *dead lover of two years kissed him and licked his way down his naked body. He loved Mitch's hard, muscled body and couldn't get enough of it. The feel, the taste, the smell—it was all so delicious. When he reached the thick, cut cock, he licked it and pulled it into his mouth.*

"Oh God, cariño, that's incredible," Mitch *said. He slid his*

cock in and out of Roman's hot mouth slowly, wanting every second to last as long as possible.

But Roman had another plan in mind. He'd watched another man kiss and caress his lover, and as much as it hurt him, it also turned him on. His cock was hard as steel and begging to get inside Mitch's hot ass. He lifted Mitch's hips off the bed, pushing his legs up close to his chest so that his ass stuck high in the air.

"Baby, you have the sweetest ass I have ever seen," he said as he licked and kissed the smooth muscular cheeks. Mitch's moans were all he needed to continue, and he attacked the quivering hole with a vengeance.

"I need you inside me, cariño," Mitch whimpered.

"Do you want me to fuck your ass, amor?"

"God, yes!"

When Roman was certain Mitch's ass was sufficiently lubricated with his spit, he moved closer to his lover's ass and slid his cock up and down the slick crack. When his cock was wet with the saliva, he positioned the head at the hole and slid it slowly inside until just the head of his cock was covered.

"Ungh," Mitch moaned loudly, and though it sounded as if he was in pain, he lifted his ass higher, taking the whole thick pole deep inside him in one slow move. "Fuck me, cariño."

Roman slid his cock in and out of Mitch's ass slow and deliberately, pulling out so that only his cock head remained inside, and then sliding the entire dick deep inside him again. After ten years together, he knew exactly which spots to hit inside his lover, and he smiled and kissed Mitch as he moaned and squirmed beneath him.

"God, babe," he said through clenched teeth, "I'm not gonna be able to hold out much longer. Your ass is so tight and sweet."

"I want you to shoot your load inside me, cariño," Mitch said breathlessly as he reached down and stroked his cock while Roman fucked him. "I wanna feel you fill me up."

"Oh shit, man," Roman panted. "Don't talk like that, baby. You're gonna make me cum."

"Fuck my ass hard and deep, cariño. Shove that fat cock deep inside me and fuck me senseless."

"Fuuuuuucccckkkkk!" Roman screamed, and shoved himself deep inside his lover, and rested against Mitch's ass and legs as he spent himself inside him.

"I'm gonna cum," Mitch groaned.

Without pulling his cock out of Mitch's ass, Roman leaned forward and sucked Mitch's hard cock deep into his throat. He sucked on it hungrily, and as Mitch emptied his load into his mouth, he swallowed it greedily.

"Fuck, cariño," Mitch gasped as he tried to catch his breath. He slowly pulled his ass off Roman's hard, throbbing cock. "That was incredible. I think that may have been the best sex we've ever had."

"How could you pick just one?" Roman asked.

"I can't, really," Mitch said, and hugged Roman close to his body. "But every time you fuck me, it is better than the time before. So this one is the best so far."

"Okay, that makes sense," Roman said. He leaned over and kissed Mitch on the lips. "I love you so much, babe. I know our relationship now isn't exactly normal, but please don't let it end. I can't imagine not being able to see you and hug you and kiss you and make love to you."

"What are you talking about?" Mitch asked. "I can't control your being here."

"Of course you can. The only reason I'm here at all, at least physically, is because you won't let go of me and move on. I'm dead, baby, and I have no choice but to let go, physically, that is. But you do have a choice, and because you want me here so badly, I can't cross over. Not completely."

"Are you serious? I can keep you here just by wanting it enough?"

"Yes."

"Then why don't more people do that when they lose a loved one?"

"Some do, they just don't let anyone know. But most people don't love their partner enough to make it happen. They don't love like you do, baby. Not that I'm complaining at all. I hope you never stop loving me this much."

"Don't worry about that, cariño. I'll never stop loving you, and I'll never let you go. How long can you stay here with me?"

"I'll be here as long as you love me and hold on to me, babe."

Mitch started crying. *"I'll never let you go. If I really can keep you here with me, just like this, for as long as I want, then you'll be here till the day I die and join you."*

"That's what I wanted to hear, babe. But you do know that that means you'll never be able to have another relationship, right?"

"I don't want anyone but you. I could never love anyone but you."

"And you won't be able to tell anyone about me. Not even Julian."

"That's not a problem. I want to keep you all to myself."

"Kiss me, baby," Roman said. *"And don't ever let me go."*

Mitch did kiss his lover, and he didn't even try to halt the tears as they fell down his cheeks and onto Roman's face. As they kissed, his cock hardened, and when Roman spread his legs apart, Mitch didn't hesitate to crawl in between them.